D1552884

HELLBENDER

THE CRUCIBLE

Michael Saxon Pikunas

LIBERTY HILL PUBLISHING

Liberty Hill Press
2301 Lucien Way #415
Maitland, FL 32751
407.339.4217
www.libertyhillpublishing.com

Printed in the United States of America.

Paperback ISBN-13: 978-1-6628-0460-1
Ebook ISBN-13: 978-1-6628-0461-8

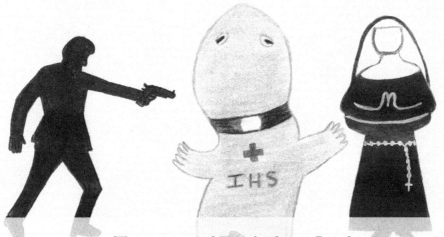

To our grandson Andrew Jacob,
affectionately known as A.J.

Marianna J Skiba

The Forest

Though it has been unusually hot this spring, down here in the glen it is cool and refreshing, the canopy of primeval hardwoods providing a natural parasol of shade as he judges the moss-covered stepping stones in making his way along the creek. It is so peaceful and quiet, save for the soothing gurgle from the tiny waterfalls and musical trilling of yellow warblers overhead. With net in hand, he is fixated on finding that large partially-submerged rock, the primary habitat that harbors his elusive quarry. He hasn't hunted in his favorite place for many years, not since his teenage years, at least. It is the memories of those happy family outings to the forest that he most treasures. He is hoping that today will be one of those rare lucky days when he might find what he is looking for.

The creature depends on clean, clear water because it absorbs oxygen in the water through its wrinkled, baggy skin, its long but flat body shape allowing it to crawl under the rocks to create perfect hiding places. It patiently waits in its secluded den for nightfall to creep out and stalk its prey.

He is back at his secret boyhood spot deep inside Cheaha State Park, surrounded by The Talladega National Forest. His secret spot is the Devil's Den, and his quarry is the hellbender.

The lizard-like eastern hellbender (Cryptobranchus alleganiensis) is one of the largest salamanders of North America, whose domain ranges along the Appalachians, from Alabama to New

York. In the Deep South, this fully-aquatic salamander thrives in clear, clean flowing streams of the Tennessee River system. The name *hellbender* probably comes from the animal's grotesque appearance. Some accounts say that the hellbender was named by early settlers who thought "it was a creature from hell where it's bent on returning." Other folklore suggests that the shriveled-looking skin of a hellbender represents "horrible tortures of the infernal regions." An ancient migrant Indian tribe of the Appalachian region had given the strange creature another name in translation...the Devil Dog.

The Indians had it as a legend that the hellbender was, in fact, something from the netherworld with whose encounters were something to be avoided. Indian youths heard tales of tribesmen coming in contact with the creature and then going mad after discovering terrifying tattoos on their bodies, the most disturbing ones appearing as a horned goat-like human face on their foreheads. The victims had last been seen running off into the forest, never to be seen again.

Long Before—The Southern Appalachians

O n these same lands, a long, long time ago, it was the Pleistocene epoch, better known as the Ice Age, it was the time of the mammoths. Along with giant sloths, saber-toothed tigers, and other mega fauna of the Ice Age, mammoths freely roamed the Southern Appalachians in herds 12,000 years ago. In 1799, German naturalist Johann Friedrich Blumenbach gave the woolly mammoth its scientific name, *Elephas primigenius*, placing it in the same genus as the Asian elephant. The name in Latin means "first elephant." An enormous shaggy-haired creature towering up to fourteen feet in height and weighing six tons, the woolly mammoth had formidable ivory tusks and a long, curved trunk that it used to scrape snow and ice off of the vegetation. A herbivore, it used its vice-shaped molars to crush, grind, and feed on the plentiful grasses.

The mammoth not only used its tusks for foraging, it also used them to defend itself against the razor-sharp flint spears and arrowheads of the hunters. Although mammoths were not naturally aggressive, they ferociously defended themselves when attacked. Hunted by the Paleo-Indian peoples who first inhabited the region, mammoths were hunted for their meat, fur, and even tusks and bones that were used to make primitive tools. Hunting the mammoth was quite the hazardous chore. In a confrontation, the hunters were in peril of being impaled or fatally struck by the massive tusks or trampled to death by an angry stomp in the mammoth's fight for its life. Upon successfully downing the gigantic beast, the Indians were at further risk of being attacked and torn apart by a hungry pack of over-sized dire wolves, which would have been watching the struggle patiently concealed inside the wood line, waiting for the right moment to pounce upon the hunters and devour their freshly-killed beast.

The earliest discovered site of Native American hunter-gatherers is the Meadowcroft Rockshelter in Washington County, Pennsylvania, which some scientists claim is pre-Clovis, the oldest human colonization, where findings of bones of wild horses imply the beginnings of American horse culture.

In the 16th century, Spanish explorers traversed the mountains of South Carolina, North Carolina, Tennessee, and Georgia, and encountered complex agrarian societies consisting of Muskogean-speaking inhabitants.

In 1540, on his expedition in search of gold, Hernandez de Soto declared that much of the region west of the mountains was part of the domain of Coosa, a paramount chiefdom centered around a settlement of villages in northern Georgia. By the time English explorers arrived in Appalachia in the late 17th century, the central part of the region was controlled by Algonquian tribes, namely the Shawnee, and the southern part of the region, in present-day North Central Alabama, was the domain of the Cherokee.

On record, the region referred to as Appalachia or the Appalachian Mountains has been a distinctive cultural and geographical area of the Eastern United States since the late 1700s. Since Appalachia lacks definite physiographical or topographical boundaries, there has been some disagreement over what exactly this enormous expanse encompasses. While the Appalachian Mountains stretch from Belle Isle in Canada to Cheaha Mountain in Alabama, Appalachia, a distinctively unique and signature way-of-life on and around them, encircles the central and southern portions of the range, from the Blue Ridge Mountains of Virginia, southwesterly to the Great Smoky Mountains.

The tools of modern archeology have uncovered some astonishing things in this region, such as the Icehouse Bottom site along the banks of the Little Tennessee River. At Icehouse Bottom, beginning in 1969, archeologists uncovered evidence of an archaic burial ritual involving the cremation of the dead. Little did they know that their uncovering would open another dimension...an abhorrent and hideous one.

Somewhere Outside the Forbidden City-Beijing

They stand in line, staring at their feet, trying to conceal their trembling. They are in the interior center of Detention Center No. 1, a dread sanctum of the Ministry of State Security (MSS)–the Guoanbu, the People's Republic of China's (PRC's) secret police agency. To their front, a red and gold-framed party banner bearing the image of Mao Zedong hangs from the rafters to the floor, flanked by two soldiers at arms. Running along the interior walls on each side of the building are rows of windowless rooms with unmarked doors, evenly spaced. Every bit of the interior space, from floor to ceiling, is painted a flat steel-gray.

They have been ordered there by their local political officer, the Zhengwei, without any particular reason given. They know full well that if they didn't immediately respond to find transport and come here, an official transport would've found them to *bring* them here.

They had feared their destination because word had spread quickly about the accidental release of a secret recruitment project. The silence is deafening before a loud click of a platoon of military boots echoes off the walls. A door opens from a room off to their left-front, and he appears, filling the doorway. Dressed in a drab khaki tunic and a peaked military visor bearing the emblem of the PRC is Ai Zian. In his late eighties, Zian is still lithe and fit. His name brings both admiration and fear; in translation, loving son of peace.

He saunters over and stands poised and erect in front of them. Zian stares straight ahead, the four-inch diagonal scar on his left cheek from the Korean conflict of the last century serves as a permanent badge of honor. Tension is rising as he continues to stand mute, as if waiting for something to happen. Then a loud gunshot rings out from an open door to their right-front that has been deliberately left open. The men in line flinch at the sudden blast. But Zian does not flinch and continues to stand erect, his steely gaze piercing right through them to the rear wall. And then movement and the smell of sulfur from the doorway, just close enough to allow the men in line to notice something being carried away on a stretcher, only the blood-dripping toes of the victim are visible, poking out at the end of a white sheet with a bright red stain.

Most had heard the rumors in their villages, the spreading anxiety of Shuangguai, the communist's bloody process of deterrence, the extreme way of administering a warning that Minister Zian has been known for. But now they know it directly, and they also know that with this warning, their own lives have been spared at the expense of one of their comrade's by this cold-blooded execution.

Ancient Origins

In the Golden Age of Greece, Lerna was a region noted for a foregone lake and fresh-water springs set near the eastern part of the tripoint region of the Peloponnese Peninsula, south of the City of Argos. Framed by the Isthmus of Corinth to the north, the Chaon Mountain to the west, and the Aegean Sea to the east, it sits on the northwestern tip of the Gulf of Argolis. Shaped as an inlet of the Aegean, its saltwater is chilled by the drift of cold waters flowing through the Dardanelles Strait from the Black Sea to the northeast. It was a caravan destination on an ancient route, from the Argolis to the southern Peloponnese, jutting into the Mediterranean Sea. Archaeological expeditions to the ancient site have unearthed relics dating it beyond the Bronze Age of ancient Greece.

It was in Lerna that the mythology of the Hydra was spawned. Its origin came from the early Greek poet Hesiod's Theogony, the monstrous offspring of the serpentine giant Typhon and the half-humanoid, half-sea monster Echidna, the mother of all monsters, who gave birth beneath the secret parts of the holy earth, in the cave of Arima. Their progeny grew to be a snake-like, poison-belching, nine-headed dragon. Covered in slime, it excreted a toxic stench. Its lair was in the depths of a dreaded lagoon, now vanished.

This bottomless swamp was professed to be a portal to the subterranean underworld. In Hydra mythology, the monster is eventually destroyed by Hercules, son of Zeus, as the second of his Twelve Labors. His was a daunting task, a heroic one. For every head chopped off with his sword, the Hydra would regrow two heads. Hercules required the assistance of his nephew, Iolaus, who used a fiery torch to burn each neck shut after his uncle beheaded it.

And this is where an ancient myth is aligning with a contemporary happening of deeper and darker forces. Antiquated storytellers spoke of an animating energy that simmered deep inside the Hydra, seen up close through its eyes, the windows to its soul seen only by its victims in their last moments. A manifestation of supernatural evil is unfathomable to modern sensibilities. Yet it is real, it is real because it was foretold in the Book of Revelation, in the prophecy of the Beast, to be brought forth from the depths of the netherworld.

For now, out of the eye of a perfect storm, the Hydra has been resurrected. Brought forth in a three-headed alliance of the most sinister ideologies on the planet, The Marxist PRC, the bloodthirsty Mexican drug cartels, and the most menacing criminal street gang in the world, the Mara Salvatrucha, also known as MS-13. Look deeply into its unnatural eyes and see the soul of this budding three-headed Hydra, animated by the same powers of unspeakable evil, but enhanced with the diabolical powers of a demon unleashed.

PRC espionage agents had, for decades, stolen US thermonuclear technologies, but the PRC has developed its own global positioning warfare capabilities unilaterally, without the aide of stolen Western science to remotely control a surgically-implanted, cyber-controlled, human robot.

The MSS has deployed a cell of highly-trained European, Mexican, and American expatriates to carry out a covert incursion through the southern US border with Mexico, specially trained for their mission of leading groups of these human-computer microchip "robots" or "hu-bots." The chips have been surgically installed

9

at a clandestine laboratory at the remote outskirts of the re-education camps in the far western province of Xinjiang, China.

Their escorts are summoned by the Communist Command Center in Central Beijing, blending in unsuspected with non-local tourist types to rendezvous inside a cleverly disguised structure outside the Forbidden Palace complex. After a cross-country visit to a training site, they will be flown to Buenos Aires to be equipped and outfitted at a remote space satellite compound in the middle of the desert. The hu-bots will be fitted with nondescript civilian backpacks wired with hand-touch detonators that will have enough explosive force to level a half-city block.

The expat operatives, the escorts, will lead cells of hu-bots using migrant caravans of refugees, like a Trojan horse, to link up with a cadre of heavily armed MS 13 in Mexico City, who will escort them to penetrate the U.S. border through cartel-controlled tunnels and bridges, from Eagle Pass to Brownsville, and other border crossings into Texas. A deafening explosion at the Juarez-El Paso border crossing will be used as a diversion. After the breach, the cells will be harbored in roadside motels near the border while the expat escorts procure rental vans for the last leg of the journey to Virginia, U.S.A.

These logistics by land and air will be executed in simultaneous timing with an amphibious assault on the Mariana Islands by a uniquely armed and equipped assault fleet of the People's Liberation Navy (PLAN).

The Chinese government has plotted their strategy for a long time, testing and fine-tuning their deadly scientific methods to the point where their calculations have indicated a high probability of success. But the project has been ramped up when spies deeply embedded in and around Washington D.C. detected the leak of an internal coup, a plot of subterfuge, to obstruct a traitorous cabal's most threatening adversary, the incumbent president of the United States, from winning a second term in office.

And now, for the PRC, the timing is ripe to coincide with the intrigues of a treasonous cabal from within the U.S., aided by and allied with foreign government heads of state, in collusion with them. But their calculations, however advanced, cannot predict from where on earth a formidable resistance would arise to rally against them...from a least likely place.

Mountains In Real Time-
Cheaha State Park

According to a recent United States census, the region is home to approximately 25 million people.

Located on the southernmost tip of the Appalachian mountain chain, the Talladega Mountains contain the Cotton State's highest peaks, as it encompasses parts of Cherokee, Calhoun, Cleburne, Talladega, and Clay counties.

Situated within the mountains is the vast Talladega National Forest (TNF), covering over 612 square miles. The forest is a mix of hardwoods and second-generation growth of pines. The forest was over-harvested for timber before it was purchased by the U.S. Government in the 1930s.

In the heart of the forest is Cheaha State Park, the oldest state park in Alabama. Imagine 2,799 acres of quartzite boulders and ancient wind-warped trees at 2,407 feet above sea level, often above the clouds and some of the most beautiful natural waterfalls and cascades in the Deep South. Virtually every stream flowing from the mountains features cascades and small waterfalls.

A park brochure warns that the hike to the Devil's Den Falls is fairly strenuous, with some inclines in both directions, and one must be aware that the area around the waterfall is extremely dangerous, with slippery rocks and a deep ravine. It warns to exercise caution at all times. A misstep could lead to a perilous dive from the Falls into the deep pool below.

He got to the Devil's Den from the entrance to Cheaha State Park, driving south on the Talladega Scenic Byway for one and a half miles to the intersection with County Road 42 (Cheaha Road). He turned right and traveled three miles to Forest Service Road 646, turned left onto 646, and drove two miles to the Lake Chinnabee Recreation Area. From there, he hiked upstream on the Chinnabee Silent Trail for one-half miles to the waterfall.

But then the loud burst of a nearby H&K MP5S5 submachine gun rudely awakens him from his daydream. He isn't in the cool forest, he is under a broiling sun up near the firing line at the new Diplomatic Security Service (DSS) firearms training range at Blackstone, Virginia, and he is covered with sweat. The head of the paper bottle target would have been severed if not for the steel staple holding it on its wood post. "Man, Tony, you are DAIN-—JER-—RUSS!" bellows Louis. Anthony Lombardozi looks like a human block of granite, as wide as he is tall, the classic five-by-five, with a bald polished pate and menacing Fu Manchu, but harboring a heart of gold. Save for their physical differences, Tony serves as Louis' alter ego.

"Here you go pards," as Tony hands the weapon to Louis. They are sharing the weapon and critiquing each other's targets. It brought back memories of New Agent's Class (NAC) and being critiqued on the firing range. Louis sets his stance, presses the butt of the weapon against the front of his shoulder, aims the front sight at the center of the target, and squeezes. Blurrrrrp! The recoil of the burst causes the muzzle to rise, sending rounds over the top of the target. He steadies himself and squeezes again this time, the rounds tearing a line of holes in the center of the bottle. No matter how much he thought he was ready to handle it, that first burst had startled him, but he calmed himself and delivered the rounds where he wanted them.

Back over his shoulder, Tony yells with delight, "Ledlow, your targets are getting worse by the day, and right now, they're looking like the middle of next week!" He is mimicking their Principle Firearms Instructor (PFI) from NAC 01-12.

Both were trained under PFI Roger Steele, an Iraqi war vet. He had saved not just one, but two of his injured Humvee crew, dragging to safety a soldier with one arm while shooting with his other, then going back for his other buddy. One soldier was cared for at Walter Reed National Military Hospital (where Louis' sister Ginnie is employed as an RN.) Tough, constantly pushing, always increasing the pressure; but he knew what they needed to hold up under extreme duress, and they admired him because of it.

Because of The Twin Towers having collapsed only three weeks prior to his EOD, *The Black Book of Communism: Crimes, Terror, and Repression* had been glossed over in his condensed New Agent's Class of October 1, 2001. The book and its contents of communist atrocities and their methods had been compressed to recommended reading. At 37 years, Louis had pretty much given up on the idea of ever becoming an agent. But then came the phone call on the Friday after 9-11, asking if he could make it to DSS NAC that Monday.

And now he has been called again to respond to Washington on short notice, but on a much bigger scale, and from the looks of things, he is in for the ride of his life.

The President

P resident George Greene cuts an imposing figure; over six feet five, with broad shoulders, a shock of thick white hair reaching down to his collar, and a set of steely blue eyes that can bore a hole right through your skull.

One admirer likened him to one of those spaghetti Western gunfighters squinting under a salty sombrero, chomping on an unlit cigar, and Colt 44 holstered beneath an Aztec-striped shawl.

The president has New York wit and blue-collar grit. He's driven to succeed, with a love of the country, shaped in old-school ethics, a product of the great American preachers with high personal expectations, demanding excellence from everyone else to a fault.

He is always impatient, doing everything in a "New York minute." But New York is also known to breed its share of extraordinary courage, like the police officers and firefighters on the morning of 9-11, hurrying up the stairwells while others were hurrying down.

A military bearing, respect for soldiers, an inner desire to honor, realizing that this country was built on the backs of well-mannered God-fearing immigrants, a time when men were men and women were women. Courageous and hopeful, they sought the opportunity for a new life in the New World. Many would be treated unfairly because they were different or didn't speak the king's English. But they were willing to work, willing to earn.

Looking out the window of his private suite on the Hudson, he sees their dreams reflected in the Statue of Liberty, Lady Liberty, the Roman goddess Libertas, who salutes their arrival with a torch in flame for freedom, freedom from tyranny and oppression.

He is bold and brash and unlike his predecessors in the Freedom Party, he doesn't just stand there and take their insults and public put-downs just to get along. He represents the American people, and an affront to him is an affront to them. So for the past three years, he's fought back, and they love him for it. Where he gets his energy and stamina remains a mystery.

But the opposing Labor Reform party and their friends in the media are out to get him.

The president can't trust the government in Washington that he was elected to lead. They hate him because he is an outsider, and he is for the free-born commoner, the everyday working citizens, who with their blood and sweat, have made this country great. He is trying to change things for them, and the Washington establishment types, the globalists who have sold the country out for self-enrichment at the expense of this generation of ordinary Americans, are feeling threatened.

Corporate giants, in cahoots with the globalists, have been given sweetheart tax and tariff deals that have monopolized the vital domestic blue-collar trades, skilled labor jobs, and opportunities. Plumbers, carpenters, electricians, and grocers, American occupations that men and women have raised families on. And this has happened over time in an inexorable, yet sinister way, all done in the shadows, in the dark shadows of corporate lobbyists.

Corrupt congressmen on both sides of the aisle had reached their palms out to be greased by the mega-monied donor establishment, with exorbitant cash-rich fundraisers, lucrative post-service retirement jobs, and sweetheart real estate gifts; all that money to buy the influence of a representative of the people who is supposed to have their best interests in mind, being influenced and enticed to use taxpayers money on whatever the mega donor's self-interest is, whether it's banking policy or overseas manufacturing of pharmaceuticals or basketball sneakers. One of the most corrupt examples, all of it carried out in the dark and unseen by the American public, was the repeal of the bill that kept taxpayers indemnified against bailouts of recklessly greedy investment banks.

The people in this president's corner are willing to pay their fair share of taxes for domestic security, a free market, and a level playing field for personal opportunity. But they abhor the thought that their representatives in Washington are enriching themselves at their expense, using their hard-earned tax dollars to fuel the global corporations with more millions, working against them to cause the erosion of their natural inalienable rights to liberty, pride in ownership of property, and a happy life... by selling them out.

This president is fighting for the American people against this onerous downward pressure that seeks to crush their spirit, to dictate how, when, and where they should worship, and how they should live their lives. The condescending mainstream media call the people names, "Billie Jeans and Jim Bobs from Jerkwater, USA" or "The Hayseeds from Hicksville." Those are the media's thinly disguised code words for *bigot*. But the president understands, as nobody else does, that these are the people descended from names on weathered tombstones who died and bled for this country and gave their lives so that strangers of foreign lands would be freed; for it is these people, the country types, who, in 1775, led the resistance against British tyranny; for it is they who do most of the working in this country, most of the building, the farming, and the fighting...and the dying, to keep this country free. For these people, in essence, are the true patriots of America.

But now he's wondering, how many are really out there in this great land we call America? Are there enough of them? If he can count on only a third of them, one bricklayer out of three, one bookkeeper out of three, one doctor out of three, one young patriot out of three, that should be enough, that should be enough to preserve freedom, a freedom that has never come free; always pain and suffering and personal sacrifice to preserve it, always at a heavy cost, and he wants the privilege to continue to serve them, not to lord over them.

And those that hate him and the people who support him have weaponized the US government in an insidious plot to remove him, to destroy his presidency and his bid for a second term.

Greene's Geeks

H is election had been like no other, a grassroots phenomenon, literally. His town hall rallies were staged on the grass, in any suitable farmer's fields that would have him and the people that flocked to see him. His podium was erected under a tent canopy next to a huge drive-in movie screen. His live image was projected on the screen while the audio set-up was supervised by a brilliant young techie campaign staffer, who rigged speakers through tree-tops, and somehow streamed in the video to attendees' smart-phones. The techie is assisted by a group of friends that wear red t-shirts with white lettering, spelled out across the top, front, and back: "GREENE'S GEEKS." It's their ungeek-like motto embla-zoned in white script in the center of their shirts, front, and back, that if you can read Latin, makes you think that maybe these nerds really *do* mean business: "*Victorus aut Mortis,*" in translation: "Victory or Death."

As news of these events swept over the land, one of the biggest attractions was the idea, by the same techie, to have an audience participation feature wherein before the introductions, an outline of The Declaration of Independence is splashed on the big silver screen. Those in attendance, from their blankets or lawn chairs, excitedly tap their smartphones to connect electronically as poten-tial under signers. After a period of tense anticipation, the names of the selected winners flash up on the big screen to be ensconced in eighteenth-century John Hancockian script under the names of Ben Franklin and the original signers. Whenever a new name appears on the screen below the immortal words: *"When, in the course of human events, it becomes necessary for one people to dissolve the political bands which have connected them with another...We hold these truths to be self-evident, that all men are created equal, that they are endowed by their Creator with certain unalienable rights... That, to secure these rights, governments are instituted among men, deriving their just powers from the consent of the governed... That, whenever any form of government becomes destructive of these ends, it is the right of the people to alter or to abolish it, and to institute new government... And for the support of this declaration, with a firm reliance on the protection of Divine Providence, we mutually pledge to each other our lives, our fortunes, and our sacred honor. ".*..Under the last, but not least, signer's name, Charles Carroll, the only Catholic signer of the Declaration, flashes: *Makayla Kaminski*–as loud cheers reverberate over the hills and dales of the countryside.

With the aid of clever ads on social media, the pastoral and peaceful festivities become the place to be to have fun and support their candidate at a big-scale drug and alcohol-free picnic down on the farm.

Keeping Secrets

T he door to the 11th-floor Executive Director's conference
room was momentarily left open as Executive Deputy Director
(EDD) Arthur Jones fast-stepped through past her desk; she heard
"then we'll go to plan B" as the door closed behind Jones. Over the
past month, these meetings with Executive Director (ED) Arnold
had become more frequent, and more guarded. Alice Brady was
within a few weeks of celebrating her 35th anniversary with the
Bureau of Federal Investigation (BFI). Arnold has been the latest
in a line of six EDs, formerly called Directors, she has served
under. And she had never seen anything like this. Day by day, she
has developed a feeling of unease. She isn't a particularly political
person, and never has been. But something was wrong as there
were constant communications with foreign intelligence agencies.

She has always taken pride in her position with the BFI. It
never ceased to amaze her of the daily–weekly accomplishments
of the field offices that came across her computer, most of them
never getting any public attention.

Spread across the country, the field offices and smaller satellite
offices is where the street agents plied their trade. Going back as
far as 1993, pre 9-11, the Bureau had thwarted and dismantled a
series of potentially catastrophic terror attempts.

It was the New York field office where Tucker Hallstrom, the
Assistant Director (AD), called the in-the-nick-of-time raid on
the hidden Al-Qaeda cell, crashing through the backroom door
to discover a bomb being cooked like "a witches brew." That raid
was carried out by everyday street agents, who, after a long day

stepping through the minefields, just wanted to get home safely to their wives and families. They were recruited from the best and the brightest in America, and most were not ambitious, climb-the-ladder types, happy enough to make cases on behalf of the good, God-fearing citizens in their communities. Since 9-11, the day former Director Bud Webster stood frozen at the doorway of the twenty-four-hour SIOC command center like a deer caught in the headlights, watching the Twin Towers collapse, they had been under increasing pressure to keep America safe. Like a hockey goalie in overtime, they could not allow even one puck to get past their pads into the net.

Since the official bifurcation that split the Bureau into two mission components, one foreign and the other domestic, Alice has noticed a change, a gradual one that has turned the Bureau on a political course, that she had never thought possible. And the likes of AD Hallstrom had become a dying breed from a lineage of professionals that harkened back to the halcyon days of the Bureau, back to the days of the G-men, back to the days when they covered their heads with fedoras and signed their work with... the Tommy Gun.

And from the bits and pieces she's been putting together, the Washington field office isn't in the plans, but foreign governments *are* in the plans.

Phil Maddox, the AD of the Washington field office has just stormed out of the conference room, not even bothering to say hello to Alice; very unusual, as Maddox was normally cordial to her.

In the corner of the spacious blue carpeted room across from Arnold's desk is a medium-sized combination safe, typical government issue, not much bigger than myriad government safes in myriad government offices across the country. Arnold has lately been spending an unusual amount of time with his door closed and increasingly more trips to the safe. The inside of the safe is divided, containing a compartment for personnel files and miscellaneous emergency materials. Another compartment holds a pile of current White Papers.

She has the combination access to his safe and frequently puts in sensitive files and retrieves items at Arnold's request. Late in the day, with Arnold and his aides out of the office at a meeting at the Australian Embassy, she gets up from her desk and enters the interior office of the ED. She approaches the safe, dials the combination to release the tumblers, and opens it. Inside, lying on top of other documents in one of the compartments is an unmarked manila envelope. She slides out the papers within, and the first one is a three-page memo stamped in red ink at the top and bottom of each page: TOP SECRET//REL TO USA, AUS, CAN, GBR, NZL, NATO. She briefly glances at the contents, seeing the word SHADE appearing a number of times within the bullet-headed paragraphs. She comprehends enough of the contents to instinctively know that this document confirms her suspicions of an international plot to remove the president from the White House, from his elected position of commander in chief. She quickly takes the memo to the copy machine near her desk and makes two copies. She removes the original and copies from the machine. She glances at the doorway before briskly walking back to the interior room. She slides the original back inside the envelope, puts it inside the safe, closes the hatch, and spins the dial.

Her friend Leslie Banks is working on the sixth floor below as executive secretary for the AD in the finance division. She will confide in her. Years ago, they had entered on duty only a few months apart from each other. They regularly spend their family vacations together each summer in Ocean City, Maryland.

"Hello, Leslie, can we get together for lunch today? Is one o'clock good for you? Wanna try the Pavilion? I'll meet you outside in front on Pennsylvania."

The BFI building, called "The Biff" by its government occupants, is a modern behemoth, spanning a full Capital city block at 10th and Pennsylvania Avenue. The buff-colored, two-wing, eleven-story superstructure is built in the pre-cast Brutalist architectural style of the mid-20th century. Consisting of exposed concrete, its facade is crumbling, which has exposed ugly rusting iron rods clearly visible to the public. Alice pushes her way through the metal turnstile and onto the sidewalk of Pennsylvania Avenue. She waits for Leslie under the shaded trees near the corner. Bright pink summer flowers fill large cement planters along the sidewalk. Looking across the street, the Main Justice Building reminds her of her happy youth and the days of Camelot. Back then, the gray stone building with high corner pillars housed the sixty-fourth attorney general of the United States, the little brother of the president, Robert Francis Kennedy.

They cross Pennsylvania, "America's Main Street," and walk a couple of blocks to The Old Post Office with its 315-foot-high clock tower. They order sandwiches from the Georgetown Deli and sit at a table under the sky-high glass ceiling of the Atrium.

"Leslie, I haven't been able to sleep lately, I think the 11th floor is running a hush-hush investigation on the president," said Alice. "What?" replied Leslie. "Do you mean that they're targeting the president without his knowledge?" she asked.

"I'm pretty sure that's what's going on," said Alice. As long as I've been around, if there was ever any serious trouble involving a threat to the White House, the president's chief of staff is the first to know," said Alice.

"I've never known you to be anything but level-headed, Alice, what are you going to do?" queried Leslie.

"Hey, I've kept in touch with Betsy Palmer, she's been promoted to a manager position at the executive office building. She runs the office over there for the chief aide to the vice president," Leslie said.

"Do you think she could get me an appointment?" inquired Alice hopefully.

"Let me give her a call this afternoon, if your information isn't urgent, I don't know what is," Leslie mused. "Weren't we sworn to something like living up to the sacred trust placed in us by the American people? I think the American people trusted in this president, and that's why they elected him, to give him a chance to do what he said he was going to do," laments Leslie.

"One last thing, would you mind coming with me, at least for the introductions, for moral support, I'd appreciate it."

"Of course, what are friends for?"

Appointment Back to the Future

Alice Brady has been granted an afternoon appointment at the Eisenhower Executive Office Building (EEOB), with the top aide to Vice President Levi Turner.

But first, Alice Brady decides that she needs to consult with God. Before heading off on her risky mission, Alice wants to spend some time before the Blessed Sacrament.

From the BFI Building, Saint Patrick's Church is a short two-block walk north along 10th Street. The church represents the oldest parish in the federal city of Washington D.C. Alice frequently attends daily noon Mass here. On this afternoon, with several city blocks to cover, she has worn her casual soft-soled shoes. Toting a nut-brown shoulder bag, she walks north on 10th, and between E and F, she glances at the gray arched-brick facade of Ford's Theater to her right, and to the left, the Petersen House across the street. In front of the theatre, a long line of high school-age students occupy the sidewalk, waiting on a public tour, laughing and chatting; some wear wireless earbuds, some unconsciously bobbing their heads to the music.

The clock turns back to Good Friday evening, April 14, 1865. A man heralded as "the Actor of the Century" waits in the shadows of the upper mezzanine. A one-shot walnut-gripped derringer pistol is concealed under his cape. On this misty night, The president is late. In the glow of the gas-lit street lamps, the open barouche horse-drawn carriage is reined up in front of the imposing three-story playhouse. The president, in a black long-tailed frock coat, stove-pipe hat in hand, extends his other hand to assist the first lady as she steps down from the buggy step onto the wood-board sidewalk. A playbill featuring "Our American Cousin" is posted in a showcase on the wall outside the entrance way. The president and first lady wait for their happily-engaged guests to alight, and together the four enter the lobby. Through the interior swinging doors, they hear the murmur from the packed audience as lines from the play are bellowed on stage. The audience and band are waiting for them, and the play is momentarily put on hold as the musical tune "Hail to the Chief" is played, accompanied by a standing ovation. The president raises his hat in gratitude. The party makes their way to their seats, house right, above the stage. The play resumes as they reach the patriotic banner-draped presidential box. He settles into his crimson-padded rocking chair and relaxes, becoming absorbed in the performance below. Looking up at the box, the audience sees the large engraved portrait of George Washington, but the president is concealed in the corner behind the edge of a flag. Laughter fills the theatre, and then a muffled bang, a blue haze is wafting from the presidential box.

Alice continues one block north to the gothic-styled church. Above the sandstone-arched entrance, a striking halo of stained glass is set between two rising turrets of hewn granite blocks. She eases into a pew next to the side altar of Saint Patrick, his image in white alabaster, chiseled with the bishop's miter and Gaelic staff. On her knees, she begs the Lord and her guardian angel to watch over her.

She makes the sign of the cross, genuflecting toward the main altar, a gold-encased tabernacle, a glittering candle there keeping vigil. On her way out, she looks up above to an assembly of lofty gold-brass organ pipes, the sun is splashing through the halo of stained glass, creating a divine spectrum of brilliant colors. She takes this as a sign, a reassuring one.

Descending the steps of centuries-worn stone, she stops on the sidewalk to say hello to a friend preparing to make a visit. Above them, looking out from the narrow stained-glass window of the north side turret, can be seen the home of Saint Patrick's former parishioner, Mary Elizabeth Jenkins Surratt.

Built in 1843, the three-and-one-half-stories-tall structure at 604 H Street NW is still there, presently occupied by The Wok and Roll Chinese Restaurant. In the spring of 1865, it served as Mary Surratt's boarding house where she hosted a band of local Confederate sympathizers. During the same night, as the chaos raged at Ford's Theatre, it was the return to the house of one of those sympathizers-turned-conspirator that sealed Mary's fate.

On the mid-summer day of July 7th, 1865, the thermometer will reach one hundred degrees. After comforting her in her stifling solitary prison cell, Father Jacob Walter, pastor of Saint Patrick's Church, faithfully climbs the thirteen steps of the gallows and stands on the platform beside his parishioner, Mary Surratt. She and three other conspirators have been sentenced to death-by-hanging in the courtyard of the Old Washington Penitentiary. Seated in an armchair as a gesture of sympathy, she's dressed in a black full-length dress and is protected from the glaring sun by an umbrella held by Saint Patrick's associate vicar. Four wooden U.S. Navy equipment boxes serving as coffins lay on the ground in a tangled patch of grass next to the scaffold. A general in uniform and dress sword reads aloud the Order of Execution. Father Walter doesn't seem to notice, he continues reading from his Book of Prayers, and solemnly administers the sacrament of extreme unction, preparing Mary for eternity. She is assisted to her feet, and nearly fainting, shuffles forward onto the trap door. Her arms, knees, and ankles are bound with tent fabric, and a white hood is placed over her head. An eight-coiled noose wound from Boston hemp is fitted around her neck and pulled snug. The crowd of onlooking spectators holds their breath. A nod from the Hangman and the trap door is sprung...

Alice users her phone to call Leslie, telling her that she'll meet her at the corner of Pennsylvania and Tenth.

Alice crosses the street and backtracks south along a stretch of glass-faced government buildings toward Pennsylvania Avenue. A stream of business-minded people in casual attire, carrying chic-colored handbags and briefcases, pass her by going in the other direction, eyes fixed to their front, in a hurry to get somewhere. Halfway to Pennsylvania, across from Ford's Theatre, stands the red-brick two-story Petersen House. Inside in a rear bedroom, the victim of the assassin's brashness laid prone on a bed far too short for his stature. At 7:22 a.m., on the Holy Saturday morning of April 15th, 1865, the 16th president of the United States is dead, passing on, belonging to the ages.

John Wilkes Booth, the assassin, will be buried secretly in the ground of the Old Penitentiary near the temporary grave of Mary Surratt. To this day, the ghost of Mary Surratt, wearing the same black dress she wore on the day of her execution, haunts her old boarding house. Passersby tell of hearing gentle sobbing from an open upstairs window, the eternal effects of her unjust conviction of guilt by association.

Hotel of the Famous

Leslie is waiting for her on the corner. On their walk to the EEOB, they cross 14th Street. On their right is erected the majestic and historic Willard's Hotel. By March 1864, the war had turned in favor for the Union. The very best hostelry in Washington, Willard's Lobby, was the foremost place to be to read the news hot off the presses and debate the latest turn-of-events. People were anticipating the arrival of the most celebrated general of the day. Traveling to the nation's capital from his wartime headquarters in the Western Theater is the president's favorite fighting general. He has gained his famous nickname in February 1862, after refusing the silly white-flagged demands of a defeated Confederate general at Fort Donelson, Tennessee. Since April 1861, this Union victory had been a bright spot amongst a miserable number of devastating defeats. He was about to be promoted to the rank of Lieutenant General to command the full array of Federal armies, east and west.

But on this night, he was being his ordinary-looking self. Chomping on a half-chewed cigar, wearing a faded ill-fitting dust-covered uniform, he made a scruffy impression, much like hundreds of other battle-worn generals who had patronized Willard's in the last three years. An onlooker might think, by the looks of him, that he might be a man who liked his drink. He wasn't recognized by the desk clerk as he stood at the counter with his young son at his side. The desk clerk casually offers him a room on the top floor, which he accepts. The clerk flippantly spins the register toward him, and then he signs the register, "U.S. Grant & Son–Galena, Illinois," as in "Unconditional Surrender" Grant, as in, Ulysses Simpson Grant, as in, the Victor of Vicksburg, as in the man who has saved the presidency of Abraham Lincoln.

But in 1864, in the American South, within the Confederate States of America, things were much different.

The outbreak of the American Civil War had come unwanted to Southern Appalachia, causing division and turmoil as fighting between North and South crisscrossed the region. Up to this time, each state was treated as a sovereign country on its own, having to equip, arm, and supply its state military force out of their own coffers.

In Southern Appalachia, sentiment for the Union remained strong, a hindrance to the Confederate's struggle for independence. However, many of these Unionists, especially in the mountain areas of North Carolina, Georgia, and Alabama, were "stipulating" Unionists, and though they opposed secession, they balked at going to war to save the Union. So when their respective state legislatures voted to secede, their allegiance switched to the Confederacy. Both Union and Confederate sympathizers engaged in guerrilla tactics that left people of the region even more fearful and mistrusting of the federal government in the years to come.

Big battles were fought involving tens of thousands of soldiers in the region, with horrific numbers being killed, wounded, or maimed for life.

Southern valor was no better exemplified than in the actions of a barefoot Alabama drummer boy at the battle of Franklin Tennessee during the late autumn afternoon of November 30, 1864. Many of the Rebel drummer boys were just that, mere boys. At Franklin, the Yankee Army of the Ohio under General J. Schofield had dug in with the winding Harpeth River to their backs. In one of those military incidents that defies belief, during the previous night, at the small southern town of Springhill, just twelve and a half miles south of Franklin, under cover of darkness, the whole Yankee army was able to sneak away from under the noses of a Rebel army that, for the most part, had them completely surrounded.

But not completely. Due to some misunderstanding of orders delivered around midnight, the Rebels had not closed the ring. The Columbia Pike, the main south-to-north road leading into the town of Franklin, had been left open, allowing over 20,000 blue-clad infantry and artillery to escape up the pike into Franklin.

The commanding general of the famed Army of Tennessee, the one-legged, one usable-armed invalid John Bell Hood, who had to be assisted and strapped into his saddle, had gone to bed that night after painfully spending most of the day lashed to his horse. He went to sleep believing that he had the Yankees trapped and ready to be crushed come morning. After the incident, Yankee foot soldiers told how they could see and hear, as they quietly tramped by, the nearby glow of Rebel campfires and the distinctive Southern accents of Rebel chatter as they cooked their bacon and played cards. The Gallant Hood, a Kentuckian by birth, one of the South's most venerated battlefield generals and former commander of the legendary Texas Brigade, had recovered from two debilitating battle wounds and was placed in command of the Western Army by President Jefferson Davis, with a desperate hope that Hood could reverse a series of military defeats and retreats in the face of the enemy.

The next morning after discovering that the Yankees had gotten away, Hood became enraged. In a wicked mood, he ordered a series of brigade-after-brigade frontal assaults against a well-entrenched enemy. The Yankees had the Confederate's approaches on the battlefield covered by the cannons of their accurate artillery battalions. Their breastworks were manned with hardened veteran infantry, their officers bravely standing on the parapets, yelling out orders to hold their fire until the Rebels came within musket range.

The "new" rifled musket of the Civil War had an effective killing range of 300 yards. In the hands of a battle line of veteran infantry firing together on command, it delivered a devastating hail storm of lead bullets toward the oncoming enemy, leaving, after the smoke cleared, a line of corpses on the ground in piteous single-rank formation, who moments before, had been some dear one's father, husband, brother, or fiancé.

The Rebels deployed their lines in an old cotton field where the soldiers could see across the open plain what they were facing, a fearsome mile-long line of glistening bayonets and musket barrels. By this time in the war, the thoughts of chivalric glory and romance had long passed. Many of their brothers, cousins, and friends lay buried under Southern sod. Under a gray late autumn sky, with their regimental bands, and one Alabama drummer boy, in particular, playing Dixie and the Bonnie Blue Flag, the butternut and gray soldiers stepped off in line, shoulder to shoulder, to meet the Yankees.

No Place For Children

It was nothing short of a slaughter. Six Confederate general officers were killed or mortally wounded, four of them being laid out afterward on the high pillared porch of the nearby Carnton Mansion. One of the generals killed near a landmark cotton gin at the Yankee battle line was Patrick Ronayne Cleburne, an Irish immigrant who was adored by his men. Cleburne led from the front, and it cost him his life, shot through the heart. A year later, at Appomattox Court House, it was for officers like Cleburne, who, only a short while before, had been trying to kill them, and they were trying to kill him, who received, from their Yankee conquerors, a solemn military salute of respect for their gallantry. These vanquished men in gray, considered by their counterparts in blue as, "good men in a bad cause."

Cleburne was the highest-ranking Confederate to advocate offering the slaves their freedom if they would take up arms to repel the invader. But his proposal had fallen on deaf ears until it was too late.

Besides the dead generals, there was that brave child musician, who while playing his drum amidst shrieks and cries and men falling all around him, had somehow made it up to the Yankee breastworks unscathed. He was sheltered up against the Rebel's side of the wall, where, from an embrasure, a Yankee cannon was firing uncontested through the acrid blinding smoke. With an impulsive idea that could only be devised from youthful invincibility, he picked up a piece of wooden rail laying there and ran to the cannon with the intention of disabling it by shoving the rail down the cannon barrel. But just as he shoved the rail down the barrel, the muzzle exploded. A few Rebel veterans hunkering nearby had been watching the boy's heroics with awe, and then horror, a shower of pink mist...an onlooking veteran bowing his head while making the sign of the cross.

Such were the terrible names of Chickamauga, Resaca, and Franklin, which became unspoken in the homes of the slain on both sides. And on the flip-side, far from home, a feeling of abandonment was experienced by tens of thousands of Union soldiers held as prisoners of war at a desolate depot on the Southwestern Railroad in Georgia called Andersonville. Amidst extreme suffering caused by the absence of sanitation, exposure to a broiling summer sun and a starvation diet caused by the circumstances of a war-strangled South, hundreds of prisoners would die each day within that swampy stockade of suffering. But even amidst this sea of misery, men of the cloth would answer their calling in disregard for their own health and safety. One priest, in particular, was a sixty-two-year-old Johnny Reb Jesuit from Savannah, named Peter Whelan. Day after day, pestered by swarms of flies and mosquitos, the elderly Confederate chaplain stood under his battered black umbrella to patiently administer the holy sacraments to the enemy, the Billy Yanks, the dying soldiers, his children.

Perhaps Father Whelan was called to follow in the footsteps of his saintly Jesuit namesake, Peter Claver, who, over two hundred years before, had administered the salvific sacraments to hundreds of thousands of ill-treated African slaves disembarking from the dehumanizing conditions of the slave ships to South America.

The destruction and desolation brought about by the Civil War, forever imprinting the region in blood and in the history books, affected not only home and hearth, but worse, it dispirited the populace in that poverty-stricken land that is Southern

Appalachia. But resolutely, they carried on in their meager existence, not having much choice in the matter.

Next Door to the
White House

N earing the White House, the women cross 15th Street, and the deep lush green of the South Lawn comes into view.

"It seems like yesterday that I took my niece to the Easter egg roll. First Lady Nancy Reagan was beaming, so thrilled to see the children scooping with their spoons and scurrying after those colored eggs. Such happy sounds, hearing those tiny voices filled with excitement," said Leslie.

"My niece was able to keep the wooden egg, she keeps it on her bedroom dresser. It has the signatures of famous Americans on it."

"Oh, yes, I saw the news clip from this past spring's Easter egg roll. Eva Greene, the first lady hostess, had the pastel-colored eggs imprinted with a sketch of the White House building on one side and the Seal of The President of the United States on the other; unique, I thought."

"She always makes such a pretty impression. She just glowed in that pastel pink Easter dress, standing on the balcony alongside her husband with the Easter bunny with those big eyeglasses, what a hoot!" said Alice.

"I'm sure you agree, the first lady has a lot more about her than the way the media portrays her. They can be so cruel. I think her National Secondary Language Program for American teens is a great idea, especially the way she wants it to be initiated, with a basic lesson in civics. Teaching the kids democracy and civic responsibility through an understanding of the Constitution-I think we need to get back to that," opines Leslie.

They stroll along the ellipse to 17th Street and turn north for a block and approach the security booth that serves as a visitors' checkpoint. The old War Department Building, taking 17 years to build, the somber gray enormity of it, gives the impression of a haunted mansion on steroids. At the booth, they give their names and appointment time with Dean Morrison, special advisor to Vice President Levi Turner. They're told to wait for an escort. In short order, a slender-uniformed Secret Service officer approaches. In black police-style peaked cap and white shirt and necktie, gold shield pinned at his left breast, he whispers into his radio receiver clipped to his shoulder tab as he greets them. He asks that they follow him down a tree-lined path lined by a black clover-tipped rod-iron railing.

The women are escorted through an interior security check-point consisting of a series of metal detectors and uniformed officers with wands. Passing through security, they enter the interior courtyard where they are greeted by a young man in a dark blue business suit. He greets them and introduces himself as Neil Donnelly, aide to Vice President Turner for Public Affairs. He takes them through the courtyard, past a bronze bust of Christopher Columbus perched atop a white marble pedestal. At a bank of elevators, they allow two men and a woman to get off, carrying white binders, serious looks on their faces, engaged in a quiet argument, ignoring them. The elevator doors open on the fourth floor where they get out and approach a set of glass doors with chrome handles stenciled with the patriotic bald eagle and stars and striped Seal of the Vice President of the United States.

Waiting inside the lobby for them is Chief of Staff Dean Morrison, who greets them warmly. He escorts them along a hallway to his executive office. Inside an inner office, a smartly dressed female aide offers a friendly hello. They walk into his main office space. The room is expansive with a set of cushion furniture off to the side of his large dark walnut desk.

At this point, Leslie excuses herself. "Thanks so much Leslie, I'll call you tonight." He offers Alice a seat in a plush black leather armchair off to the side of his desk.

Morrison seats himself across from her on a small burgundy sofa. Alice tries to conceal her nervousness.

"Mrs. Brady, I want to…" he begins.

"Please, call me Alice," she implores politely.

"Of course, Alice, the vice president has told me to extend his personal gratitude to you for coming in," said Morrison.

She places her hand bag on her lap and removes a white business-sized envelope. She stands and hands the envelope to Morrison, who takes it and places it on the glass coffee table between them.

"Thank you Alice, if I may allay your concerns. From what you told my aide on the telephone a couple of days ago, our legal team has studied and researched this matter intensely. There's a consensus here that you have acted in good faith within the guidelines of the Federal Whistleblowers Protection Act. I'm going to give you my direct cellphone number, and please feel free to contact me at any time," he assures her.

Presidents and Similarities

On her way home to the metro station, she re-crosses the south face of the White House on the ellipse. She ponders the U.S. presidents of the past. From what the nuns at Saint Lucy's had taught her, were any of them like the current president? How would any of them have acted under these trying circumstances? Or was President George Greene ordained precisely to fit this unique time in history?

She immediately envisions one American president of the past, in particular, who possessed a similar personal combativeness to respond to the calamitous challenges of his era. One president whose deeds affected the Southern Appalachian region during the forging of the United States was Andrew Jackson.

Over two centuries ago, Andrew Jackson had faced off with Charles Dickinson, known to be the best pistol shot in all of Tennessee. The two of them squared off over a disputed bet on a horse race. Jackson, counting on having a few lives left, followed the advice of his friend and dual mate and deliberately allowed Dickinson to fire first, hoping that in haste, he would miss his mark. But Dickinson fired on target, the pistol ball smashing into Jackson's chest. But the ball, aimed at Jackson's heart, glanced off a brass coat button and lodged in his ribs, inches from his heart. Jackson, somehow remaining on his feet, stuffed a handkerchief into the bloody hole in his chest and took aim at Dickinson, who, according to the rules of dueling, had to stand in place while

Jackson aimed the pistol at him. Jackson pulled the trigger, but the hammer only clicked halfway. The half-cock didn't qualify as a misfire, which would have ended the dual then and there. Jackson was able to re-cock the hammer and took aim again, this time the pistol fired, hitting Dickinson in the stomach. Dickinson suffered in agony until he succumbed that same night. Too close to his heart to risk an operation, Jackson carried the lead ball in his chest for the rest of his life.

Cabinet of State

President Greene has to find a reliable and loyal government front-line agent. At a campaign fundraiser, he has reunited with a close friend and classmate from their boyhood days at a New England military academy, who has a son in the DSS. The agent, Louis Ledlow, will report directly to the president's Cabinet member, Secretary of State Rueben "Bear" Berenger.

Berenger earned his nickname growing up in the Yukon. He was known for his even temperament, always grouchy.

It was in the middle of a workout in the gym in Blackstone when Louis received the telephone call from an aide at the State Department. He was ordered to report in person to the secretary of state's office in Washington at 10:00 a.m. this Friday; that's only two days from now. He is not provided with any details, only that his travel and accommodations have been cleared with his superiors at DSS.

It's been quite a while, Louis hasn't been inside the Harry S. Truman building in Northwest D.C. since he took a tour with the rest of his class during their final week at the Academy.

Louis is escorted through the hallways and up an elevator to the fifth floor, where the doors open to a great hall with a high-arched ceiling and a glassy two-toned marble floor. He's directed toward the end of the hall, where two large fluted pillars frame an opening to an interior room. He's thinking that this is more like a museum, *not quite like my little cubicle back at the office*, as he walks between two stone-carved female statues of antiquity, posing on each side of the wall. Above the stone-framed entrance, a colorful mural depicts a shirtless male figure on the ground, grasping at the feet of a black-robed justice, whose outstretched arm and open palm gestures to hold back a mob of angry vigilantes. A tracking dog strains on a leash while another with a bandana over his face defiantly postures with a bullwhip. Walking through the entrance, he enters the outer office of the secretary of state. A conservatively dressed woman seated at a stylish credenza stops tapping her keyboard and looks up from her computer screen to say, "Hello, Agent Ledlow, the secretary is expecting you, walk right in," she tells him.

Berenger is seated at a wide Windsor desk, reading through three pages of the latest Intel cables from the Agency. An aide excuses himself and nods to Louis as he leaves the room.

Berenger walks around the desk to shake Louis' hand. "Glad to make your acquaintance, Agent Ledlow. Please, have a seat," as the secretary points to a group of leather armchairs set around a round coffee table off to the side. Designed within the glass surface of the table, signifying the Department's custodianship, is the spread eagle with the chest shield motif of the Great Seal of the United States.

Louis sits down in a black leather arm chair. "Thank you, Mr. Secretary, glad to meet you."

"I want you to relax, I know this may seem overwhelming right now, but believe me, these last couple of weeks have been overwhelming for many of us around here," said the secretary.

"Some irregularities have developed concerning the reliability of government agencies that would normally be addressing this matter."

"From the looks of things, from the latest Intelligence reports, we've got a major national security threat brewing on our Southern border. Since last month, an Agency case officer in Mexico City has been reporting that his assets down there have overheard a strange exchange of chatter between Chinese Nationals and one or more of the drug cartels to include MS-13. Piecing things together, there are the makings of some kind of incursion at the Texas border, along the river. MS-13 has stood alone as a national priority for a while now, but this link to the PRC is alarming, something we need to get a handle on sooner than later."

"You'll be reporting to me directly through my chief aide, Matthew Rieger; he's already been briefed, knows to get a hold of me immediately, wherever, whenever."

"First thing I'd like you to do is reach out to the local county sheriffs with jurisdiction over the main international bridges on the Rio."

And, by the way, the president wants to meet you in person.

Berenger said, "Don't be nervous, the president enjoys sports, tell him about your football experiences. That'd be a good way to break the ice."

"Oh, I almost forgot, your partner, Agent Lombardozzi, he's good to go, I'll leave it up to you to give him the good news."

Interview at 1600 Pennsylvania

The interview would take place in the Oval Office of the White House. In his wildest dreams, Louis could never have imagined being interviewed by *The Man* sitting behind the one and only of its kind, a unique American legacy, hewn of nautical oak timbers, the Resolute desk.

Louis had been a walk-on safety at the University of North Alabama and was making his way up the depth chart before a serious knee injury canceled his dream to suit up on college football Saturdays. He ended up graduating with a bachelor's degree in economics with a minor in marketing. And so, he learned that the president had been watching, along with millions of other television viewers, the Los Angeles Raiders football game in 1991, when the legendary Alabamian Bo Jackson was dragged down on the field in what appeared to television viewers to be nothing serious, certainly not a career-ending catastrophic hip injury. Bo had been the top high school running back in his day.

At the time, the Head Coach at the University of Alabama was a big and burly salty-demeanor coach who wore a houndstooth hat, one Paul "Bear" Bryant. Bryant sent one of his assistant coaches on a recruiting trip to the two-bedroom house in Bessemer, Alabama, where Bo lived. The home was a little crowded, what with Bo's nine brothers and sisters living there with him and his parents. Bo got his nickname from his brothers, who shortened the word *Boar*, as in, wild boar. If you ever watched Bo play baseball, you could see how fitting was that nickname. If not hitting the ball out of sight over the fence, he could strike out after swinging wildly, and then, to the astonishment of everyone watching, break the wooden baseball bat over his knee as if it was nothing but a big toothpick.

The assistant coach offered Bo a scholarship, but he couldn't promise Bo that he'd be in the starting line-up his freshman year. So Bo, stammering and stuttering, did his best to tell the assistant to tell the most famous coach in America–thank you very much, that he'd "think about it."

So Jackson accepted a scholarship to that other school in the state, the Tigers of Auburn. He would eventually overcome his speech impediment, but for now, he would let his God-given athleticism do the talking. In 1982, with under two minutes to play in the annual intrastate grudge match called the Iron Bowl, from near the five-yard line, Bo took the hand-off, and like a rocket, blasted up and over the Alabama defense, securing the win over the number one ranked team in the country, and a long awaited victory over their bitter rival.

"Yes, Bo played baseball too, I remember watching him literally run up an outfield wall to make a catch, defying gravity, something I'll never forget," the president had remarked (Vincent Edward "Bo" Jackson became the only athlete to be named to both the Major League All-Star game and the NFL Pro Bowl).

The interview with the president, more of a feeling out and evaluation of Louis' poise and trustworthiness, had gone well. He's not sure if he had said anything much more than a bunch of "Yes, sir" and "Yes, Mr. President."

As he leaves the White House, Louis believes that he has a lot in common with the president, especially a deep-seated grit and unshakable esteem for their country.

Louis did not fail to notice during the point in the interview when the president mentioned that Louis may be asked to perform a critical service for his country. The president swiveled in his chair, seeming to look out the window. Louis noticed, however, that the president wasn't distractedly looking out the window, but instead, his gaze was transfixed on the object next to the window, the Stars and Stripes, the flag of the United States of America, he was admiring it, cherishing it, scanning it from top to bottom. And soon afterward, Louis, an ordinary front-line agent of the DSS, would receive that call, and give a response, a response, he, like Bo, really didn't have to "think about it."

A Dangerous History
in Diplomacy

The Bureau of Diplomatic Security Service, or DSS, is the federal law enforcement and security branch of the U.S. Department of State. The DSS is a relatively small department, unbeknownst to most Americans.

"A diplomatic courier is a U.S. government official who is trained and credentialed by the Secretary of State to accompany classified materials across international borders. The Diplomatic Security Service has approximately 100 diplomatic couriers who ensure secure delivery of classified and sensitive materials between U.S. consulates and embassies and the State Department."

During the American Revolution and prior to the development of a formal law enforcement agency, a network of dispatch ships, forwarding agents, and dispatch agents, working with sea captains and trusted merchants, helped ensure the safe delivery of vital correspondence. And even back then, peace was made by a show of strength, by putting a strong foot forward. To boost their maritime power, the Continental Congress and some states issued Letters of Marque, a government license to private ship owners, authorizing them to assault and seize British ships during the war. The incentive was irresistible, as they were paid a solid percentage of the value they seized. They were the privateers. And to the British and their world's mightiest Navy, they became more than a nuisance on the high seas, and to British supply ships, a nightmare, something to be feared...like the six-hundred ton, 26-gun ship-Caesar of Boston on down, to a few fearless swashbuckling mariners rowing a whaleboat.

They went after the king's vessels with a vengeance. One privateer alone was responsible for capturing a thousand of what were most likely the favorite thirty-two-pound smoothbore cannons of the British fleets. In just one victory, the privateers supplied the munitions-starved Rebel Navy with 2,000 muskets, 31 tons of musket shot, and 7,000 round shot for the cannon that was seized and aimed back at the Royal Navy. One historical accounting concluded that Patriot privateers commandeered over 2,200 British ships, valued at almost $66 million in colonial currency, during the time of 1776.

But even with 2,000 Letters of Marque issued, America's Navy was still tiny, and with no ships of the line, it couldn't face off against the British fleet. What they could do was impede British troop and supply movement in the Great Lakes and rivers of the American continent, raid English colonies, and capture British merchant ships throughout the Atlantic, the Caribbean, and even English waters. Their effectiveness was proven by the incredible quantity of supplies that they seized. But seizing British ships did more than just confiscate supplies for the war effort. The Continental Navy, bolstered by the privateers, kept an estimated 16,000 British soldiers and sailors out of the fighting while providing secure transportation of American diplomats. It further assisted with the military maneuvers of patriot soldiers and sailors, and aided in the defense of the American coastline. And, from a commercial standpoint, as with any war, there were personal fortunes to be made.

But it was a deadly and dangerous undertaking. Continental ships were constantly sinking to the bottom of the ocean; at one point, only two were left in active service, not only from storms at sea, but from a lethal salvo from the 56 broadside cannon of a

British man-o'-war, shredding the wooden American vessels into splinters. And to be blown up or drowned was a better fate than being captured, to be sent chained in the dank and dirty bowels of a prison ship. An estimated 8,000 to 11,000 colonial prisoners of war died aboard these ships because of malnutrition and the beyond unsanitary conditions, their diseased bodies dumped into what is today the Brooklyn Navy Yard. And if not to die in America, to be put in a wooden crate as a punishment to traitors, treated worse than cattle, for the two month transport to another miserable prison in England.

These privateers were led and inspired by America's most famous privateer, Commander John Paul Jones, who, in September 1779, in the vicinity of Flamborough Head, off the east coast of England, fought one of the fiercest battles in naval history when he commanded a small squadron led by his USS Bonhomme Richard frigate, named for Benjamin Franklin. He boldly attacked a British convoy comprised of the British warships HMS Serapis and Countess of Scarborough with their combined armament of sixty-six cannon. After the Bonhomme Richard was struck repeatedly, it began taking on water, and its sails caught fire. When, exalting in apparent triumph, the British captain of the Serapis ordered Jones to surrender, he famously replied, "I have not yet begun to fight!" A few hours later, the unnerved captain and crew of the Serapis surrendered as Jones boarded and took command of it while the Colonial Navy's famous battleship, the Bonhomme Richard, buried itself at sea. It had done its duty while giving birth to the father of the American Navy.

And American diplomacy and privateering would work hand-in-hand. Benjamin Franklin, from the Colony of Pennsylvania, was the very first American diplomat in Paris, a most vital ambassador in need of special protection. He would issue his own Letters of Marque over there. On October 26, 1776, exactly one month to the day after being named an agent of a diplomatic commission by the Continental Congress, Franklin set sail from Philadelphia for France, with which he was to negotiate and secure a formal alliance and treaty. During his mission, the Continentals would learn that protecting vital war correspondence was treacherous. His messages were intercepted by a trusted US official on the British payroll, Edward Bancroft, who shared Franklin's messages with the enemy, the British.

Franklin commissioned three ships to fight for Washington's Navy and operate overseas around the British Isles. One of those homemade ships, christened *The Fear Not*, sailed on British waters with private sailors aboard, gritting their teeth in the swirling smoke of their battle stations, unheralded and relatively unknown, yet they did their part in the revolt in the gaining of independence.

The DSS was evolving. During World War I, on April 4, 1916, U.S. Secretary of State Robert Lansing formally established the U.S. Department of State's first security office. From the American Revolution through the early 1900s, U.S. foreign policy focused on establishing and preserving the nation, developing international trade, expanding national borders, and asserting regional interests. Diplomacy was involved in the actualization of the Manifest Destiny policy, expansion beyond the continental United States, beginning with the purchase of Alaska in 1867.

During this early era, when American representatives overseas primarily conducted business and trade, diplomatic security was mainly concerned with safeguarding private and secretive channels of communication between Washington, D.C., and the nation's emissaries or agents, and later, staffing U.S. Consulate sites for the relief of U.S. citizens in peril abroad.

The KKK to the Knights Templar

ouis, his four siblings, and his parents were common citizens; his father an electrician, his mother a part-time special ed teacher.

The neighborhood was not the completely tranquil environment as depicted in the "Zip-It-Dee-Do-Dah" movie, Song of the South. Louis recalls as if it happened yesterday, late one evening playing ball with his friends in the schoolyard, an old Chevy sedan slowly drove past, and it was then that he saw them for the first time, those menacing white hoods, glaring; they all ran back home, shivering with fright, his first encounter with the Clan aka the KKK.

A frightful memory, that's what it would always be, a dripping burnt cross extinguished in the middle of his boyhood friend Jerome Whitlock's front yard; hearing Jerome's younger sisters crying through the front screen door. At the time, he couldn't understand what the Whitlocks had done to deserve this. Later, he would learn that it was because of something that they had *not* done, it was because of something they had been born with, had no control over-their black skin...an act of callous hatred. Young Louis had good reason to shiver because he was Catholic, another favorite target of the minacious homegrown terror.

The name of the family crest emblazoned on the ancient Coat of Arms, the Anglo-Saxon surname, LEDLOW, was first discovered in England during the 12th century. It derives from a family that lived on a hill rising above a babbling river at the market town of Shropshire near Ludlow. The terrain was a natural site to defend against the marauding raiders sent by the kings of Wales. On the Welsh border, on a promontory along the River Teme, east of the Clee Hills, stands the Norman stronghold of Ludlow Castle.

The timeless grey-granite fortress, constructed as early as the Eleventh Century, with its towering stone battlements and draw-bridge, gives a vivid impression of medieval times, of noble knights in shining armor and fair damsels in distress, fluttering silken veils, enchanting, the stuff of fairy tales.

And the most respected guests of the castle would be the "Pauperes Commilitones Christi Templique Salomonici," in English: the Poor Fellow-Soldiers of Christ and of the Temple of Solomon, better known as *The Knights Templar*, the elite warrior monks of the Crusades, the fearsome defenders of Christendom.

With the conquest of Jerusalem in 1099, Christians in Europe were free to pilgrimage to the Holy Land of The Messiah, but a perilous journey confronted them. From common bandits to the slashing scimitars of Arab raiders, the pilgrims were defenseless. And so were born their protectors.

Mounted on their snorting war horses, steely-eyed under their glinting Spangenhelms, the knights were armed with lethal three-foot broad swords and long spear-tipped lances. Their signature emblazoned on their white robes and battle shields, a fiery red cross, the red cross of martyrdom. The Knights Templar dedi-cated themselves to protecting the Christian pilgrims as well as defending the Holy City from the terror of the Muslim hordes of Saladin. They abided by a cardinal rule, never to surrender unless the Templar flag had fallen. To die in combat was for them a great honor, assuring a place in heaven.

It is believed that it was they, these knights of the Red Order, who constructed Ludlow Castle's inner circular chapel, modeling it after the shrine in the Church of the Holy Sepulchre. Today, that sacred shrine in the Christian Quarter of the Old City of Jerusalem is the most holiest of places, where exists the last five stations of the Via Dolorosa, the path leading to Christ's crucifixion at Calvary, and His tomb, ever empty since Easter morning.

The family's military tradition began with Louis' great-great grandfather, Jacob, a boy-aide and courier for Confederate General Arthur Middleton Manigault. He was blinded by a Yankee artillery fragment at Chickamauga, and his wounds were believed to have been mortal. But God had other ideas for him, he would live to marry and father five children. But this ancestor would be the reason for the family's more far-reaching identity. It was Jacob, who, in the spring of 1861, was baptized into the Catholic-Christian faith.

In the late autumn of 1859, in a decision to expand Jacob's educational and moral virtues from their farm in rural North Alabama near what is today Hanceville, his parents put him on a stagecoach to Nashville, where he boarded a train on the new Louisville and Nashville Railroad. At Louisville, Kentucky, he finished the last leg of the 329-mile journey in a rented horse and buggy to arrive at a village in Washington County near Springfield, a land known for a gritty backwoodsman, a rugged unschooled Indian fighter who once carved on a tree, "Cilled a Bar."

Trailblazers and Teachers

Jacob was following in a line of Southern Appalachian trail-blazers. They were portrayed as rugged and self-reliant as told by the reputation of frontiersman Daniel Boone. Boone was a surveyor and hunter, pictured wearing an ensemble of buckskin clothing and coonskin cap with a musket and powder horn in his hands, fighting hostile Native Indians. Settlers to the region trapped for furs and hunted wild game or practiced farming for survival. Like Boone, Appalachian homesteaders moved into areas largely isolated from "civilization" by high mountains, and had to provide for themselves against the harsh elements in their daily struggle for survival. And by settling on Native Indian lands, attacks from unfriendly tribes were an incessant danger. A Kentucky-born wilderness woodchopper and son of an American pioneer related the ruggedness of religious thinking on the subject of death in those times: "The Lord spared the fitten and the rest He seen fitten to let die." And his wit had become famous, but forever frontier-raised, an American statesman, by the name of Abraham Lincoln.

For Jacob's parents, sending Jacob to an educational institution out-of-state to Kentucky was more of a sacrifice than it was a luxury. At that time, the family lived on and maintained the Northern Alabama farm, their existence, was more of subsistence than of a well-to-do plantation of aristocrats. The family owned five slaves, but by the sweat of their brow, Jacob's father and older brothers performed chores and worked in their short-staple cotton field and vegetable gardens alongside of them. Livestock, dairy cattle, and chickens were raised for food and to make ends meet. A field of corn was maintained to feed the hogs, which were put in a pen and loaded onto a wagon for the ten-mile trip east to Blountsville, where they were sold at the market.

Founded in 1808, named after the great Dominican Philosopher, Saint Thomas Aquinas, it was the first Catholic boarding school west of the Alleghenies, ordered for the education of boys and young men. And on its grounds, a church was built.

It's Tudor-Gothic octagon tower is crowned with white spires, tipped with white crosses and magnificent long-arched stained glass windows beckoning on all sides. In the side yard, a quaint country graveyard of weather-worn tombstones adds to the eternal appeal of Saint Rose of Lima Church. Saint Rose, a member of the Third Order of Saint Dominic, is the patroness of Latin America and benefactress of those ridiculed for their piety.

Jacob studied Latin and Greek, and under the subject matter of natural philosophy, the brothers taught him the disciplines of chemistry and physics. And young Jacob, along with his school-mates, would have served as a field hand on the surrounding farm of six hundred acres. The Dominican's down-to-earth practice of toil in the soil was intended to impress upon Jacob the importance of the simplest yet greatest spiritual practice of humility.

And the one Dominican who made the most profound impression on young Jacob Ledlow was an immigrant who had followed his calling from Cuba, Father Timothy Rock. It was Father Timothy who taught him the dynamic that is at the center of Aquinas teaching. That it was Christ Himself, The I Am Who I Am, the Truth, the Way, and the Life, who proclaimed at the Last Supper that the bread and wine that He was about to share with the remaining Eleven was His Body and Blood.

And soon thereafter, Jacob received the inexplicable, the inexplicable gift of faith. Because he came to believe that the Holy

Eucharist, the celebrated transubstantiation, the supernatural changing of the bread and wine at the hands of His priests is the Body, Soul, and Divinity of Christ, simply because Christ, the God-man, said that it *IS*, and whoever eats this bread will live forever.

Saint Rose is also venerated for another intercession, for the resolution of family quarrels. In a lamentable irony, Jacob would withdraw from the Dominican institution to enlist in the Confederate Army, to serve under a most notable former alum of Saint Thomas Aquinas, one Jefferson Finis Davis, president and commander in chief of the government of the Confederate States of America. Davis would be elected to lead one of the two sides in a bloody nationwide quarrel between families, North versus South, a bloody strife over age-old moral and economic traditions and ideals.

Blood on the
Classroom Floor

L ouis first Googled info on the DSS and read:

"The Basic Special Agent Course is an intense 29-week program that prepares newly appointed Diplomatic Security Agent candidates for domestic duty with the Department of State. Upon entry on duty with the Department of State, all Special Agent candidates attend a three week orientation at the National Foreign Affairs Training Center followed by 12 weeks of training at the Federal Law Enforcement Training Center at Glynco, GA, (now Blackstone, VA) for the Criminal Investigators Training Program. The course culminates 13 weeks of specialized training in the Washington D.C. area that includes two weeks of introductory training, deliberate planning, leadership, tactical medicine, personnel recovery, weapons, small unit tactics, and movement and static security procedures need to operate in non-permissive environments."

Louis got a kick out of the "Need to operate in NON-PERMISSIVE ENVIRONMENTS," as in "YOU'RE NOT WELCOME HERE." What a bargain, he thought.

It was during his first week in New Agent's class that he realized that it wouldn't be all fun and games. The basic sidearm of the DSS is a GLOCK 17 Gen5 pistol. To clean the weapon, the trigger must be pulled to release the locking mechanism and allow the gun's upper frame and barrel to be taken apart for cleaning.

After an adrenaline-filled day on the combat range, he and his classmates were at the tables inside the gun cleaning room, the air filled with the pungent odor of Hoppes solvent, gleeful that they had made it safely through another day. And then, a deafening BANG, a warm liquid on the back of his neck, then loud screaming and shouting, a small pool of blood on the floor. The new agent working behind him had been hit by an accidental discharge. The momentary chaos that ensued was quickly subdued by three firearms instructors who rushed to the aid of the wounded agent who was laying on the floor with a terrified look on his face, holding a bloody hand over his arm. The injury turned out not to be life-threatening, a flesh wound to the upper left tricep. A week later, after getting all stitched up, the agent was able to rejoin the class, a living example of how not to be careless in handling deadly weapons.

His New Agent's class of 45 newbies included a group of cocky sit-and-lean-back-in-the-last-row kind of guys. Although seats were assigned in alphabetical order with those with last names beginning with A and up in the front row, those lean-back guys stood out. During evenings, they congregated in the Board Room, the built-in Academy's watering hole. By the second week, they had nicknames for just about everyone, minus the handful of females.

They gave him the name "Moonshine," which he could live with, those names never taking hold beyond the New Agent's class.

He knew, from the government website, what was required before he applied, "Special Agents are required to perform protective security assignments with physical demands that may include, but are not limited to, intermittent and prolonged periods of running, walking, standing, sitting, squatting, kneeling, climbing stairs, quickly entering and exiting various vehicles, pushing, pulling, dragging objects or people, wearing heavy body amour and gear, as well as carrying and fully operating a variety of firearms. Agent must also endure long or unusual hours, inclement weather, lack of sleep, rest, or meals, jet-lag, extremes of heat and cold, and wet or polluted environments. Applicants must pass a thorough medical examination, which includes a cardiovascular stress test conducted or authorized by the Department of State's Office of Medical Services."

An Exercise at Blackstone

Todays in-service training itinerary features the latest Personnel Recovery exercise, if you want to call it that. Props for the exercise are set up around a serpentine track at the Tactical Vehicle Operations Center. His class is broken up into squads. For this exercise, they are dressed in field gear, Kevlar helmets, and ceramic-plated vests. Area locals are hired and paid by the hour to play-act roles in the live practical problems at the Academy.

An instructor briefs Louis and his squad mates with the scenario: the embassy housing the Ministry of Foreign Affairs has come under attack by the enemy. The enemy is storming the compound, armed with small arms and rockets; a simulated "vehicle kill" is part of the situation. As he finishes, a thunderstorm is brewing dark clouds in the sky.

Louis has "volun-*told*" to be the driver of a desert camouflage Humvee and crew of six. Under an ear-splitting barrage of AK-47s firing blanks, Louis is behind the wheel as the vehicle is "hit" by enemy fire. He "crashes" into a roadside ditch. An instructor, a former Marine drill-master, a purplish vein flaring on his bulging neck, blasting an AK-47 in the air, screaming at the top of his lungs, "Your vehicle is dead, what are you going to do?!!" Louis grabs the radio, shouts at the crew, "Contact left, bail right." In this situation, just this week, he's been trained to reach out for the Quick Response Team. Into the receiver, he yells, "Mayday, mayday, under attack!" He shouts their coordinates into the mic. A rumbling of thunder adds to the noise of simulated gun fire as another instructor rushes up to the ditch. He points and shoots a paintball round into one of the crew's thighs. A hefty female play-actor, she is ready for the sting of the pinkish red paint round that splatters into a leg of her blue jeans. The instructor screams, "You've got wounded, take cover!" Reflexively, two of the crew who have bailed, help their wounded crew mate to the protection of the front wheel well on the opposite side of the vehicle.

"You're being flanked from the south," he points his AK-47 to the top of a hill, "make it to that tree line, your squad mate is disabled, can't move her legs!" The "wounded" knows, at this point, to go dead weight. Louis and an old classmate from Illinois, grab hold of the "wounded" from under the top edge of her vest and begin dragging her up the hill. "Go, go, go!" rings out. Grunting and sweating over sharp rocks, prickly burs, and unseen deer ticks are making their task anything but pleasant. With their red-handled Sig-Sauer 226 pistols, the remaining crew provide rear-covering "fire" as they make it to the top. "Code red!" an instructor yells, and they catch their breath. Louis only now feels a burning sensation as blood oozes out of a long thin cut on his forearm. The "wounded" play-actor chatters cheerfully on about the excitement of the exercise, mindless of the spider web of scratches on her lower back. While they applaud themselves by patting each other on the back, a cloud bursts overhead and the crew is doused in a refreshing summer rain.

A Visit to Father Joe

A benefit of training in Blackstone is being within a three-hour drive up Interstate 95 to Washington D.C. where Louis' brother, Father Joe, is assigned.

Louis' brother, Father Joseph Michael Ledlow, was ordained a priest after attending Catholic University and Mount Saint Mary's Seminary in Emmittsburg, MD. He is assigned part-time to the Catholic University's philosophy department in Northeast Washington D.C. He is also active in what could be described as a special ministry at the Franciscan Seminary nearby.

Father Joe is tall, dark, and handsome, with a touch of gray above his temples. As a school boy, he had been a hard-hitting Free Safety for the Bulldogs of Hanceville High. With the good looks of a matinee idol, he had dated his fair share of lovely young belles. He received several offers from elite SEC schools, notably the University of Tennessee and Mississippi State. He turned them down to follow a higher calling.

An old-school caricature, like an image of Saint Michael brandishing his gleaming sword, his brother is cast out of the mold of gritty vicars in combat. Father Joe brings to mind the famous Civil War chaplain, William Corby, who, on the 2nd day at Gettysburg, stood upon a boulder on Cemetery Ridge to give general absolution to soldiers of the famous Irish Brigade, who were about to face that ferocious onslaught of General Lee's Rebels, before cheering them on to do their duty.

Genuinely humble, but not shy to display an uncommon other side of the Alter Christus, Father Joe has the humility of Saint

Joseph, the foster father of Jesus, and the fighting spirit of Saint Michael, the great warrior prince of heaven. He could, like Father Corby, erupt and upbraid any yellowbelly who failed to do his duty, or if he caught anyone mistreating one of his flock, he'd not think twice about knocking their head in a creek.

Louis invited Tony along for the ride, and Tony was happy to go; he'd had enough of the buffet by Marriott. As they drove north along I-95 in Louis' five-year-old Dodge, they're making good time. A simple roadside breakdown at this hour of the morning didn't cause a miles-long backup of rubberneckers. As they approached the exits for the Quantico Marine base, they noticed a vehicle up ahead on the shoulder and its driver standing next to it. They slowed and saw that it was a stranded marine in green khaki uniform with a cell phone up to his ear. As they eased onto the shoulder in front of the broken down Jeep, Louis pulls over not too near to the guardrail so Tony can get out of the car.

As they approach the Marine, Tony, once a Marine, always a Marine, blurts out "Oorah! Looks like you can use some assistance, eh, Marine?"

"Hey, thanks for the support, guys, I just talked to my buddy who said he's ten minutes out."

"What outfit you in?" asks Tony.

Twenty-fifth Post Security Detachment, here to prep for deployment to Baghdad, my unit's got the rotation for perimeter security for the Baghdad Embassy Compound (BEC)," said the Marine.

"Nice, I saw the zombies hit the front gate with a Toyota brand bomb-on-wheels a couple of weeks ago," said Tony.

"Yep, we were briefed about that a couple of days ago; they strengthened that area, moved out the checkpoints, and added almost a platoon, installed a couple of 50-caliber machine guns too," said the Marine. They exchange goodbyes. "Keep your head down," adds Tony.

They continue on I-95, and within forty minutes, they are crossing the Potomac on the 14th Street Bridge, the circular colonnade of the Jefferson Monument appearing across the river. Even at this hour, the lanes on the bridge are already filled with early sightseers trying to avoid the weekend tourist traffic.

"Father Gabriele Amorth, the prominent exorcist, has left an apprentice successor who was consulted about the demonic phenomenon occurring at the Franciscan Monastery of the Holy Land in America...across from the National Shrine down the street...and that candidate would be Father Joe."

They park in the driveway next to the pale-brown brick and stained-glass church. The sweet floral fragrance of honeysuckle fills the air. They walk along under an open red tile-covered portico of stone arches and manicured hedges. Out in the brick-paved courtyard, a white stone statue of the child Jesus stands atop a marble pedestal. They descend a flight of cement steps down to a lower level framed by shady hardwood trees, and see Father Joe sitting on a green wooden bench under the shade. The stone statue of a little girl kneels in the middle of a circular patch of bright yellow daffodils. She is gazing at a statue of the Blessed Mother placed to the right of a stone cave. He asked them to meet him here, the Lourdes Grotto. It's his favorite spot to clear his mind and meditate.

"Hey brother, you remember Tony from Sis's wedding?" said Louis.

"Good to see you again, Tony, taking good care of my little brother, I hope?" as Father Joe reaches and shakes Tony's hand.

"Great to see you again, Father Joe, and I'm sure you know better than most, with your brother, it's never-ending," replies Tony.

"Louis, I didn't want to say anything over the phone, but there's something going on here that maybe you can help us with," said Father Joe.

"Yeah sure, what's going on?" asks Louis.

"Well, you know it, Louis, but to let Tony know, I've been recently appointed as the exorcist for the diocese. I haven't had a real case yet, but I've had a bit of training and studied it more on my own time. So this individual made several appearances at our homeless shelter and soup kitchen. In addition to the shelter, after supper, we offer programs for people coming off the streets, one especially for the youth, teenagers, young adults. It's been well attended lately and we felt we were making progress with five to six kids at least, maybe more."

"So this spooky-looking guy shows up, Hispanic, really rough-looking, covered in tattoos. Funny thing is, he won't look me in the eye. He mingles with everyone else, including a few of the brothers, Brother Arthur in particular. And as best I could, without giving it away, I watched him, and I think he put a curse on our place. He was making weird bewitching gestures in front of the pictures hanging on the walls of the hallway leading to the activity room. A couple of days ago, one of our volunteers spotted him leaving the chapel. The next day, one of the brothers noticed that the gold-plated crucifix we've had on the side altar for as long as I can remember was missing. Soon after that, I'm trying to think, maybe a couple of days, things started going wrong with the program. A few of the kids got sick, and it seemed like the group, including a few of the brothers, became despondent, like a malaise; couldn't put a finger on it," Father Joe explained.

"And?" prompted Louis.

"And then about a week ago, one evening, in the middle of one of our programs, the room felt cold, a chill in the air, and all of a sudden, books and stuff started flying across the room. A few of the kids just got up and left and we haven't seen them since. That night, I detected a lingering odor, so I went to work, giving the rooms a thorough expulsion," explained Father Joe.

In addition to his basic exorcism kit, Father Joe carries with him a unique object, mounted in a tiny glass and gold-framed locket, a splinter of the cross, the sacred cross of Golgotha. When in the presence of a demon, he wears it around his neck.

Tony is unaware of the wide-eyed look on his face. "Can you give me a detailed description of the guy, any vehicles, did he give a name by any chance?" asks Louis.

"Let me think, medium height, really dark skin..."

"The one thing that stands out the most, in the middle of his forehead, a tattoo, a goat-like face with horns. And I think I should tell you guys, Brother Arthur came to me the next morning, white as a sheet, he said he had this terrible nightmare. In the dream, he was up close face-to-face with this guy in the chapel, and one of the goat's eyes *winked* at him!" exhorts Father Joe.

"Hey, wait a minute, that tattoo on the forehead," exclaims Louis, "I saw a cable come in from the Mexico City agent in charge, he had some blurry surveillance photos. A group of MS-13 were seen with one of the big-time Narcos and what they think, strangely, are a few Chinese Nationals."

"They've put together a timeline of major incidents along the coast, from Veracruz up to Matamoros. Evidence points to an alliance between MS-13 and the Narcos. Really bloody stuff, double trouble," estimates Louis. "I swear, that goat-face tattoo was mentioned in the police files from more than one of those places, maybe from threatened witnesses. We'll dig into it when we get back to Blackstone," promises Louis.

"One last thing, Father Joe, are there any surveillance cameras on the grounds that may have recorded something?" Tony asks. "There are none, sorry, and if what I suspect is correct, it might not show up in the same way on camera anyway. But you could get lucky. I'm praying that you do. These things, being otherworldly, appear in different forms in different places and are not photogenic to say the least. They can sense when their identity is being threatened. At this point, it would be dangerous to attempt to subdue this thing and try to submit it to tests, finger prints, blood, saliva, and all that," cautions Father Joe.

Following Father Joe's personal tour of the church and chapel, they walk to the university, taking 14th Street to Perry, along the shade trees of Fort Bunker Hill Park to Michigan Avenue NE, where on the corner, a street vendor, smiling under two blue and yellow beach umbrellas, tempts Tony with steaming redhots boiling away. Down the block at Murphy's Grill, they have burgers and steak fries served by a staff of bustling students. The agents just can't get used to how young college kids look these days.

Fastballs and
Father Amorth

Father Joe has scored tickets to the Nationals game this evening. Lucky for them, the big righty, number 37, is slated to take the hill against the Dodgers. The Nats are in first place, making a run for the pennant. Drafted as the first player taken in the 2009 draft, his was a talent that comes along once in a lifetime. Nine years ago, in early June, there had been a perceptible buzz in Nationals Park. It had started early, soon after the gates were opened. Every seat had been purchased well in advance. The 21-year-old phenom was making his major league debut. And on this night, it just wasn't the Pirates batters that were overpowered, even the radar gun blew a fuse. Stephen Strasburg struck out 14 batters that night, the last seven looking so helpless as if they couldn't even see the ball. A performance like that always brings back quotes and memories from the former greats. Reggie Jackson, the one and only Mr. October, said of fire baller Tom Seaver, aka Tom Terrific, of the Amazin' '69 Mets, "Blind men come to the games just to *listen* to him pitch," It hadn't always been effortless for Strasburg. In California, as a high school junior, he won only one game in 11 starts. It was his grandmother who encouraged him not to give up.

Louis, Father Joe, and Tony thoroughly enjoy the warm summer evening, sipping on Blue Moons, cracking peanuts, finding the aroma from the hot dog vendor irresistible; thirty-thousand people all in a happy mood. Their third base box seats are close enough to hear the thwack of the ball popping the catcher's mitt. In the third inning, a foul ball heads right at them, Tony stretches backward, the ball glances off his hand, bouncing down in front of a little girl wearing a pink Nats hat. She scoops it up, face ecstatic at her surprise gift souvenir.

Louis gleefully yells "error on the big kid!" By the time the moths fluttering about the light stanchions get tired, Strasburg has struck out 10 with one run unearned, leaving the last inning for the bullpen to finish off LA for the win.

On the drive back, Louis and Tony discuss what had been disclosed by Father Joe and the manifestations of the demonic. Louis relates some of the spooky details of real possessions he has read in Malachi Martin's acclaimed book: Hostage to the Devil: The Possessions. Louis tells Tony that after reading that book, for a whole week, he slept with the light on and rosary beads around his neck. This was a topic that Tony thought was ancient folklore. He searches his smartphone and finds on the Libero website a first-hand account of the supernatural by Father Gabriele Amorth. It happened during an exorcism:

> "Suddenly, I had the clear sensation of a demonic presence before me. I felt this demon that was looking at me intently. Scrutinizing me. Moving around me. The air became cold. It was terribly cold. Father Candido had also warned me ahead of time about these sudden changes in temperature, but I tried to concentrate. I closed my eyes and continued my prayer by rote. 'Leave, therefore, you rebel. Leave, seducer, full of every kind of fraud and falsehood, enemy of virtue, persecutor of the innocent. Cede your place to Christ, in whom there is nothing of your works.'"

Tony finds an excerpt from Father Amorth's book, The Last Exorcist, wherein Father Amorth reports an entire dialogue he had in his role as exorcist with the devil, on the topic of the Mother of God.

Father Amorth: "What are the virtues of the Madonna that make you angriest?"

Demon: "She makes me angry because she is the humblest of all creatures, and because I am the proudest; because she is the purest of all creatures, and I am not; because, of all creatures, she is the most obedient to God, and I am a rebel!"

Father Amorth: "Tell me the fourth characteristic of the Madonna that makes you so afraid of her that you are more afraid when I say the Madonna's name than when I say the name of Jesus Christ!"

Demon: "I am more afraid when you say the Madonna's name because I am more humiliated by being beaten by a simple creature than by Him "

Father Amorth: "Tell me the fourth characteristic of the Madonna that makes you most angry!"

Demon: "Because she always defeats me, because she was never compromised by any taint of sin!"

During an exorcism, Father Amorth remembers, "Satan told me, through the possessed person, 'Every Hail Mary of the Rosary is a blow to the head for me; if Christians knew the power of the Rosary, it would be the end of me!'"

Eva Greene and a
Luminous Linen

The first lady of The United States of America had her own life story when it came to handling adversity. Her given name, in Hebrew, is pronounced EE-VAH, meaning "Life;" in the Old Testament, "The First Woman." Born in the ancient town of Ptuj, on the Drava River, which, at that time, was under the communist rule of Tito's Yugoslavia. When it came to religion, Statism was the only government-approved option. But the natural conflict flowing through her veins had originated far back in her people's fight for life and human dignity. Beginning their struggle in the Middle Ages under the Roman Caesar, then run over roughshod by the Franks, it was during the barbaric rape of their women and pillaging of their towns by the Ottoman Turks that a culture hewn from a fight for survival, a fight for everything, a *take nothing for granted* mentality was forged. And yet, in contrast, the Slovenians embraced Christianity as their national religion.

And thus, they were an austere people taking on a stoic approach to life, a wait-and-see attitude. Revolt, only if necessary.

And Eva was no different. Her family faithfully practiced their faith like all of the other Catholics in town...underground. She remembered the fear she had as a child, the recurring nightmares of her best friend and family having been forced out of their house next door, taken away in a large ominous van in the middle of the night. Seeing her own parents shaken and knowing they were equally guilty of having that same illegal, government-condemned priest in their home to celebrate Mass. Her uncle Vit (pronounced VEET), on her mother's side, fled the country to join the Franciscan Order in the United States.

By the grace of God, Eva was able to use her natural beauty and unshakable spirit to make it out of there. Aided by an education in cosmetology, she was able to develop her own commercial makeup line and face-model it herself. Her horizons expanded.

In her twenties, as part of a sightseeing trip to the United States, she visited Father Vit at the Franciscan Monastery of The Holy Land in America in Washington D.C., a beautiful place with acres of rose gardens and a replica of the catacombs.

Before moving into the White House, she had the buildings and grounds exorcised. She had been searching for a suitable Catholic priest when someone at the Franciscan Monastery highly recommended Father Joseph Michael Ledlow. After the ritual, they had a nice chat, Father Joe informing her that he had grown up in Hanceville, Alabama.

"What a small world. Years ago, my Uncle, Father Vit, took me there to see the monastery," said Eva.

Back then, Father Vit had taken her to the Shrine of the Most Blessed Sacrament and Our Lady of the Angels Monastery in Hanceville, Alabama (the site is visited by pilgrims from around the world, and is consecrated to perpetual adoration of Our Lord Jesus in the Holy Eucharist, and dedicated to the advancement of the Gospel).

She'd never forgotten it. The nuns filing into the chapel, soundless, their brilliant white under veils framing their radiant young faces, all clothed in a striking dark habit; a stunning sight, a joyous sight, a penitential sight, a sign of the world to come. It was there that her uncle introduced her to the abbess, Sister Helen of The Unborn, whom she had kept in touch with over the years by mail.

She had become a regular viewer of the Eternal Word Television Network, and was looking forward to visiting nearby Irondale, the place where it all started. And Father Joe would become *her* priest, always there for her when she needed him.

The first lady is hosting an inaugural Easter gala at the Willard Hotel, featuring special guest speaker Father Joseph Michael Ledlow. Father Joe will give a lecture on a special piece of cloth; the cloth that Father Joe will be discussing is actually a shroud woven from Syrian linen about 14 feet in length. And on it is imprinted an ancient image of a man.

Father Joe has a reputation for delivering solid sermons on Sundays. Not being a polished professional orator, Father Joe, it could be said, was a very basic speaker. He had no desire to be thought of as a brilliant jawsmith. He got his message across, and it was the substance of his messages, not his style, that served him well. He had a knack for making the New Testament relevant to the modern-day challenges of everyday living.

But on this night, it's not only the message and subject matter that is creating the buzz, causing what had previously been anticipated as an interesting topic to ripen into an extraordinary one, it's also being delivered with a magnetic presence of the priest speaking in front of them. The audience has become riveted in their seats. As word begins to spread throughout the building, people begin to stream in through the rear doors-maids, waiters, and wandering guests lining up three deep against the back wall. For the first time in anyone's memory, the famous hotel lobby is deserted. The audience becomes spell-bound, the fidgeters stopped fidgeting and the clock-watchers forget to look at the watches on their wrists, a feeling as if...outside of time.

Father Joe, with certitude, explains the bountiful evidence revealed during the 1978 examination of the shroud by a team of scientists: the unique botanical trail of microscopic pollen, naturally proving its trans-century journey from the hands of Saint Peter in Jerusalem to Edessa, what is today, Istanbul, Turkey; to its discovery in 944 and delivery by a Byzantine army to Constantinople; then, in 1204, to its capture by the European Knights of the Fourth Crusade and bequest to France; its travel through Northern Greece to Romania and Hungary before returning to the House of Savoy in France, and finally, in 1578, to Turin, Italy, where it rests today.

He adds that the cloth contains micro-specimens of twenty-eight plants and flowers from Jerusalem, some which still grow there today.

There is a footprint on the fabric, a dirt sample taken from the cloth that matches precisely with dirt removed from the Damascus Gate of Jerusalem.

What of the remarkable imprint of a Roman coin placed over one of the man's eyes that's consistent with the Hebrew burial custom? Not just any coin, but the unique 1/32 of an inch-sized letters of a coin issued during the years 29 to 36 A.D. A coin issued by a Roman governor by the name of... Pontius Pilate.

And let's not forget the wounds on the image of a man with Jewish-style side-locks on the side of his face; the wounds of torture. The image shows 120 wounds inflicted by a Roman flagrum, a short-handled whip with three leather straps, each tipped with small lead dumbbells. There were forty lashes inflicted, satisfying the Hebrew maxim of punishment by flagellation, and a wound on the side that matches precisely the dimensions of a Roman spear, the Spear of Destiny.

As Father Joe steps toward his laptop on top of a table, he points out that "a most astonishing discovery was made...of the absence of any paint pigments or dyes. But the cloth did test positive for traumatized-clotted human blood, type AB, which continued to bleed after the man was being gently wrapped inside of it. And defying all logic, it, the blood stain, still to this day, retains the color of red."

In the end, the team of scientists could not explain how the image got on the cloth; there was simply no earthly explanation for it.

"But, wouldn't you know, there are those, even though they see, they will never believe."

With that assertion, he presents the "scientific results" of tests on the shroud conducted in 1988. At what turned out to be an earth and heaven-shaking press conference, the team of so-called experts claiming that, upon examination, they could conclusively prove that the cloth wasn't real, that it was a fake, made sometime between 1260 to 1390.

He purposefully pauses, then satisfied, he illustrates what was thought at the time to be a forlorn attempt to deny reality, a hypothesis offered by an ordinary couple, a husband and wife from Ohio, who refused to believe the findings of the experts, that the cloth wasn't real, that it wasn't what it is supposed to be; after looking at photographs on their home computer, they just didn't believe the scoffing experts who concluded that the cloth was made in the fourteenth century. They resolutely believed it had been stitched and woven... in the first.

Father Joe steps closer to the audience. "Well now, how could the faithful have been defrauded, not by experts anyway, how could they? They tested a piece of the full intact cloth, did they not? So what about the three inch piece of the cloth they sliced off from a bottom corner of the shroud and submitted as the carbon test specimen? Well, it has everything to do with that specific piece of cloth. Because that specimen, it was later discovered in a follow-up examination, contained cotton fibers. What of the cotton fibers, you might ask? It was because the specimen piece had been part of a lengthwise re-woven and dyed-to-match strip, added twelve centuries later as a repair, made with cotton, and so, in a re-test, with predictable results, it tested as a foreign fragment, not original to the principle cloth made of pure Syrian linum usitatissimum.

And so the hypothesis of the faithful couple had been true, proving once again, that fact is sometimes even stranger than fiction.

But that's not all. One of the experts selected to examine the cloth in 1978 was a Jewish photographer who analyzed what is the positive and *not* what was thought for centuries to be, negative image on the cloth. He compared it to all known photographic possibilities. He determined that if produced in the fourteenth century as the "experts" claimed, whoever or whatever made the image would have had to have perceived the concept of photography 650 years before it was invented. But there's still more. His advanced equipment has revealed the image to have a three-dimensional quality to it with the wound marks having atomic laser consistency, being *only* visible under ultraviolet fluorescent light. He was astonished with the realization that no medieval human artist could have possibly created something like this. Before traveling to Turin, he was the least likely of all of the authorities to be a believer in Christianity, but that all changed, for he began then and there to recognize a higher authority."

Father Joe approaches the table and taps the keyboard. An image appears on the screen, an image of a man on a burial cloth. The man appears to have been tortured by scourging, crowned with thorns, crucified and pierced with a lance, the legs unbroken; the crowd becomes hushed and still, tears begin to stream down cheeks as people reach for tissues and handkerchiefs. Father Joe's eloquence and mastery are having an effect on the audience. His prologue has brought them to a point where, having imagined the image in their mind's eye, when they see it, it becomes deeply personal, as if whoever this man on the cloth was, he was something beyond words...something divine.

And now they do believe, for it is truly holy, the burial cloth of Jesus, the God-Man, a megawatt miracle of illumination, searing instantaneously, His divine image into the linen at the moment of His resurrection.

A Book of Evil

When Louis and Tony return to Blackstone, they find positive information in response to Louis' inquiries that causes
them to make an appointment with Sheriff Augustus McClaws
of Cameron County, Texas. The sheriff has some urgent information with respect to recent events that sound just like what they
are looking for.

Under a glaring mid-day sun, Louis and Tony enter the Rio
Grande Valley of South Texas, a landscape dotted with black-
brush and scrub mesquite. In Olmito, they turn off of Texas Route
511 onto Old Alice Road. Within the high security fenced-in
compound of the Carrizalez Detention Center is the Cameron
County Office of Sheriff Augustus McClaws. They enter through
the razor wire-topped swinging steel gate and park in the rear lot
in the corner, finding scarce shade under a green ash near a utility
shed. As they get out of the car, a family of blue-capped Green
Jays scolds from the upper branches.

Sheriff McClaws is a descendant in a bloodline of Texas
lawmen. On his mother's side are two generations of the storied "Los Diablos Tejanos, the Texas Devils," better known as the
Texas Rangers. In 1823, Stephen F. Austin wrote that he would "...
employ ten men...to act as rangers for the common defense" of the
Texas frontier; "the wages I will give said ten men is fifteen dollars
a month" payable in land, to counter the attacks of the Mexican-
Texas border tribes, the fiercest, being the Comanche.

They were the true have-gun-will-travel types of John Wesley
Hardin and Bonnie and Clyde fame. They were the legendary

lawmen of America's Wild West. Before the firepower of the Browning Automatic Rifle, the long gun that tore apart Clyde Barrow's stolen Ford V-8 with he and Bonnie Park in it, a Ranger of the late 1840s relied on his horse. He wore a full beard, knotted neckerchief, and tanned cowhide chaps under a soft wide-brimmed sombrero. He more resembled a Vaquero, a Mexican cowboy. His one-shot Hawken flintlock rifle was backed up by a pistol tucked in his belt with a bowie knife. He had to rely on his horse because without it, against the Comanche, his carcass would be left for the vultures.

And when it was called for, they had to be mean, as mean as John Wesley Hardin who once killed a man because he was snoring. The snorer was one of 40 men killed by Hardin. After a pursuit covering three states, a Ranger cornered Hardin and four other bad men on a train. In the ensuing shootout, he killed one of Hardin's boys and captured Hardin, with an outlaw's bullet through his hat to prove it.

Sheriff McClaws hasn't carried a gun in years, not everyday, at least. If he is out in the field and trouble presents itself, he allows his young deputies to handle the deadly force business for him. But after seeing that crime scene, he is reconsidering.

A tall blond deputy with a full-flared mustache greets them in the lobby. The laces in his tactical boots match the color of his coyote-colored shirt, a five-point silver badge, finial gold acorns fixed at the ends of a black and silver hat cord down around the crown of his black campaign hat. The deputy seats them in the conference room, in black leather recliners, a large wood plaque of the State of Texas outlining Cameron County in shiny brass hangs on the wall. Propped in the corner side-by-side are The Lone Star State flag of Texas and the Stars and Stripes. Pictures of famous Western lawmen adorn the walls: Earp, Masterson,

Hickok, Garrett, Tilghman, and Texas' own Roy, "The Hanging Judge" Bean.

Sheriff McClaws, in his late fifties, appears in his crisp uniform, a navy necktie pinned in the center with a miniature silver five-pointed badge. A robust, stoutly-built man with a full head of white-silver hair and tidy groomed mustache; his face is care-worn but congenial, reflecting decades of bearing the weight of responsibility on his shoulders. He extends his meaty hand, and with a firm handshake, he offers coffee and homemade peach cobbler to the agents.

"Since I invited you down here, I felt I better have something special waiting for you." It is the very best Texas-style cobbler in the state made from scratch by my loyal assistant." Maggie, his secretary, smiles from across the other side of the meeting room as she places a fresh pot of coffee on the side table. Smart-looking and in her early thirties, with layered shoulder-length auburn hair, she's dressed in Southern Living style, a sleeveless color-blocked cactus green Alfani, tied in front with chic matching pumps .

"It's my great grandmother's recipe. The batter is a family secret; that way, this is the only place you can enjoy it. I'm hoping it brings you back. We've got vanilla ice cream in the break room, may I bring it in for you gentlemen?" she asks politely. The agents look at each other.

"Why not, sure might not have this opportunity again," said Tony. They share a pleasant exchange of small talk, enjoying the great-tasting hospitality before the sheriff brings them around to the business at hand.

"Gentlemen, I've been in this business for over thirty years, but never in my life have I seen anything this bad. It's downright evil; nothing random or routine about it," said the sheriff. He reaches for a brown accordion folder on the table. "This activity on both ends of the bridges appears to have started about three months ago. The Tamaulipas State Police, who have been fairly cooperative lately, have shared their incident reports with us. I think this is a new level of violence even *they* haven't seen, and that's saying a lot. They're aware that some of it has washed up over here with evidence pointing back and forth across the border," he advised. "Just look at these three cases going back to the beginning of spring, and this last one, across the river in Matamoros; I see it in my mind when I *don't* want to see it."

"They got across the river to our side somehow, someway. It's probable that some crossed upriver onto the ranch lands and made their way east back to here. But we *do* know that they are using the trains, boarding them somewhere outside Matamoros. I talked with the Border Patrol, they've made multiple arrests on commercial crossings at the old bridge," the sheriff explains. "The MS-13s are more slippery, and it appears that they've taken complete control of the day-to-day smuggling of the migrants. For some reason, there seems to be an escalating degree of MS-13 activity around here," he adds.

The more fear that you show, the more they will attack. And then, they will eat you to the bone. 'Mata, Viola, Controla,' translated to kill, rape, control-the mantra of Mara Salvatrucha, MS-13, the most dangerous gang on the planet. Named after a colony of Amazon army ants, they tattoo themselves with the letter M, the 13th letter in the alphabet, Los Emes. Like a voracious column of ants marching across the jungle floor devouring all living things in their path, so the criminal gang of MS-13 wreaks havoc on anyone who gets in their way. The gang originated in 1980s Los Angelos, immigrant Salvadorans, some military-trained, fleeing a bloody civil war. From El Salvador, at first, but now gang members come from all over South America.

From the folder, the sheriff pulls out a packet of crime scene photos and passes them across the table. The agents take several minutes to look them over, unconsciously grimacing and groaning at what is in the photographs.

The sheriff takes the black binder and opens it to reveal its contents, a stack of on-scene incident reports.

"The chief over there has a witness that they're doing their best to protect. He told them that he was in the final stages of initiation to become a "Home Boy" and become one of them. In detail, he laid it out that the murders were planned to take place at midnight as part of a drug-cash exchange outside in the parking lot of the Del Sol Plaza Fiesta on Cardenas Ave-101. Three machetes were kept in the back of one of the SUVs for the initiation. The ranking leader's plan was to vest-up around the corner and distribute the blades.

Besides the leader, there were ten gang members, and him, the witness, who was one of three to be initiated. The witness was somehow able to remove himself from the scene before it went down and didn't stick around for the attack. But a bank surveillance camera across the street captured it all on tape. It's hard to watch, even from a distance. If these photos of the crime scene aren't enough, you're welcome to watch the video," offers the sheriff. "It's by far the most gruesome we've seen yet. Our incidents over here involve more typical MS-13 assaults, but they're definitely MS-13, all lathered in tattoos. We arrested two of them. We had Deputy Lopez question them in Spanish; they didn't talk. I didn't expect that they would."

"The witness did provide a good description of the leader, though. What stood out, a tattoo of a goat face with horns on the middle of his forehead..."

"This decapitation stuff, how should I say it, has been happening at and around the border for some time now, the Cartels, and now, MS-13. I hope the people around here aren't becoming numb to it," sighs the sheriff. You men are welcome to use the office inside the Cameron County Jail in Brownsville; it's on East Harrison between 10th and twelfth."

"That would work perfectly for us if you don't mind, we won't cause any trouble for you, Sheriff...I hope," says Louis.

"Excuse me, Sheriff, one last thing, that description of the goat face tattoo, this isn't the first place we've heard about it. I'll keep you informed," said Louis.

"What do you think, Tony, good enough for now?" asks Louis.

"Yep, I'm good to go."

Mothers and Monasteries

They stay the night on South Padre Island at The Peninsula Island Resort & Spa, a 4-star hotel, which accepts the government rate. From their private balcony, they have a spectacular view of the Gulf. Their nostrils catch the invigorating scent of sea salt in the air-a postcard picture of sailboats floating out on the water with colorful sails filled by the wind-the lure of the sea.

They order Ceviche Peninsula with shrimp for an appetizer. A gull lands on a fence post-wrapped in nautical rope, eyeing their dinner. Piña Coladas frozen with maraschino cherries are a perfect choice after the heat of the day. Based on the waiter's recommendation, Tony orders the blackened fish tacos. After a few bites, he is pleased at the authentic Mexican taste, while Louis enjoys an entre of red snapper Acapulco.

"I'm beat, Tony, no swimming pool for me tonight, although it sure looks inviting. I better call Hannah before she puts the kids to bed." "What do you think about watching the river tonight, just to get a feel for the area?" suggests Louis. "Sounds like a plan," concurs Tony.

Louis' wife, Hannah, has a master's degree in library science. At this point in time, she is a dedicated stay-at-home mom to their oldest daughter, Teresa, who is ten, and their two "Irish twins", Joshua, a boy of 4, and Jaida, a girl, age 3, who are less than a year apart. After an extremely difficult pregnancy, they were told by the doctors that the baby would most likely be their last. But they prayed for more children, if only one more, and so God gave them "twins".

Teresa was a Down syndrome baby, who has become the beating heart of the extended family. When first diagnosed, they listened to suggestions from medical professionals to "terminate" the pregnancy. After getting up from their knees, they chose to embrace the spirit of the remarkable Mother Teresa of Calcutta, the baby's namesake, and her famous saying, "I know God won't give me anything I can't handle. I just wish he didn't trust me so much." They decided to entrust the infant's life and well being to God, and as a result, it was this special baby's life that enriched *their* lives; she became a joyous family rallying point. Teresa's birthday is a must-family get-together. She never tires of playing Lynyrd Skynyrd's, Sweet Home Alabama, and playing it loudly.

> "Bee-ig' wheels keep on turnin',
> carry me home to see my kin,
> Singing songs about the south-land,
> I miss 'ole' 'bamy once again,
> And I think it's a sin."

Her favorite saying is, "Nothing happens by accident." She has become a frequent playmate of three children at the Shrine in Hanceville.

Hannah and Louis have made their home in Hanceville, Alabama, which is her husband's hometown. She grew up in Birmingham, about forty miles to the north. They met as students of the University of North Alabama (UNA) in Florence, noticing one another while visiting Leo the Lion III in his on-campus habitat. They are both Alabamians to the core, a "How y'all doin'" friendliness, finding simple pleasure in such things as a serving of country-fried steak and butter beans. Louis had once dreamed of preppy sophisticated girls from the northeast coast of New

England, but it was Hannah's voice with that syrupy warmth of the Deep South, that claimed him in the end.

"Hello Louis," she beams, so happy to speak with her husband. "Hello honey, how was your day? Missing you and the kids, it was a long day," he said.

"Well, we had a good day today; it was hot, so we were in the pool a lot, and had story-time out in the back on the swing. I'm so glad you put that up under the trees, we've really enjoyed it this summer."

"We attended Mass this morning at the monastery, and after Mass, we said hello to Sister Helen. Did you know that she corresponds with Eva Greene, I mean *the* Eva Greene, as in the first lady of the United States! Can you *believe* it, isn't that exciting? Sister is so modest she would never have mentioned it unless I brought up the visitors that travel here. The first lady had an uncle who was a priest who took her to the monastery, and during her visit, she became acquainted with Sister Helen, and they have corresponded by mail ever since. Amazing, what a small world. And she was able to meet Mother Angelica at the Shrine. The first lady had been a big admirer from watching her on EWTN," Hannah relates happily.

When people mention Mother Mary Angelica, they talk about her in the present tense, as if she is still alive; people do that because they believe her presence is alive and well, that she is with and around them every day.

"Holiness is not for wimps and the cross is non-negotiable sweetheart, it's a requirement." Mother Angelica had a way of telling it like it is, that is, right from wrong. She wore a full traditional habit, her beaming bespectacled face framed in white under veil, wimple and coif, her signature mini-gold monstrance, a receptacle of the Blessed Sacrament, hangs down from her neck. Using a direct no-nonsense style, a natural comedienne, along with her endearing sense of humor, she was fearless. In a sweet way, she could figuratively hit you in the teeth with a baseball bat to let you know if you were getting too caught up in yourself. She saw the big picture, the big picture that carries on into eternity, and eternity is a very long time. And those who she most helped, most loved: sinners. She sold the thing that nobody wants, better than anyone, suffering. She gave it meaning: redemptive. Suffering from injustice, are you? No better example than the Son of God.

Born Rita Antoinette Rizzo in Canton, Ohio. The Rizzos' community was an example of the rough-hewn small towns sprinkled across mid-America. She learned at the School of Hard Knocks. But maybe it led to one of her popular sayings: "You must laugh your way to heaven because tears won't get you there." At an ordinary church and school in Northeast Ohio, that only God could have arranged, at Saint Anthony's, the patron saint of lost things, is where Rita Rizzo was found and baptized into the faith; and what a faith it became.

During one of her live on-the-air TV shows, Mother illustrated faith and imperfections, the common inconveniences of life by demonstrating, "if God gave us a nose, sometimes we have to blow it." Naturally, without hesitation, she used her handkerchief at that moment, saying "some TV producers would faint if I did this, but if l didn't, I'd have a runny nose." She was for real. "We can only find perfection in love for one another," she'd say. Her explanation for a mother's Herculean effort to lift an automobile off of her child...love.

In real life, she was a friend of Hollywood celebrities. To old men who leave their spouses: "Hey, Mr., your bald head is no morning sunrise, sorry!" or the absurdity of going to hell for a family fight over something as petty as a fancy inlaid commode. "Imagine," she said, "someone already there asks, 'And what are you down here for?'"

She said, "The self-righteous liked to put the period in the wrong place, prematurely, they like to pick and choose the parts of the Gospel that justifies their behavior. But there is usually much more to complete the words uttered by Jesus, so one has to read on. Yes, the woman caught in adultery was forgiven, her soul cleansed by the Lord's admonition to those who would condemn and then stone her to death: 'who of you are without sin'? Do not judge or you, yourself will be judged,' was His message. But let us not forget the second part: 'Go and sin no more...' *Period*."

"We have been given wonderful freedom of will to be 'for God or against him,'" she said. The angels had this one choice. And so Lucifer chose the latter. Man goes to hell because he wants to, because he loves evil. Like a thief in the night will come Lucifer. Admittedly, she was there to scare you, scare you straight, straight off the path to hell. She wanted, or should say, *wants* you to get to heaven, she still does.

And how much did she value prayer? "If you have a problem in your life that you can't fathom or understand, you have to examine your prayer life, *not the problem.*" That's how much.

She mentioned that she is glad that people don't know her IQ-didn't do too well on the test, said she, thought it was dumb, scored a 90, but then, she joked that the results showed that it was *she* who was the dummy. She then went on to mention that in these competitive times, having to be always on top, to be important, then explaining what is truly important, the virtue of humility, and that it is the children and the child-like who will inherit the world. Imagine this saintly nun grading out to an "average" IQ, and yet, being responsible for over 300 million viewers in more than 145 countries, the foundress of the Eternal Word Television Network, better known as EWTN; just a tad better than average, wouldn't you say?

And Mother Angelica's illumination would have prophetic meaning for events taking shape. "There will be hard times when your faith will be attacked and when your doubts will be increased. What will you do? Persevere in prayer now."

New Frontiers of Old

Clarissa Turner could have gone to any university in the country, but she intentionally chose a place where her ethnicity would not be in the demographic majority, but, nonetheless, she chose a relatively safe place to get an education. That place would be in the City of San Antonio, in South Central Texas. A plump and freckled strawberry blonde, she grew up in a sheltered bedroom community just north of Atlantic City, New Jersey, and when she realized that the competitive swimming times she posted fell well short of scholarship material, she settled on being a scholar. Her name is derived from the Latin word *Clarus*, which means "bright, clear, or famously brilliant." She never expected to be famous, but bright she is. During her junior year in high school, to strengthen her social background as a college prospect, she volunteered to be a counselor in a summer camp for underprivileged kids at the Jersey Shore. With many of the campers being the children of local hotel and casino workers, the experience inspired her to pursue a liberal arts degree featuring Mexican American studies. The best place to receive an authentic education in that field, she decided, was at an institution in a practical locality, preferably, in one of the border states with Mexico. Hence, she chose UTSA.

She had won the battle with her parents to reduce the U.S. Secret Service protection detail assigned to her to a minimum. With reservations, her parents agreed to regular monitoring of her well-being, but unimposing from a discreet distance. She wanted to be treated as normal, to be an anonymous college student pursuing her education, and not as the privileged daughter of the vice president of the United States of America.

Following her second year, she and three of her friends have been able to find a more spacious and suitable place at a rental house just outside the edge of the main campus.

When, on a free weekend, she and her friends visited the site of a famous battle, only fifteen miles south of the campus, they were not aware that about three hundred years ago, a special statue of a saint had been sculpted to fit inside a niche carved into the face of a limestone block, comprising one of four statues gracing the face of a historic chapel there.

Way back when, before college kids made the area their temporary home, a variety of wild game-bear, cougar, and wolves lived here. Herds of buffalo occasionally roamed into the region to graze. Alligators and unique fish, like the long-snouted alligator gar, big snapping turtles, and blue catfish swam in the clear streams. Many species of birds, green parakeets and blue and green macaws, fluttered about the grassy river banks amongst the cacti, prickly pear, and mesquite. And the diamondback rattler has continued to thrive here, blending in with the loam and clay landscape.

The uniqueness of the landscape is framed by the magnificent grandeur of silvery-gray trees, the bald cypress trees that bring awe and beauty to the waterways of this part of the Lone Star State. In early summer, their fine fern-like leaves give a soft and graceful appearance. These deciduous conifers are a member of the redwood family, among the first trees in Texas to shed reddish orange needle-like leaves in autumn, and the last to show bright, lime-green buds in April. Their prodigious domes provide nesting sites for ospreys, bald eagles, and the great blue heron.

Here, fresh water springs gushing as high as twenty feet in the air were the source of life-sustaining water from the natural aquifers underground. The Native People, the Coahuiltecans (kwa-weel-tekens), sleek and sinewy experts with the bow and arrow of the Payaya tribe, had a great reverence for the fresh water springs, calling them "Wan Pupaco."

The Coahuiltecans considered the springs to be divinely sent because, as they saw it, the water came out of the womb of Mother Earth. In ceremonial festivities, the thriving wildlife along the streams and tributaries of the waterways had always played a symbolic role.

They believed in the Great Spirit, a supernatural force ruling the universe. Twinklings in the celestial skies, the rain, the thunderstorms, and the droughts were believed to be signs from heaven, or faces, of the Great Spirit, through which he manifested his moods to show his favor or his displeasure.

On June 13, 1691, Spanish General Domingo de Teran led a small expedition of Spanish explorers traveling north from Mexico, advancing some 150 miles into present-day Texas. Their brown-robed chaplain, a Franciscan friar by the name of Damian Massanet, met with the Coahuiltecans near the headwaters of the river. A native interpreter translated Father Massanet's question to the Indians, seeking the name of the waterway. He wrote of their response in his missionary diary; they called it "Yanawana." However, playing his role in the "discovery" era, with a New World Christian mindset, Father Massanet named the river "San Antonio de Padua," because on this day, the joyous feast of the Catholic Saint Anthony was celebrated.

The Franciscan would teach, and the Coahuiltecans would come to believe in a true Great Spirit, the Holy Spirit of the Trinity, One in the same with the First Person of the Trinity, the Father, whose indignant wrath would make it rain for forty days and forty nights to flood the face of the earth. The same divine Spirit of the same divine Father would soon show His favor to a boat-load of people and creatures floating on top of the waters on a big wooden arc. These were the divine Father's faithful children who would release a dove over the flood waters, and that dove would return with a sprig of green to usher in a new beginning.

In May 1718, the settlement that preceded the main campus of UTSA had begun as a fort built near the San Antonio River, designed for protection of the Spanish mission San Antonio de Valero. The new Spanish governor of Texas, Martin de Alarcon, and his Presidio soldiers, constructed the fort with barracks and huts to house the soldiers and their families of the expeditions. This complex was located in what is now San Antonio.

In the middle 17th century, after acquiring horses and ponies from the Spaniards, mounted Apache bands rode from the southern Plains of New Mexico and moved southeastward to raid the lands of the Payaya tribes. They attacked and drove these hunting-and-gathering tribes into a haven of protective structures erected by the Spaniards.

And on the Apache's heels, there came the threat of another more ferocious tribe, an off-shoot of the Shoshone. Wearing red and black face paint, brandishing European armor and flintlock muskets to bolster their own lances and bows, the Comanche brought their unwelcomed aggression upon the Apache to drive their chief rival away in conquest of the San Antonio region of Texas.

To support the needs of the missionaries, de Alarcón deemed necessary the construction of a way station between the settlements along the Rio Grande and the new missions in East Texas. Temporarily constructed out of sticks, straw, and mud, the new mission was developed near the headwaters of the San Antonio River, and was near to the community of Coahuiltecans, which these natives would find a safe haven. The mission served their souls, and at the same time, it protected their skins from attacks by the Indian raiders.

In 1758, the chapel, which still stands today, was constructed out of four-foot thick limestone blocks, cut and shaped in an ornamented cruciform, with a long nave and short side transepts extending outward. The new mission, called San Antonio de Valero, was named after Saint Anthony of Padua.

At some point, probably derived from the Spanish name for a nearby stand of cottonwood trees, the formerly ecclesiastical place came to be known as the Alamo.

In the early 19th century, after the religious purpose of the mission was abandoned, the surrounding walls of the mission were installed with cannon, and the former convent was converted into military barracks. From 1821, a series of struggles between the Republic of Texas and Mexico, called the Texas Revolution, came to a boiling point. In December 1835, Mexican forces surrendered the Alamo to a force of besieging Texans and retreated across the border. The Texans thought that their struggle with Mexico was over, but it was not to be.

In January 1836, believing that the complex would not hold up to a siege, General Sam Houston ordered a contingent of Texans to take away the artillery pieces and destroy the fortress. The soldiers, after realizing the strategic importance of the place, individually voted for a resolution to stand up and defend the Alamo rather than abandon it. On February 23rd, the Mexican Army recrossed the border and laid siege to the Alamo in an effort to recapture it.

The chapel proper would serve as the last bastion in a desperate battle where eleven of the last living defenders manned two twelve-pounder cannons and fought beside them to the end before being overwhelmed and bayoneted to death.

March 6, 1836, is the shared date of death registered for William Travis, James Bowie, and Davy Crockett and their compatriots. President-General Antonio López de Santa Anna ordered that their bodies be stacked and burned.

Sisters Throughout the Centuries

The statue of note in one of the four niches displayed the sculpted image of Saint Clare of Assisi, the 13th-century saint; she, of striking beauty and finery, who turned her back on those worldly gifts to found the Order of Poor Ladies, a monastic religious order for women in the Franciscan tradition, commonly referred to today as the Poor Clares.

It was in 1234, at the convent of San Damiano in Assisi, that Saint Clare, with a spiritual and physical act of faith, unnerved a rampaging invasion of murderous cutthroats hired by Emperor Frederick II of Sweden. The rapacious horde had surrounded the town before breaking through the gates when her cloistered virgins summoned her from her sick bed. Crying and trembling with fear, they pleaded with her to defend them as they were about to become violated and sexually feasted upon by a regiment of vicious Saracen mercenaries.

Moved by the Spirit within her, she prostrated herself before the Lord in the tabernacle and tearfully implored the Son of God for protection, begging Him not to deliver His handmaids into the hands of ruthless pagans. Suddenly, a clear child-like voice emanated from the holy receptacle: "I will protect you!" Then, regaining her feet, with her face streaked with tears, she comforted her nuns: "I assure you, daughters, that you will suffer no evil, you need only to have faith in Christ."

Breaking into the chapel, the intruders confronted the sisters, expecting frightened submission, but what they saw before them unnerved them: a nun holding high a ciborium, possessing a faith-filled fearlessness. Abruptly, they recoiled and scattered like a flock of geese, high-tailing it back over the walls from which they came. When the threat had passed, their abbess, their mother, instructed those present to, "Take care not to tell anyone about that voice while I am still alive, dearest daughters."

Though the statue of Saint Clare had been removed from its niche before the Battle of the Alamo, her spiritual guidance would be sought, over two hundred years later, in an even greater struggle sought by another convent of Poor Clares nearly one thousand miles away, worshiping in silence, at a monastery in Hancevile, Alabama.

The wrought iron gates swing open underneath an arch atop which two angels kneel, holding a shield and coat of arms between them. It is the entrance to a different world, a place of genuine serenity, a place where the afflicted can find relief, an oasis for the thirsty to dip into a fountain of forgiveness to find that elusive inner peace, a respite apart from the chaotic demands of the modern world.

They began in a garage in Irondale, Alabama with only $200 to their names. Earlier, in May of 1962, Mother Angelica, Sister Raphael, Sister Joseph, Sister Michael, and Sister Assumpta had left Santa Clara Monastery in Canton, Ohio for God's new groundwork in the soil of Northern Alabama.

The nuns embraced the network from the beginning, taking calls at the telethons, giving tours to visitors, opening mail, printing programs, they even began a fishing lure business, named St. Peter's Fishing Lures, to raise funds for a monastery. But most of all, praying for the work God had surprisingly entrusted to these cloistered nuns!

In 1995, while visiting the Sanctuary of the Divino Nino Jesus in Bogota, Columbia, Mother Angelica received a vision while praying before a small statue of the divine child Jesus. The statue came to life and said to her, "Build Me a Temple, and I will help those who help you." Following this experience, Mother Angelica looked at sites for about four months before settling on a 400-acre property in Hanceville. According to Mother Angelica, the spot was chosen because she "felt the presence of God here."

In December 1999, the shrine of the Most Blessed Sacrament at Our Lady of the Angels Monastery in Hanceville was consecrated.

The once unimaginable dream had become a reality. It would become the great media apostolate that it is today.

These humble little cloistered nuns, the Poor Clare nuns of Perpetual Adoration are contemplative nuns with a unique missionary vision, and with solemn exposition, are dedicated to perpetual adoration of our Lord in the most blessed sacrament. With the privilege of solemn vows, they are a part of the Second Order of Saint Francis of Assisi.

Fittingly, the shrine is a place of worship for people of all faiths, offering opportunities for visitors and pilgrims to find peace and rest in the presence of our Lord.

Little Ones and Outlaws

The monastery sits near the banks of a natural loop in the southwest flow of the Mulberry Fork, a tributary of the Black Warrior River. The Mulberry Fork drains part of the southernmost end of the Appalachian Mountains north and west of Birmingham. The winding tree-lined stream provides fish and wildlife a habitat of deep pools, channels, and sandy shoals.

Lately, three children, a boy and two girls, have been seen catching sunfish and frogs in the Mulberry Fork. The youngest is known as the The Little One. She and her two cousins appear to live in a nearby trailer park. They are often seen laughing and singing on the rusty swing set in the adjacent dirt playground. The Little One wears a bright blue dress, which never seems to lose its brightness, and a deeply fragrant scent emanates from her person. The Little One moves with a concentrated effortlessness known in Italy as Sprezzatura, her exertions are unforced and graceful. Her facial expressions capture the joy of youthful innocence.

From a distance, she and her two cousins have been seen playing with three little white dogs, but one observer could have sworn that he saw three little white sheep. The nuns at the monastery are reluctant to reveal the youngest's name, but that doesn't seem to matter to anyone, calling her "The Little One" is perfectly charming.

Another train whistles its approach from the Mexican side. Louis and Tony sit in their vehicle, staring across the river to the Mexican side, blinking, trying to stay awake; caffeine only works up to a point.

Louis dozes off, dreaming at the secret spot at the creek in Cheaha State Park...the piercing shrill of a red-tailed hawk circling below a patch of pure white clouds...

Progress would find its way to Southern Appalachia because of its one valuable and plentiful resource coveted by a rapidly developing nation, trees. Combined with the lengthening of the railroad system, the dense forests made for a profitable lumber industry. The railways allowed enterprising capitalists to meet the insatiable demand for an ever-growing nation.

But not all young and able Alabamians of those times could be successful being a logger or a farmer. With no skills other than what they learned during the Civil War, they had to make a living somehow, someway, and thus emerged the outlaws.

And one, in particular, Reuben Houston Burrow, had made an honest effort to make a living as a farmer, but a plague of yellow fever came from the Caribbean. It was spread by ravaging mosquitoes, which took the life of his young wife, Virginia, and left him with two small children. When his second attempt to raise crops failed, his outlook on life changed. He turned to robbing banks.

He was called the Robin Hood of Alabama because he never took from the poor. This was before the days of sports heroes. The celebrities of those days were the outlaws and the lawmen who pursued them. The best-selling dime novels of those times featured bank and train robberies and shootouts between bad guys and good guys. Others would eventually cash in on their fame, but not the outlaws themselves. The instant wealth they had stolen would be of no use to them, nor were the profits generated from the sale of merchandise produced in their memory, macabre commercial photographic postcards of them laid out with the tools of their trade in their coffins, briskly sold to a mesmerized public.

With his little brother Jim, he recruited some acquaintances to form the Burrow gang. Express trains of those days were slow moving and could be derailed by placing rocks and logs on the track, but they were also robbed by outlaws sneaking on board at train stations and then waiting for the right moment to rush the conductor and stick their six-shot hoglegs in his face, encouraging him to hit the brakes. With ear-piercing wheel metal on rail metal, kicking up a shower of sparks, the train would come to a screeching halt, and the bandits would go about their work.

On December 9, 1887, at Genoa, Arkansas, Rube and his gang boarded a train and drilled the Southern Express car door full of lead, causing it to be opened from the inside by the Express man.

Inside, the bandits gathered up more than $3,000, about $75,000 in today's currency. But unwittingly, they had won big in another way, they had scooped the winning ticket to the Louisiana Lottery. They never did cash in, rather, they rode into Texas, where the long-arm-of-the-law tracked them down. They got in a gunfight, but before galloping away, they left behind some personalized horse tack that led the lawmen to a gang member who squealed on the whole bunch.

The trail of evidence led to Alabama, where Rube's brother Jim was arrested. Rube was able to use the backwoods of Southern Appalachia to carry on his looting ways until he was caught in October 1890. On December 8th, with a concealed gun, he made a successful jail break, locking two deputies in his cell. But instead of running for the hills, he took another by gunpoint to a nearby store where he tried to recover his confiscated money. But his taste of freedom ended then and there. A gunman named Dixie Carter walked up and shot him dead. His career, which had begun in Arkansas and ended in Alabama, lasted one day short of four years.

But his legacy lives on. His postcard, gobbled up by the public at fifty cents apiece, shows him laid upright in his wood coffin, bareheaded, eyes closed, wearing the same outfit he died in, his cowboy hat planted on his chest, his stiff hands grasping his pistol belt and six-shooter, a lever-action rifle at his feet, prominently propped up on public display.

Through their night-vision scopes, they watch in amazement as an armor-plated armadillo casually waddles its way out of a patch of wild sunflowers near the water's edge. They are parked on a beige pebble road on the railroad side of the old bridge spanning the Rio Grande. They have been parked there since midnight. During the night, across the river in the distance, they hear the occasional sound of the balazos, the ominous bursts of automatic gunfire from the drug cartels known to the local Mexicans as Los Manosos, to everyone else...the Narcos.

Nurses, Narcos and Army Rangers

"Tony, I checked with Sheriff McClaws. He knows Sheriff Ramirez well; that team out at Eagle Pass has two Texas Rangers that served together in Afghanistan. Both were severely wounded during an airborne assault on a remote Taliban stronghold. When he told me about them, something triggered in the back of my mind. My older sister Ginnie had trained as a triage nurse at Walter Reed National in Bethesda. She had told me about these two Army Rangers she was nursing back to health. They were in the same combat unit, both of them had been seriously wounded in Afghanistan on the same day. One was a captain who had been shot through the top of his skull, causing him to literally fall off the top of the mountain, breaking his back in several places. The other, a specialist, had been shot clean through his chest and upper arm. She had developed a fondness for them, humorously relating how the captain would yell across the ward to the specialist: 'Specialist Seymour, I need you to procure me a Dr. Pepper, on the double!' The specialist would reply, 'Sir, that's against doctor's orders.' '*Bleep*' the doctor's orders, Specialist, *bring it*!' Ginnie told me how she would sneak the cans of soda pop to the specialist for his captain."

"Both of them, these two, are gentlemen, and kept in touch with her by phone, following, to her amazement, their return to active duty only months later in Afghanistan. She asked the captain what was the reaction of their commander to his return. He said that the colonel said to him: 'Captain, you've just been shot in the head and fallen off a mountain, we're not putting you back in.' Wherein the captain replied 'But *I'm* fine, Colonel. *You're* not scared, *are* you?' The captain told Ginnie that he would've cleaned out the latrine just to get back to his men. He was soon reassigned to his old platoon, and privately, the colonel could not have been more proud of his captain."

"Yeah, and her other patient, the specialist, told her, over-the-phone, his own experience of getting back to his band of brothers. Reporting to the forward base of operations in Kunar Province, he confronted his platoon commander, stood at attention, and promptly saluted. His commander abruptly ordered him to recite the second stanza of the Ranger Creed. The specialist had to respond that he 'didn't know it, *Sir.*' 'Then hit the ground and give me pushups, *Specialist!*' his commander barked. At that point, Ginnie said there was a pause on the other end of the line, and she could sense that he was getting emotional. 'Doing those pushups were the happiest moment of my combat service,' he said, 'because it was what I had signed up for, to be treated... like a soldier.'"

"Where do we get people like that anymore?" marvels Louis.

Surveillance on the job can be excruciatingly boring until it's *not*. There's movement across the river, a lonesome coyote? Probably the same one they'd heard howling since before day-break. "Tony, that's not a coyote, there's a *bunch* of them...*people!*" exclaimed Louis. "I think you're right, where the hell did they come from? Did they just jump off that train?" exclaims Tony. Through their binoculars, they could see that they are wearing black, making their way to the riverbank, inflating a raft, carrying what looks like grappling hooks and rope.

But then they got "made," law enforcement speak for being unintentionally discovered. From somewhere nearby, it could have been their side of the river or the other, an unseen lookout had spotted them. In the blink of an eye, the train jumpers melted away into the thick green foliage. "That kid on the bike, I thought he seemed just too interested in us." Tony remarks with a frown.

Was this a practice run, a diversion?

With the break of dawn, a chorus of chirping crickets and serenading cicadas is fading away while a reddish sun is rising over the Gulf. In the morning coolness, a flurry of early morning foot and bicycle traffic begins as Mexican workers make their way across the pedestrian bridge from their homes in Matamoras to their job sites in Brownsville.

Here at the bridges, you can easily toss a rock across the Rio Grande. But this narrow stretch of river is a boundary dividing safety versus danger, serious danger.

"Bienvenidos a Mexico" reads the large gold lettering on the upper face of the Mexican border gate . At one time, not too long ago, people did feel welcome. Taking the pedestrian footbridge to Matamoras was an everyday path to a bright and festive town in the Mexican State of Tamaulipas. But today, the bright blue, green, and pink pastel-colored shops and sidewalk cafes are faded. Here, the word "Feliz" does not follow Casa anymore, the homes no longer happy. And lately, people who have walked across the bridge into the town have never walked back. Because today, the town is a battleground between the Gulf Cartel, in Spanish, Cártel del Golfos or CDG, and Los Zetas.

Motorists driving south on Matamoros-San Fernando Highway (Mexico Route 101) out past the hotels and commercial district, the landscape becomes a picture of classic southwestern desert, tumbleweeds, and cactus. Looming up ahead, growing larger, spray painted on the face of a small mountain, a giant scorpion, fiendish. Like a royal tiger spraying his scent to mark his territory in his jungle domain, Los Escorpiones spray paint the hills along Tamaulipas highways to mark these drug-running routes as theirs. And woe to anyone or any group that doesn't heed to their warning. Los Escorpiones are the most ferocious of the factions within the CDG. Like the five New York families of the Italian mob–La Cosa Nostra, there is constant infighting between CDG factions for supremacy.

A former Gulf Cartel, Don Antonio Cardenas Guillen, better known by the locals as "Tony Tormenta," was taken out in a fire-fight by the Armada de Mexico, armed to the teeth with grenades and automatic weapons. But not before his and another one hundred corpses littered the ground near the border.

And lately, a dreaded rival cartel has built an empire with its own deadly force of Sicarios that don't scare all that easily. Uniformed in jungle boots and cameo, carrying new AK-308s, are Los Zetas. They are the elites, former military types, professionally trained, who began as hired guns for the Narcos and then violently forged a regime for themselves; they spray paint their mountains... with a Z.

Once a carefree and happy place, where people who imagined spending their money on grilled fajitas and sizzling costillas, now anxiously dread losing their money to armed robbers or being escorted at gunpoint to an ATM to make a forced maxed-out withdrawal. That's if they're lucky. Sexual assaults, ransom kidnappings, and murder happen now all too frequently. The people have become numb to the violence. And to expect the local lawmen to respond to a crime in progress, there is a reason for their hesitation.

A short distance downriver, floating in the Gulf of Mexico's Laguna Madre, a fisherman spotted what he thought was a loose buoy tangled in seaweed. But when he used an oar to poke at the clump, he discovered in horror, a headless body, its empty neck still dripping in blood. This was no boating accident. It looked like the head had been severed with a sharp blade, a machete. The Narcos' version of payback for knowing too much.

You decide, "plata o plomo," do you want the silver or the lead? This is the choice thrust upon police officers, prosecutors, and judges that would dare uphold the law. So many choose to take the money, and thus, the Narcos reign. And victims and witnesses don't dare talk, for fear of their lives.

And even across on the US side, especially at night, stray bullets from the balazos pay no regard to the border checkpoints.

A Señorita Has A Date

"Do we know if the Nationals are guarding contraband on this Union Pacific route?" asks Tony. "Our consulate rep over there said that things have died down over there since the big round-up," said Louis." I heard the task force collared the sheriff here in the States, the dad of the Narco, taking his cut on this side; can you believe that?" asks Louis.

"Hey, man, being from South Texas, no it doesn't, nothing surprises me around here anymore," said Tony.

"But I've got some good news, our agent in Matamoros says that a señorita walked into the Consulate last week and offered to provide some information to the Drug Enforcement Administration (DEA) on CDG. She's motivated, her twin brother disappeared last month, he was last seen at the Restaurante on Calle 3ra and Libra. Thinks a cousin had something to do with it. She works at the university here. She just wants protection, wants it explained to her," Louis says optimistically.

Except for the security attendants booth at the entrance, the U.S. Consulate building in Matamoros is nondescript in appearance as it is supposed to be. Across the street, a gated, tree-lined, well-to-do residence with manicured landscape and a stone-figured fountain of a fish spouts water into the air, cascading down and around it into an aqua-blue wading pool beneath.

Louis rolls down the window as they approach the gate. Both agents show their credentials to the guard who gives them a serious looking over. The guard acknowledges them with a "Buenos dias" before opening the gate and lowering the steel spikes in the pavement for them to pass. They are greeted at the door by a smiling young clean-shaven DEA agent. The agent leads them through a hallway into a briefing room. The agent seats them and asks them if they'd like some bottled water, they accept, and he walks out to retrieve his material. "I've got socks older than that kid," whispers Tony while shaking his head. Louis laughs out loud at the fitting remark. The agent re-enters the room carrying two bottles of spring water and a notepad. "Thanks for coming, guys, I was hoping somebody would be interested in this. From the look of things, this might have far-reaching impact," notes the DEA agent. "With what this Confidential Human Source (CHS) told me, I was able to find some matching Intel pointing to a terrorist incursion from South America. I reviewed the agent's reports about similar activity along the Gulf," said the DEA agent.

"And, about the witness, I met with her when she came in, she seems legit...and fearless."

After reviewing the reports and taking notes, the meeting is wrapping up. "The book, KILLING PABLO, your guys' case on Pablo Escobar, good stuff, read it twice," remarks Tony. Shaking Tony's hand, "Dude...that's what I signed up for".

Walking to their vehicle. " I dunno Tony, this stuff from the CHS and the rest of the stuff going on south of the border, could this be just one big coincidence?"

Re-crossing the Rio Grande on the International Bridge, a U.S. Customs agent glances at their credentials and waves them through the gate, they turn east at the U.S. Border and Customs building onto palm tree-lined East Elizabeth Street, crossing the bridge over the horseshoe of mustard-brown water of the Fort Brown Resaca. Just past the buildings of the Catholic Diocese of Brownsville, a road sign spells West University Boulevard as they drive onto the campus.

The main entrance to the University of Texas Rio Grande Valley is picturesque, with water fountains, palm trees, manicured lawns, and symmetrical red brick walkways, all framing an impressive main building in Spanish architecture. Like a lookout tower guarding the approaches to the snaking Rio Grande nearby, a portholed, blue-domed cupola rises to its apex.

Maria Joan Menendez walks out from under the neat Sahara-buff bricked arch. She is drop-dead gorgeous, a luxuriant complexion, the color of creamed and sugared coffee. She's wearing a bright yellow sundress, red strapped heels, with designer sunglasses propped on top of her gorgeous jet black hair. Flashing a full-toothed, dazzling-white smile, she extends her hand to the two wide-eyed, gaping-mouthed agents. They each sheepishly shake her hand and show her their government credentials.

"Come with me, guys, I want to show you something." They follow her loping athletic strides to a nearside building.

"Look up there under the top window; do you see that?" They look up to where she is pointing and see a small hole in the brick with a piece of lead protruding. "Narco bullet," she tells them, "It's a way of life around here. You can't imagine what's happening to my country. Seems like overnight, the whole territory across the river is under assault. As you can see up there for yourselves, the evidence shows that it's spilling over. And now it's just not the drugs. Avocado rancheros are being extorted. Pickers are being held at gunpoint all day; can you believe it? For a truckload of avocado! It's just not one gang, there are so many of them that they shoot each other down to see who's going to get to hijack the trucks and trailers for whatever is in them. They chased away a Coca-Cola factory last month. The company gave up and moved out of the country; got no help from our government to protect them."

"I believe they've kidnapped my brother Juan, but I'm not giving up, me, and many more who love our country aren't giving up. We hope and pray that God will provide us with someone, a courageous and honorable leader who will stand up for freedom to take our country back, to take it back from the violent cartels and their colluding politicians."

"It's all about a submission to fear...we once had General Enrique Velarde, who led La Cristiada in the fight against the atheistic tyranny of President Plutarco Calles. Many suffered torture, and many martyrs paid with their lives before a truce led to the reopening of the church. The war was fought with bullets backed by faith and courage. On the eve of battle, General Velarde said to his soldiers: 'Men will fire bullets, but God decides where they land....Viva Cristo Rey!' was their battle cry."

Louis and Tony just stand there with blank expressions, they're not used to hearing anything like this.

"My family is wealthy, my brother and I grew up in an avocado plantation home outside of Uruapan in Michoacán. My parents are devastated, the kidnappers are demanding a $500,000 cash ransom in exchange for my brother," laments Maria.

"I would hope to have the courage to do my part in any resistance to these killers. I have studied the life of my patron saint, Joan of Arc. At nineteen, she followed a voice from God, riding a white steed, wearing a suit of armor, she led the French Army to victory over England's tyranny. She said: 'I am not afraid...I was born to do this.' She was burned to death because of her faith."

Phone Calls and Beggars

It is past midnight, and Maria Menendez is in her bedroom sound asleep. In her dream, she is hearing chimes ringing somewhere off in the distance. She is startled awake. Her cellphone is ringing on top of her dresser.

In a voice barely audible, "M.J...it's Juan...I'm okay," her brother whispers.

"Juan, is it you?" she chokes up. "You're safe?" she implores.

"Yes, I'm good, one of the guards is helping me; can't explain why, I'm not sure, but I think he recognized my scapular. So it's Los Escorpiones, they blindfolded me, drove about two and a half hours to somewhere near a commercial operation. I can hear something like brakes screeching. But listen, there is something bad going to happen; these dudes are plotting something with MS-13. Gotta go, I'll try to call again soon. Viva, love you, sister." Juan breaks off.

"Juan, I love you. Viva, may the angels protect you," she sighs, thankful that her brother is alive. Maria immediately goes into her contacts and finds the number for Agent Ledlow.

Crossing the river into Mexico, on his smartphone, Tony is reading about Father Miguel Agustin Pro. Father Pro was one of the Catholic priests that defied the Mexican government's decree that any clergy caught celebrating Mass or offering the sacraments would be subject to being shot on sight or hanged in public. Father Pro refused to ignore his obligatory duty to the Catholic faithful.

He turned into a master of disguise and escapes. With the police suddenly appearing at a wedding reception, he gently took the arm of a young lady and asked her to dance with him, the police failing to recognize him, they left the premises. He would dress as a beggar in the middle of the night so he could celebrate Mass and perform baptisms and marriages. He impersonated a police officer and entered prisons to bring the sacraments to imprisoned Catholics who had defied the government's shutdown of the churches. Father Pro even dressed up as a fancy businessman and went door to door, trying to collect money for the poor. He did all of these things in obedience to Christ, his King. In 1927, he was arrested and falsely accused of an assassination attempt against a government official.

On November 23, 1927, President Calles ordered the execution of Father Pro by firing squad. Father Pro was marched from his cell into the courtyard where soldiers with rifles were waiting.

Tony stares in awe at the photographs of the public execution. Father Pro blessed the soldiers, and then, with an impatient officer standing nearby holding a blindfold, he kneeled down to pray in silence.

Declining the blindfold, with his back against the log bulwark, he faced his executioners, with a crucifix in one hand and a rosary in the other. He stretched out his arms out in imitation of the crucified Christ and shouted, "May God have mercy on you! May God bless you! Lord, thou knowest that I am innocent! With all my heart, I forgive my enemies!" He then shouted the defiant cry of the Cristeros, "Viva Cristo Rey!"

And then, wilting under a ringing fusillade of bullets, he was martyred.

President Calles knew the assassination attempt charges against Father Pro were false, but he worried about the success of this priest in evading his henchmen using the clever disguises. So Calles had the execution well-documented by journalists and published the photographs in newspapers throughout Mexico. He thought this clear warning was a good way to send a message to anyone else who dared defy his ban on the public practice of Catholicism. But Calles' graphic attempt to deter further defiance backfired. It was reported that around 40,000 people lined the road for the funeral procession, and another 20,000 waited at the cemetery to pay their respects to the slain martyr.

Father Pro's courageous witness to his faith rejuvenated the Cristeros, and many carried the newspaper clipping of his execution on their persons as an inspiration of what it means to live and die for the phrase, "Long Live Christ the King! Viva!" His blood droplets have created a blossoming trail for others to follow in his footsteps...the seeds of the Church.

The outside of Maria's house is painted in a cheerful blue pastel. The interior is even more festive, a kaleidoscope of color. On the wall of the entry hall, Tony sees a picture that makes him feel better, in a gilded frame, Our Lady of Guadeloupe, the banner of the Cristeros.

At her kitchen table set with bright Fiestaware, Maria offers, and the agents find it hard not to accept the iced sweet tea and Crab Rangoon with tangy dipping sauce she has prepared for them. They enjoy the refreshments while Maria tells them about her work at the university. But it is time to get down to business; with steady composure, she tells them about her recent, abrupt, and guarded cellphone conversation with her brother.

"My brother was able to call me again late last night, very briefly, he's still okay, he had to end the call quickly, he said he overheard them talking about caravans," explains Maria.

Did he mean the caravans of refugees trekking from South America to the U.S. southern border?" asks Louis.

"I think so," surmises Maria. "Can I see your phone for a minute?" Tony asks. With Maria's consent Tony uses his smartphone to take a snapshot of Maria's phone history.

Re-crossing the bridge into the U.S., "Wonder what the caravan connection is about," Tony wonders.

"It's right out in the open, perfect cover for someone or some group to blend in," Louis suggests.

"She sure was making eyes at you, Tony."

"What? When? No way."

"*Really*, Tony? At the end, you didn't notice? C'mon man, are you really that oblivious? It was so obvious."

"I guess I was thinking about what to say next. But that Crab Rangoon was delicious."

Recruits of the Red Menace

The PRC has received the results they were hoping for, an in-country trial test of its sinister computer chip implanted in inmate Uyghurs to carry out remote-controlled assaults and murders of Catholic priests and nuns, those who protested the bulldozing of Marian Shrines in China.

The oppression, an underpinning of Marxism, is nothing new. "Transformation of Society," a political slogan, a state-sponsored slogan spoken in 1930, the slogan of Loseb Besarionis dze Jughashvili, also known as Comrade Joseph Vissarionovich Stalin. Stalin means "Man of Steel." He would forge a "new" socialist society. Stalin's new society would be a society of the people. The people that Stalin favored would be the right kind of people, ordinary, industrious, and loyal...loyal to the State. These people, as preferred by Stalin, were more commonly known as peasants.

Actually, Stalin, like his predecessor and benefactor, Vladimir Ilich Lenin, were students of Karl Marx, the German philosopher who produced "The Communist Manifesto."

And Marx, himself, had been a student of Franois-Noel Babeuf, better known as Gracchus, whose era in French history was best known for its casual use of the guillotine.

Lenin, exiled to Switzerland, appointed Stalin to serve on the first communist committee, known then as, The Central Committee of the Bolsheviks. Having seized power by overthrowing the Russian tsar, November 1917 would be a date that history would never forget. It wasn't the first large-scale social revolution that used force and violence to obtain its utopian theory of equality. That distinction belonged to Gracchus and another notable of the French Revolution, Maximilien Francois Marie Isidore de Robespierre, whose own fate ironically ended on July 28, 1794 with his own date with the guillotine.

But the Red Terror in Russia lives on to this day. Massive high rise-sized portraits of Lenin and Stalin were not only displayed on the streets in Moscow, but later in communist China's Beijing, as ruled by a former peasant, Mao Zedong, also known as the Red Emperor.

Both regimes featured three things in common: relentless class warfare and the obliteration of private ownership, and the only method to maintain these dictates: State-sponsored terror.

Both regimes had large-scale projects like Mao's, the Great Leap Forward, designed to produce food for the State. Both involved the forced collectivization and harvest of staple crops for the State, and both resulted in the mass starvation of millions.

Those that resisted were rounded up to be put through what the Chinese called "Cheng feng," a brutal process of "reeducation" by starvation and forced labor.

And the State created a habitat of terror that was designed to maintain control over the populace, which, in the USSR, were the Gulags, and in Red China, cloaked in secrecy, the Laogai.

And the regimes needed a systematic method, an organized detachment of cold-blooded killers to implement and carry out wide extermination and forced internment. In the USSR, the State political police were called the Cheka, and within the PRC, they are the People's Armed Police.

The Ministry of State Security, the MSS, the State Intelligence organization of the PRC, has devised a devious scheme utilizing social media to evaluate, select, and cultivate a group of expatriates for the special secretive mission. The recruits share one thing in common, an unshakable certitude about The Communist Manifesto. Global harmony and social justice for all, most importantly, equality for the ordinary man. Seductive. To them, the sins of Communist forefathers are a thing of the past. It is true that communism and Judeo-Christianity have historically not mixed very well, but those selected today are better suited with enlightened education and tolerance to make it work, they believe. But things will remain blurred because the PRC's rationality is that the end justifies the means, while a key commandment of Judeo-Christianity is, "Thou shalt not kill."

The expatriates have gleefully accepted a friendly invitation extended by PRC operatives to serve the State in a special way, to participate in what they are told is a special mission. They are a versatile, multifaceted group with Ph.Ds., consisting of biologists, sociologists, psychologists, electrical engineers, and high-level computer hackers. And they are multilingual, fluent in English and Spanish. As directed, they have completed a series of courses in international cultures online at HarvardX, with emphasis on cultures encompassing the geological span of the mission.

But this State initiative is unlike China's publicly showcased Thousand Talents Plan, a universal recruitment program featured at Wuhan University, aimed at advancing China's economic, scientific, and national security interests. Because it is top-secret and those chosen have a deep-seated resentment toward the United States as the beacon of Western civilization, with its foundational philosophy illuminated by Christianity. They would prefer that America be spelled with a "K." They have called to be important participants in the People's War on Terrorism, and they are all motivated. They are instructed to bring one suitcase of clothing and personal essentials.

They interconnect on ex-allegiant.com and share with each other their surprise and excitement. They are more excited about the opportunity to prove themselves, as many of them feel a shadowy presence, always seeming to be looking over their shoulder. The radius of their residences, in their preferred national sanctuary, span from Shanghai to Beijing. The expatriates from Mexico and the U.S. are the PRC's most prized recruits.

The recruits are given the location for the meeting place. A nondescript State building on South Xinhua Street in Beijing, on the edge of the largest town common in the world, is Tiananmen Square. Dominating the view is the Great Hall of the People, which the recruits are suggested to enjoy and visit before the meeting. It is one of the Ten Great Constructions and a tourist favorite. Built in the Soviet neoclassical style, it opened in 1959, and required 8,000 workers to complete in time for the tenth anniversary celebration of the PRC and the Great Leap Forward.

Inside is the Great Auditorium. A space of three million cubic feet, it holds ten thousand seats for people to attend the annual session of the National People's Congress of ten thousand delegates. And it plays host, on special occasions, to commemorate the leaders of the past.

The 154-foot-high ceiling is a constellation of lights with the PRC's great symbol at the apex, a colossal red glass star. Surrounding the star are glistening waves of gold shells or petals that represent the People, the People of China.

They are lodged in the upper floors of the Shangri-La China World Summit Wing Hotel on Jianguomenwai Avenue in the Chaoyang District. From the sixty-fourth floor, they enjoy a stunning view of the Imperial Palace complex, three and one-half miles to the southeast.

But first, they are given a tour of the Forbidden City.

They board a reserved double-deck tour coach bus painted in lime green with curtains on the upper floor glass windows. Though many of the group visited the ancient site before as tourists, they are excited to see things they may have missed.

Tiananmen Square is dominated by Tiananmen Tower, a massive two-tiered, ten-columned pagoda, meaning: the Gate of Supreme Harmony. It is the PRC's showcase of modern China. A few recruits have arisen early, taking taxis or Didi to hear the long drumroll and watch the mesmerizing Red Military hoisting of the Chinese National flag above the square.

But there are those who will never attend the flag hoisting ceremony, no matter how impressive the event. They include a unique group of forgotten matriarchs, the heartbroken mothers of the hundreds of unarmed college students massacred on "June the Fourth", shot down on Tiananmen Square and crushed under the military tank treads for daring to protest government persecution and control.

The group of twenty-five recruits has gathered at the biggest attraction: Chairman Mao's Memorial Hall, the tomb of Mao Zedong. A pretty college-age tour guide greets them. Her white long-sleeved top is embroidered with a blue outlined patch of Beijing Normal University. She introduces herself as Lin. During her opening remarks, she cordially inquires if any of them have experienced the Peking duck at Quanjude Restaurant in the Dongcheng District on Qianmen. She also warns to watch out for pick-pockets.

At the museum storage depot, they mimic their guide as she deposits her green khaki shoulder bag at the counter. They follow her to a long line of tourists quietly waiting outside the tomb. The group files past the surprisingly small glass-encased corpse of Mao, tucked under a red blanket, and they are astonished at its life-like state of preservation. The guide waits patiently as they peruse the crowded memorial gift shop loaded with souvenir knick-knacks of the embalmed emperor.

She assembles the group outside of the Mao Memorial building and they head for the Tower and Gate. Together, in a tight group, they cross a footbridge flanked by fierce-faced stone lions believed to protect humans from evil spirits. Hanging on the wall above the archway, the large portrait of Mao awaits them. Concealed police surveillance cameras watch them as they gawk at his iconic baldheaded likeness clothed in a buttoned-up drab-gray tunic. They walk under the portrait through the Meridian Gate, a twenty-six-feet thick red stone-walled passageway, and enter the palace courtyard to the ancient dynasties of the Forbidden City.

One of the recruits named Lucas remarks that "If this was 1492, we would have been executed by 'death by a thousand cuts' for trespassing," as he chuckles to himself. Others don't appreciate his feeble attempt at humor, diehards.

They move through the exhibits in silence, imagining the palace grounds with god-like emperors and countless other consorts and concubines, mingling around and about these acres of colorful edifices. After an afternoon of sightseeing, they cross the stone-railed bridge back over the moat. They depart through the Gate of Divine Prowess to the north of the museum. They have seen the grandeur of the ancient dynasties, and they are satisfied.

Throughout the tour, the subject of "June the Fourth" was never brought up, even though the slain students were roughly the same age as the touring recruits. It was not only because any mention of the bloody affair is prohibited, it is also because they have fully bought into the PRC's talking points: 'The central government took decisive measures. The troops took measures to prevent and stop the upheaval. This is a correct policy. As a vaccination for the Chinese society, the Tiananmen incident will greatly increase China's immunity against any major political turmoil in the future.'

The PRC's procurator-in-charge, is Qi Yingjie, which means "rising hero." At six feet five inches, Qi towers over everyone. His handsome chiseled face is striking. But it's his foreboding reputation that stretches far beyond his physical stature.

The interior of the building has been painted in a charming mint green, imparting an atmosphere of welcome. Floral arrangements flank a marble stairway. On the second floor, in the middle of a spacious bright room, is an overlong conference table; the legs are sculpted in a motif of snarling dragons, its surface a sparkling mirror-like finish inlaid with mother of pearl. The wood-carved chairs are upholstered in red fabric, conspicuous five-pointed stars adorn the top rails above the padded headrests.

As they are seated, two attractive females enter the room pushing wheeled carts. They are dressed in white silk tops, black skirts, their hair braided in buns. Dangling from their ears are jewels of tiny red stars enveloped by diamonds. Like United Airlines flight attendants, they wheel their carts down each side of the table to collect their smartphones. One of the recruits named Bram asks, "I've got all my personal stuff stored on my phone, what are you going to do with it?" The assistant, with a smile, responds in perfect English, "For your safety, we are enhancing it with a long-range component to keep us interconnected during the mission."

The women push their carts out of the room all the while smiling. A military-dressed assistant closes the door behind them. Out of sight, the women push their carts to the end of the hallway to an open freight elevator door. The elevator takes them up one floor to another hallway where they get off and push toward an open double door. As they enter, a team of cyber technicians take the smartphones off the carts and briskly install the latest BXAQ malware. Like flypaper, the mobile software instantly snags their texts and phone calls and transmits them in live-time to the MSS.

Procurator Qi greets them warmly in several languages. They are transfixed. To their surprise, his light-hearted humor is disarming and they begin to relax. He mentions the refreshments prepared down the hall and then points a remote device to the end wall, which causes a large motorized screen to drop into place. He walks around to the other end of the table and stands behind a podium, which features the gold-encircled National Emblem of the PRC; the large star in the design represents the Party, the four stars below are the four social classes of the people. And emblazoned below the stars, the Tiananmen Gate, the entrance to the Forbidden City, all in a field of red. The red of revolution.

A projector beams a bold white-lettered greeting on a bright red background: WELCOME GUESTS.

The projector clicks the next image, a bold geographical drawing of a country, instantly recognizable. Inside the perimeter, in bright red, a hammer and sickle. And underneath in bold black letters, "TARGET: UNITED STATES OF AMERICA."

Before dismissal, the recruits are each presented with a silver cased laptop burnished with a personalized name plate. Embedded in these devices is a malicious State-sponsored software application, which will monitor their keystrokes.

Back at the Shangri-la Hotel, they enjoy drinks on the house as announced by a pair of friendly bartenders, who seem to know each recruit personally as they treat each guest with a personal touch.

Train Ride to a Massacre

They are ordered to get to bed early, they've got a train to catch. Arising at the crack of dawn, the group starts the day at the in-house Delicatessen, enjoying a delicious variety of cakes, pastries and pralines set about an arrangement of crystal vased orchids.

As they get off the bus at the south side entrance to the Beijing West Railway Station, they can't miss seeing the big landmark abstract sculpture of the Red Dragon.

The station is one thousand feet long with a giant red pagoda on the top middle of the roof and smaller pagodas on each corner. Big red Chinese characters stand alone above letters in English: BEIJING RAILWAY STATION. Just below the letters, a conventional mega-sized clock shows the time with its big and not-so-little hands.

They walk by a black SUV with tinted windows marked POLICE. In line behind a constant flow of travelling tourists, they pass through two metal detectors and are wanded up and down by a smiling uninformed woman security officer. The central corridor of the station is designed with a high glass skylight. People are everywhere, crowded and noisy, but this is normal. Marching smartly ahead of them, a single line of soldiers in khaki green outfits and glowing red armbands with bright yellow markings. The soldiers are led by an officer in blue shirt and necktie, his authority made obvious by his gold-corded military visor. The group stops and waits for the soldiers to pass across in front of them, with eyes sternly fixed to the front. They continue toward a massive electronic arrival-departure board looming over a ticket counter.

Their assigned assistant directs them to a specific window where an agent has twenty-five tickets ready, passing them out individually with each recipient getting a smiling "thank you." They take a bank of elevators down to the lower corridor. A band of custodians carrying giant-fronded whisk brooms over their shoulders is going up one of the seven escalators next to them as they are going down.

Four passenger cars are reserved for the group for their two-day train ride to the southwest City of Khotan, the Xinjiang Uygur Autonomous Region. The MSS has arranged for a two-day train ride in a spirit of team-building. The recruits will also be accompanied by two of the PRC's most accomplished psychiatric experts.

Peering through the invisible glazing on their widows, the recruits seemed hypnotized by the seemingly endless expanse of moving sand dunes of the Great Asian tundra. A few squint in vain looking for a speck of vegetation. The railway follows the route of the ancient caravans. In olden times, merchant caravans called this unsparing region the Land of Death. Their train is heading for the same destination of relief as the ancient caravans, the southern and most ancient branch of the Great Silk Road linking China to the West, the ancient oasis town of Khotan.

This is the ancient Kingdom of the Uyghurs.

Away in the distance, south toward the Kunlun mountains, a few recruits notice a circle of military trucks painted in desert cameo, soldiers at attention facing out at the train; behind them, a few heavy backhoes at work as if they are guarding something.

As the train roars on, leaving the scene in the distance, they are unaware that the embedded malware in their laptops and smartphones has screened out a UPI article covering the *massacre* of 15 Uyghurs by National Police in the desert near Khotan for illegal religious activity. "The bodies were buried on the spot using bulldozers. Six pocket knives and a shovel were recovered from the scene."

It is a small world, and as much as things appear to be rapidly changing, much of human nature remains the same. Far away from this train ride in the Western China Desert, across the globe to North America, an area has been chosen to carry out a mind-boggling plot on a scale yet to be measured. But going back in time, there is an interconnecting link to what has already happened and what is being planned to happen, an atrocity involving extreme bloodshed on the very same lands.

During the 1700s, the Appalachian Region was known as the "back country" or the Appalachian frontier. White settlements on lands occupied for centuries by various Native American tribes created tension leading to a brutal and bloody tug of war as Native tribes attempted to hold onto what they believed was their territory to keep. And the boiling point was known as the Indian Wars.

And this is where the word *massacre* appears in the American lexicon.

On August 30, 1813, a force of about 700 Creek Indians attacked and destroyed Fort Mims in present-day Baldwin County, Alabama, killing 250 defenders and taking at least 100 captives in the first major battle of the Creek War of 1813-14. Some 400 American settlers, U.S.-allied Creeks, and enslaved African Americans had taken refuge inside a stockade hastily erected on the lower Alabama River plantation of Samuel Mims, a wealthy resident of the Tensaw District of the Mississippi Territory. The Creek attack on Fort Mims, and particularly the barbaric execution and mutilation of civilian men, women, and children at the end of the battle, outraged the U.S. public, thus prompting military action against the Creek Nation, which controlled what is now much of modern Alabama.

The Creek men who carried out the massacre were members of the Red Stick faction (named for the red wooden war clubs they carried). They were followers of Shawnee leaders Tenskwatawa (the Prophet) and his famous War-Chief brother, Tecumseh, who threatened death to any Indians who accepted white culture over the ways of the tribe. In 1813, as the Creek Nation became fractured by infanticidal civil war, the Red Sticks determined to destroy a community of Creeks, black slaves, and a group of four hundred white settlers who had established plantations in the Tensaw District and had taken refuge from hostile Creeks inside Fort Mims. The fort was garrisoned by a small contingent of Louisiana militia commanded by Major John Beasley.

The militia was armed with smoothbore flintlock muskets burnished with bayonets while the Creeks carried bows and flint-tipped arrows.

The muskets fired a one-ounce, round, lead ball and had an effective killing range of one hundred yards, but much of this battle would be fought hand-to-hand with the militia using bayonets, and the Indians, their painted wood-handled war clubs, the blades forged of iron.

This legion of 700 Red Sticks was led by Chief Red Eagle, who had been born William Weatherford, the son of a Scottish trader. Though only one-eighth Indian, he chose to cast his lot with the Creeks as he had been inspired by the legendary combat feats of Tecumseh. In company with Far-off Warrior and the prophet Paddy Walsh, Weatherford 's men leapt, whooping out of the tall grass and through the fort's main gate, which had been carelessly left open without posted sentries.

In the chaotic opening moments of the surprise attack, Major Beasley and nearly one-half of the garrison were slain. But Captain Dixon Bailey, himself a Creek, and his forty-five U.S. and Creek Indian militiamen were able to turn back the Red Stick onslaught.

For four hours, Bailey's men successfully defended against the relentless attacks with the hundreds of terrified settlers huddled inside the flimsy, one-acre stockade. Only when the attackers set the fort's buildings ablaze with burning arrows did resistance collapse. All but thirty-six militia who managed to escape, perished in the attack or were taken captive. As a memento of the fight, some Creek warriors cut scalps of skull with hair from the heads of the slain. A woman and child's scalp was a most coveted trophy, as it proved that the warrior had fought and defeated an enemy inside his stronghold.

The Red Sticks' assault on Fort Mims ranks as one of the great successes of American Indian warfare. The massacre of civilians, however, had rallied U.S. forces to the battle cry: "Remember Fort Mims."

When word of the massacre reached Nashville Tennessee, the legislature authorized an army of 3,500 militia to seek revenge and destroy the warring Creeks. Their commanding officer was a profane, hard-nosed fighter and horse breeder named Andrew Jackson. The general had been informed of his appointment while bedridden, recovering from serious gun shot wounds sustained in a pistol duel. The general had the nine lives of a tomcat, and with a habit of challenging his adversaries to pistol duals, he needed all nine of them.

Jackson would win a decisive victory in the Battle of Horseshoe Bend, which led to the Creek Nation's subsequent surrender of their lands to the U.S. government by the Treaty of Fort Jackson. A few years later, Jackson, nicknamed Old Hickory, led a motley contingent of militia, frontiersmen, slaves, Indians, and even swashbuckling pirates, to withstand a series of frontal assaults by a bigger British force to become the hero of the Battle of New Orleans, and seventh president of the United States.

Continuing outrage surrounding the massacre at Fort Mims would contribute to one of the saddest chapters in American history, the forced uprooting of the Creeks and Cherokee tribes from their native homelands in what became known as the Trail of Tears.

As the train approaches the Southern Xinjiang Railway Station of Khotan, they see a convoy of open military trucks packed tightly with men dressed in blue jumpsuits. The trucks are following the flashing lights and sirens of two fire brigade search-and-rescue vehicles while police motorcycles fixed with ballistic hand shields ride beside the trucks. The motorcyclists are clothed in black uniforms, and florescent green safety vests, their black Kevlar military helmets labeled with the police insignia of the PRC.

The convoy is headed to a secret government medical building nearby where "forced organ harvesting from prisoners of conscience, including the religious minorities of Falun Gong and Uighurs, has been committed for years throughout China on a significant scale, and that it continues today. This involves hundreds of thousands of victims," explained a China Tribunal lawyer to the United Nations Human Rights Council. The lawyer continued, "Victim for victim and death for death, cutting out the hearts and other organs from living, blameless, harmless, peaceable people constitutes one of the worst mass atrocities of this century."

As the train starts to slow, those sitting at the north side windows can see what looks like a walled fortress with overlooking octagon turrets of tinted glass. The outer perimeter is a steel chain-link fence, its top secured with razor wire. On the ground in front of what appears to be the front gate, a sign reads: "Khotan County No. 1 Vocational Training and Education Center." A group of raggedy-dressed civilians is standing across the street, staring at the building.

Arriving at the Khotan Train Station, they gather outside for instructions from a serious-looking police lieutenant. Looming in the distance is a towering statue of Chairman Mao, chiseled in a long military overcoat and cap, his right arm extended, hand pointing forward.

The group is given today's itinerary, lunch at the officer's dining hall, and afterward, a visit to a local garment factory and tour of a vocational training center. The main attraction: a student dance performance at one of the vocational centers.

After a freshening up and showing of their rooms and facilities at the police barracks, all are served a local dish, soupy noodles with chopsticks. They climb aboard a drab green bus with windows of steel mesh under glass.

They travel through a neighborhood with red-starred plaques on the doors and National flags flying from posts along both sides of the street.

As the bus turns a corner onto a commercial strip, people and scooters are everywhere, a cacophony of honking cars. At a stop sign, a few see a man in a white shirt follow a young family of three through a brick, arched entryway with a Christian motif. Above the arch, hung on a crucifix, a sign bears the National message: "Love the Party." The man comes back out, holding a frightened child by the arm, and sits the child down on a bench outside the building. On the bus, two expats turn and look at each other and shrug.

Surveillance cameras mounted on long white poles seem to be a fixture on every building in town. As they file into the garment factory, Lucas gives a friendly wave to a camera above the doorway, wondering who is watching on the other end of the CCTV. His facial recognition data has been digitized, it's already in the system. As they enter a large open room, they hear a loud buzzing, sounding like a giant swarm of bees. Entering the room, stuffy air, a thick web of electrical wires extending from the ceiling, they are given an oral presentation by the director of the operation.

They see perfectly-arranged lines of workers seated at a long table of sewing machines and large spools of thread, men on one side, wearing yellow-green shirts, and women on the other side, wearing red. The workers are concentrated on the task in front of them, seemingly absorbed in their work. Around the outside of the room, men in uniforms stand erect, their arms and hands hang behind them holding metal batons.

The high mechanical gates adorned with Chinese symbols swing wide open with two crisply-uniformed soldiers, one on each side. The bus rolls down a long driveway, a tiny white picket fence off the curb and grass between ten-foot-high walls on both sides. A huge white five-story building giving the impression of a chain hotel grows larger as the bus gets nearer. Across the top of the building, in five-foot-high red Chinese lettering: "Listen to the Government."

The director of the center explains that the students are being rehabilitated from religious extremist thoughts. And she makes it a point that they all chose to come to the center freely with a desire to be re-educated. It is here that the students are given proper guidance on how to LOVE THE PARTY.

The tour at the Vocational Training Centre begins with a visit to a classroom of co-ed teenage students engaged in the study of Mandarin. Seated two to a desk, in a bright room with poster boards filled with Mandarin symbols and characters, the students are cooled by a portable fan mounted on a wall. The next classroom serves as the highlight of the day. Dressed in bright ethnic costumes, the girls wear bright orange and yellow skirts, the boys in wearing helmeted warrior outfits, the students perform three traditional Chinese dances and one modern jazz piece for the group, receiving enthusiastic applause. The dancers bow and return the applause with bright smiles, bright smiles that have been forced. Not a part of the scheduled tour, three floors up, is the student's dorm. They sleep on bunks, ten cramped into a room, sharing one toilet.

They return to the barracks, their assigned rooms in the officers' quarters.

On their way to dinner in downtown Khotan, they pass a woman street vendor on the sidewalk wearing a black protective vest, selling eggs in crates. A few paces away, a man peddles bright hand-made carpets. The bus turns onto Renmin Road, heading to Khotan's popular Night Market. They park a block away on a crowded street. Walking toward the market, one of the group attempts to ask one of the people walking past about the menu at the market, the man abruptly turns his head away and hops down onto the street. They dine on stuffed nang with rose jam and enjoy the rest of a pleasant summer evening.

Creation and Destruction

The desert camouflage bus is idling in front of the Khotan People's Government Building, flanked by four Chinese Provincial police on motorcycles. With the exception of a ten-foot-high clock tower with tinted windows on each of its octagonal sides extending from the roof, the front of the two-story building facing Wulumuqi North Road looks ordinary. A government sign with red Chinese symbols stands out on the access drive in front. A supermarket across the street hosts a normal activity of shoppers carrying groceries in the parking lot.

Unseen and hidden by a fifteen-foot-high wall topped with razor wire that extends behind the building is another building at ground level. Its black roof has pairs of evenly-spaced vent fixtures on each side. The wall, interspersed with surveillance cameras, actually surrounds a whole complex of cement block buildings with gray corrugated steel doors resembling a storage facility. White cement driveways provide access throughout the squared-off grid. The rear of the complex is accessed off of Beijing West Road through a heavy steel two-wing mechanical swinging gate. The access drive is spaced between an agricultural Bank of China branch building and a Xiaoxiao Cold Noodles shop.

Several times a day, the gates swing open and closed for Red Cross ambulances arriving and departing.

In 2007, an experiment had been administered in the industrial City of Shenzhen. The State named it the: Shenzhen Residence Card Information Management System Project, which mandated all citizens of this prominent hub of electronics manufacturing to carry chip-imbedded identity cards detailing extensive personal information. Employment history, marital status, number of children, social welfare status, and the likelihood to engage in armed insurrection was among recorded data. Following an evaluation of the beta-tested results, a government official commented that the pilot project had been deemed "a residual success."

Then came the Games of the XXIX Olympiad, more commonly known as Beijing 2008. It was China's first public utilization of a radio frequency identification device (RFID) on a world-wide scale. It was then and there that each one of China's Olympic athletes carried a first-generation RFID implant under their skin for the official purpose of ensuring their safety, security, and social welfare. At that time, according to China's Minister of Information Industry: "The devices help make sure athletes get to correct event at correct time, receive food when needed, and not by mistake enter diplomatic zone of unfriendly foreign nation."

And then China made plans for each of its 1.4 billion citizens to be a recipient of a long-range, high-frequency RFID transponder because, explained China's Minister of Public Security: "Identity cards can be lost or stolen. But RFID chip implanted in spine is very hard to gain access to without sharp knife or other cutting tool. After the operation, every citizen of free, democratic Republic of China will feel more secure, and citizens' rights and continued upward progress of our great nation is assured."

"They are means for which government assure every citizen can be quickly located, day or night, whether they be gathering in small groups to express support and admiration of Communist party, working every day to strengthen China's economic output, or limiting their reproduction to a single child per family. It is for the freedom, happiness, and prosperity of all citizens. It will be the first known application of the technology toward the tracking and management of democratic citizens. It is for the freedom, happiness, and prosperity of all citizens."

He continued, Chinese citizens would need to be reminded that "they will be required to report to the RFID charging center in the city at which they are registered as resident every fourteen days for recharging."

Immortality, longevity, and The Fountain of Youth-the perpetual pursuit of conquering death. In the ancient religion of Hinduism, earthly immortality is celebrated by the celestial imagery of the avatar.

A virtual world is a computer-simulated environment, which may be populated by many participants who can create a personal avatar, and simultaneously and independently wander over an imaginary world. It is when the avatars become human and their controllers become sinister that the metaphysical line between good and evil is obliterated and civilization is transformed into a world of fanaticism. And it is achieved with the experimentation and empirical outcomes of Molecular Neurobiology, more simply known as "Brain Science."

From laboratories throughout the country, from Shanghai to Peking, a team of the most highly educated neuroscientists has been summoned from the PRC command center in Beijing, located off of the west wall of the Forbidden City. For the past five years, these scientists have conducted interdisciplinary biological, physiological, and cognitive neuropsychological research to understand how humans think and behave.

The Command Center is constructed with impenetrable anti radio-wave containment walls. It is designed with a spacious control room, with neuroimaging apparatus to include the most advanced positron emission tomography (PET) and functional magnetic resonance imaging (fMRI) scanners for real-time visualization of the human brain. A complimentary array of auditory, visual, and physiological equipment is in place to monitor the pulse, blood pressure, and heart rate of human subjects.

But most ingenious of the high-tech equipment are the sensor cameras loaded with biometric body and face identification software to identify and monitor "mobile targets" embedded with microchips. And a built-in GPS function to keep them in sight.

Under the government program title of *The Peoples State Security System*, scientific experiments in deep brain stimulation have succeeded in developing a secret two-way radio channel of communication and command between a computer and the human brain. Artificial Acetylcholine (ACh) has been developed that acts as a neurotransmitter to send a chemical message released by molecular nerve cells to transmit signals to other cells, such as neurons, muscle cells, and those that effectuate functions of the human body.

They have implemented a system of synthetic telepathy, wherefrom satellites in outer space, brain functions of microchip-implanted human beings are controlled by microwave radio signals and manipulated by changing frequencies. And they can be followed anywhere on the face of the earth, remotely monitored by ground-based supercomputers.

The first step involves the surgical installation of a silicate glass-encased computer microchip, one-tenth the size of the diameter of a human hair. Implanted into the optical nerve, when activated, it draws neural impulses from the brain and overrides the function of the neocortex to command attention, arousal, and motivation. And then, the electronic altering of the supply of ACh to the hippocampus and subcortical areas of the brain to produce retrograde amnesia, in essence, a neural physiological erasing of a human's blackboard of memory; to create a new clean slate and a ready-made memory bank to accept sensory input deposits of Communist re-education and control.

Cryptically secure high-volume data storage facilities have been strategically placed in various provinces of China to provide redundancy in the event of foreign compromise. And a sophisticated computer modeling showroom is furnished to digitally configure, demonstrate, and display live on-screen, "The Wonder of Cybernetics" to official visitors.

Through a secure cyber link-up, these revolutionary scientists have been able to coordinate experiments in neural circuitry to unlock the secrets of mind reading and mind control, to replicate human consciousness, and create "hu-bots" of brain, flesh, and bone, in essence, the perfect human avatar.

In a remote facility, carved into the ground-level wall in the Valley of Discipline, ten of the hu-bots are seated in a small sense-a-round theater, where they are watching an animated training lesson, a practical exercise. And they are hearing voices in their heads. Their lifetime of memories and skills in herding goats or weaving carpets no longer exist, nor do their treasured thoughts of loved ones at home.

While they watch, PET images of their thought patterns are being monitored by the scientists on floor-to-ceiling computer screens from an adjacent room. As a quality-control measure, on a split-screen, their thoughts have been converted to digitalized neural blueprints, which are being juxtaposed next to a set of algorithms integrated within a novel genetic code. The comparisons are to assure that the subjects are "learning" in the way they have been designed to learn... like a robot.

Recent field studies have determined something else when things don't go as smoothly as planned: the need for a steady remote-controlled delivery of high frequency radio-wave shocks of electricity to the brains and spinal columns of hu-bots having misbehavior problems. Simultaneously, specific visual reminders are administered to them from a set of artificially-delivered hallucinations: "Love the Government," "Joy in Obedience," and "Your Family Is the State."

Their facial expressions and groans of pain are monitored with each jolt of electricity to ensure that the corrective procedure is working. A scientific computer log is created to quantify the degree and number of doses needed to gain control of a non-compliant hu-bot. It's purely a State-sponsored, state of the art system of cyber torture.

The object of today's trial exercise is telepathically delivered to the hu-bots in a soothing artificial voice. The subject: "Synthesizing Christianity: A Unification of the People." The master scientists use the computer keypad to increase adrenaline flow into their bloodstreams.

The deafening din of jackhammers hurts the ears as a dingy-yellow mechanical monster is in the process of demolishing the church of Our Lady of Mount Carmel, which has stood for over one hundred seventeen years. A caterpillar traction excavator with a massive jointed arm with a steel-teethed bucket on the end is ripping away at the wall of the church.

This is happening at the popular Catholic shrine in Tianjiajing village in Henan Province. The sanctuary was designed and dedicated to the Mother of God in gratitude for protecting missionaries during the Boxer Rebellion and it has hosted thousands of pilgrims during each of its years of existence. It is the latest government-sponsored attack on Jīdūjiào, i.e., Christianity.

An elderly woman wearing a white silk veil rushes out from behind a government police cruiser, she is waving and crying for them to stop, her hand grasping a set of carved teak rosary beads. She hobbles to the front of the steel monster as it loudly tears at one of the side walls. The operator, sitting high in the cabin, doesn't notice her, doesn't seem to care, he has a thousand-yard stare fixed straight ahead on his task of destruction. He is listening to voices in his head. The monstrous machine turns, catching the bottom of the woman's dress, she shrieks, there's no reaction from the operator in the cabin, it keeps turning, companions hiding nearby are watching her, in horror, they read her lips "My Jesus Mercy," she bows her head moments before the steel treads suck her underneath and crush her.

The stone statue of Our Lady of Mount Carmel tumbles down from its place on the upper corner of the collapsing wall. As the statue thuds to the ground in an appalling upheaval of dust, the head of the statue, the head of Our Lady, detaches and rolls to a stop at the site of the bloody martyrdom. Its face, Our Lady's face, is looking squarely at a remnant of the woman's muddy dress. One of the victim's companions is astonished to see tears dripping from its motherly eyes while the eyes of the men in the white laboratory coats, remotely observing the scene from hundreds of miles away, remain callously dry.

Set back from a street corner nearby within the settling dust of the demolition, but within plain view for all passersby to see, a large bonfire is burning, a small group of State police are tossing books into the flames, but no one comes close enough to read the covers on the books: "Shèngjīng," in English: Holy Bible.

No one comes close enough, not close enough to the sacrilegious fire used as bait to lure them in to be arrested and detained under the dubious State suspicion of "gathering a crowd to disturb social order." Detained if only identified as "socially dangerous persons" as Jīdū tú...Christians.

All the while, the demolition crew continues to operate with precision; they are listening to voices in their heads. And throughout China, Catholic priests and believers are being jailed or "disappearing" while the dictates of a new gospel is being spread, which is nothing but the old manifesto of Chairman Mao and the State Political Directorates of General Secretary Stalin who preceded him.

To the Valley of Discipline

The itinerary has only one destination on today's agenda, a special training camp, one that will be a major factor in their mission to America. The recruits change buses for the journey south toward the Kunlun Mountains of the Tibet Plateau.

The provincial road runs parallel to the Jade Dragon Kashgar River, or more commonly, the River of White Jade. The river is fed by the melting glaciers of the mighty Kunluns to the south. But this is the dry season, and in the near distance, they can see people prospecting for precious jade in the riverbed.

Past the ancient City of Mallikurwatur on the west bank of the river, from a distance, they look like a scrambled pile of boulders, but getting nearer, coming into focus, there can be seen characteristics of human design. The eroded sand-blasted irregular-shaped stone ruins, buried up to their necks in flood silt, were built 1,500 to 1,600 years ago under the laws of the Buddha. The snow-covered peaks of the majestic mountain range loom in the distance. Turning onto a forgotten fork in the Ancient Silk Trade Route, the bus begins a winding upward climb.

Scattered about the rocky terrain are rugged sun-bitten shepherds tending flocks of sheep and goats, their primitive stone-walled villages looking like three-dimensional puzzles crawling up the bottom edges of the steep knobby hillsides. Ascending and twisting between barren cliffs and canyons, it is a treacherous road with harrowing blind turns, fallen rocks in the road unseen until right up on top of them. Far below, on the sands of the thirsty desert floor, is the wreckage of a tractor trailer. The soldier driving the bus seems unfazed, slowly swerving around the danger as if he's been doing this for a while.

Rounding a bend on the mountain, the road comes to an end and then it comes into view; a secluded basin, an enormous natural pit. Over the rim, it is enclosed by confining rock walls. Embedded in the walls, halfway down, they see a ring of overlooking caves. Inside the mouths of the caves, glinting steel, small colored objects are seen moving about. Looking further downward far below, on the floor of the prodigious pit, they adjust their focus to a seething motion of activity.

It is called Shan-qu Xue-sho-ke...the Valley of Discipline.

In a corkscrew descent, the bus winds down a road paved around the interior face of the basin walls. The passengers begin to see what from above had been making the motion and movements in the caves. Descending, they also observe what had caused the glint from inside the mouths of the caves, mounted machine guns pointed at the floor of the basin, manned by military personnel.

Part of the floor of the basin is a complex of buildings consisting of long barracks in precise rows. Outside of the buildings is a sectioned-off training ground with multiple rectangular fields, each three hundred by one hundred yards in size. Fifty-foot-high watchtowers with antennas protruding from the roofs are spaced around the perimeter. From a distance, several of the fields appear to be obstacle courses with people climbing over and under high-steel walls and spike-topped black steel fences. There are others in military visors looking up at people straddled over the top of the fences.

As they get closer, they see that a group of people are at the bottom of the fence, unrolling what appears to be simple Teflon baking sheets. They observe them tossing the sheets up on top of the spikes. They see them pull up and grab the top bar of the fence, hoist themselves up, and straddle the fence over top of the sheet before dropping down to the other side. At another station, they see people hanging from ropes using wire cutters to remove razor wire from the tops of fences as small groups are watching and waiting on the ground below. On the far side of the grounds, hard to make out, a group of soldiers restraining German shepherds on leashes.

Reaching the bottom of the basin, their bus crosses over a small bridge spanning a canal of water where they see a bunched up group on one side, watching two people swimming across it, to another group of military personnel waiting on the other side with a taller fence constructed to their rear.

Swimmers who already made it across are taking up firearms to shoot at small black targets affixed to the top of the fence, the sounds of the gunshots echoing off the walls of the basin. The expats watch as the shooters sling the weapons across their backs and toss up ropes with grappling hooks, catching the claws around the top, then pulling themselves up and over and down the other side.

Continuing onward, the bus comes to a stop in front of a swinging steel gate, which is pulled open by soldiers on each side. The bus drives through the gate and parks in front of a building guarded by soldiers in desert-cameo uniforms. They file off of the bus and are directed by a soldier to gather under the shade of an outside pavilion. The hum of generators is heard coming from behind a building next to the pavilion. A military-dressed officer comes out to greet them, the commandant.

He stands before them framed by a large white-board. He mentions that they will be shown their living quarters to be followed by a schedule of physical training.

The commandant uses a red Sharpie to illustrate the training program they are about to experience. He calls them "the expats," young leaders-in-training, drawing on the left top of the board the Chinese symbol pronounced as "li," the shape of a plow for strength and guile. He explains that they will be trained to lead alongside the best of the State's officers, the MSS's elite, the elephant, the symbol of power, and draws that Chinese symbol across from the expat group's symbol of strength at the right top of the board.

Together, he explains, they will lead a cell of loyal servants, the trainees, who they observed on their way here, to spread the message of the State to the Western Hemisphere. He draws the feng shui symbol of the horse, the symbol of conquest, below the two symbols making an inverted triangle to complete the official insignia of the mission. He explains that there will be risk and danger, but they will be guided and protected by a group of friendly foreign fighters throughout the mission. He uses the Sharpie to draw a circle around the symbols together as one.

He goes on to explain how they will develop skills alongside the trainees and bear witness to their commitment to the mission, which will serve to strengthen the confidence and morale in each of them.

They are fitted with exercise gear, an assortment of Nike cross-training shoes. They are all issued with a short-sleeve tee shirt, sky-blue with a bold yellow disc printed on the front, symbolic, meaning that there is only one sun in the sky, and this one flaming planet is...the country of China.

After being outfitted, the group is led out to the training grounds. One of the group looks up at the top rim of the basin and realizes, for the first time, how isolated and removed they are from normal human civilization. As a midday shadow casts its cloak on the north face of the steep basin wall, far above in the clouds, what at first looks to be a group of flies, is actually a small flock of vultures circling around the perimeter of the basin.

Out in the field, the group is astonished at the synchronized precision-like discipline the trainees display in changing stations, as if they are all responding to a singular inner voice.

Seemingly out of place, one figure stands out, tall with muscular bronze skin, a bright red bandana wrapped around the top of his head. He's standing outside of a steel razor-wired gate, he is conversing with a group of Chinese military personnel. On his forehead, the top half obscured by the bandana, a tattoo of a goat-like face with horns.

Soybeans and a Desert Hiding Place

The Chinese name for it: 家常豆腐 (jiā cháng dòu fu), is said to have originated in the Western Han Dynasty in the years spanning 206 years BC-Before Christ to AD-Anno Domini, in the year of the Lord 24.

It was discovered by the grandson of a Chinese emperor in pursuit of immortality. Trying to discover something to eat to keep him alive forever, he climbed to the top of Jiuhua Mountain, where he mixed bean juice with gypsum to make a fragrant and delicious "bean curd," or in Chinese, "tofu."

Soybean, also known as the "miracle crop"; it's valued for its versatility in growing in different climates for use to feed the animals that feed the people; poultry, pigs, dairy cattle, and even fish farms.

The Chinese are the world's largest importer of soybeans, importing 3 billion bushels a year, a twenty-five year increase of 16,600 percent. Why this staggering increase? Because it takes 1500 tons of water to produce one ton of soybeans. And due to pollution and waste, the Chinese are running out of water, which threatens their very existence.

And so China is building a railroad through the jungles of the Amazon because it needs to buy up every soybean grown in South America.

And, the People's Republic of China's Minister of Water has said: "To fight for every drop of water or die, that is the challenge facing China."

And so China's survival depends on Argentina's soybeans to feed its people, and Argentina's survival depends on China's wealth to keep from going bankrupt. With a friendly trade arrangement and an $11 billion loan to make solvent Argentina's Central Bank, China has also satisfied its military ambitions by financing a prime hidden-away location in Argentina for a modern space-age project. Along with other cash advances for hydrologic dams, this 50-year lease is made tax-free. It has a long-term purpose and a short-term one designed to bring the United States... to its knees.

It is bounded by the Andes Mountains to its west, and the Atlantic Ocean to its east. To the northwest, the landscape gradually shapes into the foothills of wine country, and to the northeast are the fertile lowlands of the Pampas. To the south, in the Province of Neuquen, the Magellanic Steppe, also called the Patagonian Desert, is the largest desert in Argentina and the eighth largest desert on earth, all 260,000 square miles of it. And it is cold. It is a winter desert. But not all is desolate. In a scattered existence, the heart of the steppe is alive with shrubby and herbaceous plant species. Mate negre is a dense, coarse bush with yellow flowers and small succulent leaves. The plant thrives in the cold, dry climate of the desert as the unusual foliage holds moisture near to its branches. The cold strong winds restrain the plant from growing over two feet tall.

And another plant looking like something that came from another planet nestles in the rocky Magellanic landscape, the cushion plant. It appears like a lime-green lumpy blob on the terracotta-tinted rocks of the Steppe, its specially adapted tap roots siphoning nutrients from the stubborn soil.

Amidst these strange forms of life, framed by a remote ice-covered expanse of the lower Andes Steppe in the distance, a behemoth satellite dish materializes seemingly out of nowhere. A glaring white dish-shaped reflector with fifty-thousand square feet of the surface and weighing three thousand tons supports the 17-stories-high antenna, capable of tracking a spacecraft in orbit tens of billions of miles from earth.

Threatening KEEP OUT! warning signs are fixed to the middle of a ten-foot high razor-wired chain-link fence, marking the entrance to the People's of China Satellite Launch and Tracking Control Base. And these warnings are meant for the Argentinean government. It is China's first deep-space installation on foreign lands, lands outside of the motherland.

That is what can be seen above ground, the tip of the iceberg. Below ground, it is vast. It took two years and hundreds of Argentinian workers commanded by a Chinese military contingent to have completed the cement casing just for the above-ground antenna. It is not known when the construction commenced or how long it took the Chinese to complete the subterranean sections of the military space station.

One room below ground is a fitting room with racks, a vast selection of hip sportswear, ranging from New York Yankees ball caps to Rata Blanca Band tee-shirts to Nike basketball shoes.

From Argentina, the PRC has guided a Chinese spacecraft, a Shenzou, to the first ever touchdown on the dark side of the moon. The lunar explorer that made the moon landing, Chang'e 4, is named after a legendary Chinese goddess who has reigned on the moon for millennia.

A confident deep space taikonaut spoke to a Beijing News correspondent: "The far side of the moon is a rare quiet place that is free from interference from radio signals from Earth. The launch of a new relay satellite sends back data from Chang'4." The taikonaut went even further: "This probe can fill the gap of low-frequency observation in radio astronomy and will provide important information for studying the origin of stars and nebula evolution."

The biggest challenge of operating on the far side of the moon is communicating with Earth. Already, China has launched a specially designed relay satellite so that Change 4 can send back information.

Hours after the landing, the general secretary of the Communist Party of the People spoke of the nation's dream of becoming a leading space power; from their base in Argentina, China has obtained a new direct and open field-of-fire to use ASATS, direct-ascent ballistic missiles with guidance system-equipped "kill vehicles" that detach from the missile to destroy satellites in low to medium Earth orbit. And to deploy airborne lasers to blind sensors in image-producing satellites in geosynchronous orbit used to provide cyberspace command and control intelligence to the U.S. military...and to predict hurricanes.

The ongoing project of the Chinese is to develop missiles capable of destroying the ASATs themselves. But the Argentinean desert location, supposedly purposed for crucial deep space monitoring in the Southern and Western Hemispheres also provides a hidden nuclear launch site. But the most ominous of the subterranean installation is a critical piece needed to carry out a top secret operation in the Southern Hemisphere, a subterranean human avatar control room.

So the Chinese are left alone to maximize their South American-based global coverage of outer space and other endeavors, for the nearest Argentinean town of Las Lajas is 31 miles away on the Rio Agrio River.

And Argentina's politicos are satisfied with their end of the bargain. They have been able to replace their obsolete military airplanes with twenty Chengdu JF-17 "Fierce Dragon" fighter jets.

Powered by WS-13 Taishan turbo-afterburner engines, the stealthy sharp-nosed single-seat jets fly at altitudes of 55,000 feet above and beyond the clouds and can obtain speeds of Mach 1.8 with an upgraded combat radius of over 1,000 miles. They are loaded out with laser-guided bombs and long range air-to-air ballistic missiles. Presently sheltered under hangars at Tierra del Fuego airbase in southern Argentina, trimmed in yellow, the Chinese color that symbolizes neutrality and good luck...and the Falkland Islands of the United Kingdom are only a 945-mile flight away east by seagull's wings.

Parked on the single concrete runway of Hotan Airport is a commercial airplane. From the outside, it looks like the Chinese version of the Boeing 737 Max-8 passenger jet airliner, a Comac C919 narrow-body twin-jet marked, as such, with the lengthy China Eastern Airlines nameplate painted over top of the passenger windows in red Chinese symbols. The jet's tail is painted Kelly green with big white C919 numerals tilting aft on the stabilizer. A royal blue stripe wraps around the rear of the fuselage.

But the inside of the cabin is designed uniquely, partitioned off with steel grates. The high-tech military cockpit will be manned in shifts by twelve of the most fit pilots, copilots, and navigators.

The 23,612-mile 56-hour flight is achieved with a re-fueling stop in Auckland, New Zealand, 20 in-air hours from Hotan away, where only the flight crew and expats deplane for refreshments; the other passengers are kept guarded on the plane. Flying over the Pacific on the final leg, the flight plans dissect the skies of Easter Island and Tahiti to land at Ezeiza Airport in Buenos Aires, Argentina.

Back at the desert space compound, from a seamless outside wall, an automatic bay door yawns open like something from a science fiction movie. A tan commercial-looking Toyota Land Rover leads a motorized column comprised of several mid-sized passenger buses with tinted windows. Two guards, dressed in off-white khaki uniforms and pith helmets, operate the outside gate and stand erect as the column passes through before mounting their ATVs to return to the building through the bay door as it closes soundlessly behind them. The convoy is heading toward Ezeiza Airport. They will return to the station with a human cargo for an outfitting.

Returning to the desert station, each hu-bot is refitted with a micro adapter to connect to the radio frequencies compatible with the monitoring computers in the underground control room. The expats are equipped with a touchscreen smart watches fitted to their wrists. The devices have a built-in GPS and a unique telemetry communication system linked to the desert ground satellite control room. The expats are also issued impeccable false identification cards to include photo driver's licenses from various states in the U.S and Avis-Preferred Hertz Gold and Enterprise Plus Rewards cards.

The 700-mile, 13-hour cross country drive back to Buenos Aires is filled with optimism, the MSS have achieved one more patient step towards the goal...Destination America.

At 500 miles per hour, the flight from Buenos Aires to Belize City will take 8 and one-half hours.

The flight plan from Buenos Aires to Belize, then into a convoy of deceptively-marked tractor trailers, saying "Avocados-Soybeans," and a highway route taken to meet and mix with the caravans headed towards Mexico City.

Caravans Moving North

The International Bridge at Tecun Uman which separates Guatemala and Mexico is a mass of humanity. They are one thousand miles away from the Texas border. The stifling haze of heated air creates a roadway mirage as the shimmer reflected off the asphalt cruelly fools them to believe they are seeing rippling pools of thirst-quenching water in the distance. They are overwhelmingly young males, of military age, their throats are parched, and they are becoming angry. They are carrying national flags, but the national flag of the United States is not to be seen. Mixed in, a small number of innocent children are suffering from the heat and dehydration. Their progress has halted at the Mexican end of the bridge where a line of police in riot gear is standing in the way. A group of teenagers try to swim across, but several of them, including a few brave souls swimming out to save those that have panicked in the water and can't swim, get swept away in the current.

Days later, for those who have successfully crossed the border and moved so many miles northward, the Mexican police, who were supposed to stop them, are now acting as escorts. At intervals, they are climbing atop trucks and tractor trailers as they move northward at 20 miles per day. A small group detaches from the crowd and in front of a cameraman, sets fire to a U.S. flag with a black Swastika spray-painted on it.

And this swarming mass of people is providing the perfect cover for tactically-placed cells of invaders moving north with them. From the Command Center, The master scientists are watching every step on large screens powered by satellites. Messages of praise and reassurance are periodically streaming into their heads. The expats are acting like shepherds, keeping one eye on their flock and the other on the lookout for danger or hostile interference. The expats are following the protocol, aiding the hu-bots with fluids and nourishment, if necessary. They march evenly spaced, no more than ten feet apart, with tightly packed migrants in between, within the predetermined intervals enough for the expats to control and the marching cells to fit into the LED viewing screens of the master scientists.

At Mexico City, they will step away from the migrant caravan to link up with a contingent of heavily-armed MS-13 wearing Mexican National police uniforms. A fleet of black Humvees marked POLICIA FEDERAL await to escort them on a series of parallel routes to the Texas border.

Juan is confined in a warehouse district, his holding cell is part of a subterranean safe house connected by tunnels to a larger complex, which serves as a cocaine and heroin operation for the cartel.

He's calling Maria while his sympathetic guard and another stand close by, watching. When the other guard pokes his head through the doorway to investigate something outside, Juan punches in a Wi-Fi hotspot.

"Maria, they moved me last night, blindfolded again, quite a distance, I think, I nodded off for I'm not sure how long, so I'm really not sure how far the distance was from the last place. I'm being held in some kind of permanent compound; from the musty smell and lack of sunlight, I think I'm underground. Fortunately, the same guard, he's more like my guardian angel...cigarillo."

Maria hears another voice, "*va'monos*, got to go."

From the cell phone number intercepted by Maria's caller ID in conversation with her brother, the DSS command post is using the latest in cell tower triangulation techniques in an attempt to find the precise location of Juan's cellphone emissions.

The phone he has been using has a built-in GPS, but it only acts as a GPS receiver. A device with GPS isn't actually 'contacting' satellites to determine its location. Instead, it's just listening for the radio signals that are being broadcast from one of the four of twenty-four GPS satellites visible in the sky that are in constant orbit around the globe, constantly broadcasting data in a direct path down to the device on Earth.

The device's GPS receiver 'listens' for signals from the four or more satellites. Signals from the closer satellites will arrive sooner while signals from the farther satellites will arrive later. Each transmission includes the location of the GPS satellite and the time the signal was sent. Each satellite has an atomic clock onboard, so the time of the emission is very precise. By comparing the time the signal was broadcast and the time the signal arrived, the receiver can estimate its relative distance from all four satellites. Using trilateration, the measurement and analysis of the separate distances in relation to each other, the receiver can then fix its location.

But GPS is useless if the signals are being blocked in a subterranean chamber...it won't work.

So they must have the coordinates in longitude and latitude of three or more land-based cellphone towers that have received radio signals from that target phone. A python algorithm is used to process the data generated in signal strength and time delays that the roaming radio signals take to ping back to the towers from the target phone.

The DSS task force has entrusted Colonel Manuel Cortes and his Special Weapons and Tactics Unit of the Mexico City Police with the responsibility of a highly unpredictable hostage rescue operation. A wiry bronze-skinned veteran of the Michoacán drug wars, Colonel Cortes is the only one they can trust. He, himself, has dodged a recent attempt on his life for refusing a $50,000 bribe to look the other way, the other way opposite of the cartel's blood-thirsty business. The colonel is dressed in a sharply pressed uniform, and despite the pressure, his steely demeanor appears intact. His men are as untouchable as he is, and when they remove their visor-tinted combat helmets, they neatly resemble each other. They look alike because they *should* look alike. They are all someway related, brothers and cousins, all handpicked by the colonel. He trusts them with his life, and they are willing to risk their lives for him.

Santa Muerte

The SWAT team has assembled in the colonel's conference room adjacent to his office, they have been told that a DSS analyst from the Consulate has results from the command post trilateration efforts. The walls of the room are replete with flaking dark walnut paneling. The colonel is seated at the head of the small, scuffed, and stained rectangular table, his chair is about the only one that is sure-proof sturdy that can be considered relatively new. The other chairs, which have been around for a couple of decades, have rips and tears in the orange vinyl, and have become a bit wobbly over the years. The officers choose to stand, they know better, none want to become the latest unwitting victim who ends up splayed on his back to lay prone on the faded worn-out carpet with an embarrassing look on his face.

The DSS analyst, standing at the other end of the table, begins the briefing in Spanish. He says that he appreciates being here and that he's been in his assignment for going on three months now. More than one SWAT officer wrinkles his lips and rolls his eyes, it's a knee-jerk response, meaning, "Yeah, sure you do!"

He points to a map pinned up on an old bulletin board behind him. He uses his finger to circle an area that an analysis of the cell signal data has narrowed it down to. It's a ten-block area in a market place in the north-central part of the city.

All at once, their heads drop, and they begin to shift and fidget, some use their thumbs to rub the leather on their police belts. They were all hoping that it wouldn't be in that area, but they had a feeling that it would be. In this area, there is an open-air market place where the regular customers wear ballistic vests...the Tepito District.

The place is an unrestrained above-ground celebration of the black market. It teems with a frenzy of underworld activity where customers can freely purchase a "high" from roaming street vendors, calling out the type of drugs they're hawking, "We-e-e-ed!" or "Doe-oe-oe-oepe!" as casual as peanut vendors at a ballpark. Or you can buy just about anything from one of the tented stands, from counterfeit DVDs to automatic assault rifles. That's only if you are willing to risk the high possibilities of being mugged, extorted, or hit by stray bullets.

There is no real order to the place, but if one would guess which characters might have rule, it would be the Extorsionador se tatu'a el logode La Unio'n Tepito, the vicious gangsters who extort, kidnap, or violently beat the merchants of the marketplace who refuse to pay them the tribute price, or the "Right to the Floor." These thugs proudly sport their wreath-encircled red and green 'U' tattooed on their chests.

The colonel's men are most unwelcome at this market place, not because of their badges and police uniforms, Lord knows there's enough of those around, it's because the criminal element in the marketplace knows that the uniforms and badges worn by the colonel's men are worn with honor.

From a distance, it looks like an ordinary statue of the Virgin of Guadeloupe dressed in a bright blue mantle with hands pressed together in prayer below her chin, a sparkling full-length aureole around her, sprinkled with blooming roses. But as one gets closer, it is not the face of the Virgin, it is the fleshless face of a skeleton, it is the Santa Muerte to commemorate... the Day of the Dead.

The idol is, to newcomers, frightening and appalling to look at, an image of the macabre. But in the marketplace of the Tepito District, or "Barrio Bravo," a powerful cult prays to this strange image of the Goddess of Man, seeking worldly favors of all sorts. It is an idol that is worshipped as an alternative to the living God.

With a prepared street-by-street grid, the SWAT team has been at work. Their surveillance van is equipped with a removable rooftop radio antenna. They've been driving around in the area, measuring the strength of Wi-Fi signals from a variety of access points. There is a consensus that Juan, a non-smoker, used the word cigarillo as a Wi-Fi hotspot for them to zero in on. They are getting close, but they need more phone calls, more emissions to work with.

At the university, Maria has kept busy, putting in several hours of overtime. Keeping busy helps keep her mind off other things.

After work, she's having dinner with a couple of friends at Gazpacho's when her phone rings. She recognizes the number and asks to be excused for a moment, stepping away from the table. "Maria, hello, sister, I've heard more caravan talk, they're talking as if some of them are going to find it and see it, I'm not sure. But, listen, one guy passed by the door, covered in tats, has to be an MS-13. Have you talked with Mama and Papa...can I get a cigarillo?"

A long pause, "Juan, are you there?"

A Treacherous Plot
and a Rescue

He had just been briefed for the ninth time by the BFI's ED John Arnold, and he's still holding his briefing book. He had been given a summary about the lay-of-the-land in respect to intelligence reports of foreign activities concerning the upcoming election. He was shown bold political advertisements taken off of the internet that stated false but plausible claims about his recent presidential opponent. It didn't surprise him that foreign-paid political commercials could be disguised so well to resemble any one of many legit political attack ads.

A secretary on the 11th floor of the BFI had stuck her neck out and put her job on the line by making copies of the ED's notes and memorandum against the president. And he knew what Arnold was telling him was a crock of s***!

He held his temper and bit his tongue until Arnold left the room. He thought to himself, "How stupid do they think I am?" In walks his Attorney General (AG), Sam Patton. With his voice rising, "What the hell, Sam? They've been playing me." "Yes, sir, you're right," the president cut him off. "Those dirty sons of bitches. If not for Arnold's secretary, who I'd like to give a big hug to..."

The attorney general was a tough guy, but even he didn't want to face what he knew was coming. He was sick to his stomach, he should have figured it out, he should have had the president's back.

"Mr. President, just got word they've subpoenaed Deputy Chief of Staff Hunt over trumped-up allegations of fraud. They claim that he accepted bribes in exchange for information related to the contract on the new M1A2 Abrams," said Patton.

In 2006, during Operation Iraqi Freedom, Sergeant Lucius Hunt of the 82nd Airborne Division was awarded the Silver Star for valor when, serving as a combat engineer, he used his rifle to hold at bay an enemy unit of sappers who had just detonated a car bomb to knock down part of the wall of his Forward Operating base. The explosion injured and disabled several fellow soldiers. Rushing to a nearby bulldozer, he shoved together debris, making a temporary defensive barricade at the breach. Sergeant Hunt had been part of the 9-11 generation, and at the award ceremony, his commander called it the *next* greatest generation.

Following his military service, he joined the Federal Bureau of Investigation, where he led its National Hostage Rescue Team in one of the most dangerous and challenging hostage situations in Bureau history. In a small town located in southeastern Alabama, a psychopath had kidnapped a five-year-old boy off a school bus after shooting and killing the driver. The kidnapper, armed and dangerous with a Ruger pistol, held the child in a deep sound-proof underground bunker he had excavated next to his leftover trailer from a federal disaster relief program. Besides a working television set he installed to watch the events of his own making on the local news stations, he had rigged a lethal bomb in a PVC pipe sprouting from the bunker that could be triggered by the kidnapper pulling on a cord from within. The kidnapper demanded that a television reporter join him in the bunker to broadcast what was his fanatical manifesto.

The standoff was approaching a week, and with negotiations, via a throw-phone failing, Hunt and his rescue team were facing a complicated life and death decision. Sleeping gas could cause the kidnapper to set off the bomb or shoot the victim and himself as had happened in a catastrophic hostage scenario in a Moscow theater.

From a monitor feeding images from a concealed camera they had been able to slip in amongst other supplies to the bunker, the kidnapper was seen to be at a boiling point, yelling with rage, threatening to die, and rehearsing steps to detonate the bomb.

Make a desperate gamble and hope for the best; it was the only choice, but a tortured one, with a five-year-old's life at stake. A decision was made to storm the bunker. Hunt assigned himself to be the first one in, the first in file to rush down the narrow 12-foot long laddered shaft into the bunker. The plan was set. Hunt would be followed immediately by two fellow agents clinging to each other's shirt tails.

As he dropped through the opening, on the way down, he got stuck and entangled in a steel coil barrier that the kidnapper had devised in defense against a surprise assault. The agent following him dropped on top of him while the kidnapper fired several shots at them as they hung suspended in the shaft, incredibly missing them.

After he and his teammate were promptly being pulled out, a breaching team stepped in to cut the cables, allowing another chance to try it again. This time, using stun grenades, Hunt made it down through the shaft, but during the plunge, his hand holding his weapon struck a ladder rung, knocking the pistol out of his hand. As he hit the floor, in the smoke and chaos, he lunged forward, groping blindly when he felt the five-year-old victim. He instantly grabbed the boy and covered him under his body. The two agents dropping behind him fought briefly with the kidnapper before shooting and killing him. Embracing the child with an emotional release of adrenaline, Agent Hunt whispered in his ear that "everything will be all right now."

Patton went on "And, I'm afraid, Sir, it gets even worse. A grand jury in the Southern District of California, supposedly under seal, indicted his daughter on federal charges related to her peaceful protest outside of an abortion mill. My sources say that she was with a local pro-life prayer group, legally joining in prayer across the street on the sidewalk when a truck pulled out of the driveway. As it was turning onto the street, the rear door flung open and a plastic storage bin fell onto the middle of the street before driving away. His daughter innocently walked into the street to move it safely out of the way of traffic. The lid had come off, and you can only guess what she saw inside. Horrified, she and her friends didn't know what to do. No one came out to answer the door, so they took the bin to their church rectory where the young associate priest put them in touch with a local funeral home. The funeral home took care of it.

So then an anonymous phone call was placed to the abortion mill saying, according to them, that she had stolen the grisly thing from the truck with the purpose of using it as a political device to smear them. There hasn't been a press conference to announce any of this yet," Patton said, his eyes fixed on the blue carpet.

And now, at this critical time, the president needed the wise and prudent council of his deputy adviser. He needed him unencumbered, but he *was* encumbered and neutralized by a purposeful plot set against the president to weaken his abilities to lead the country against enemies within and without.

Arnold and a cabal of the heads of multiple intelligence agencies have colluded to concoct a subversive scheme involving the president's campaign to regain the White House by fixing the results and manipulating the votes from key states of the electoral college to include Florida, Pennsylvania, Wisconsin, and Michigan.

An anonymous tipster had warned the AG's Office that a nefarious backdoor program called SHADE has been created by a cabal of international government globalists embedded in the Five Eyes Alliance. The program has been installed in the firmware of voting machines and connects to secret state servers to "spoof" the voter's choice, tabulating to the globalists' preferred candidate, Erasmus Floyd, a cunning one-world government type from Berkeley, California. These voting machines are specifically delivered to key swing states through supply chain manipulation in collusion with willing corporate cronies. The cabal's asserted alibi, which defies credulity, is a classic ploy of transference-that the president and his staff conspired with Eastern bloc communist nations to use foreign-designed computer software to change voter tabulations; all in exchange for U.S. oil.

It was hard to determine at this time how many executive heads were involved, what with 17 active intelligence agencies operating in and outside the country.

A Dream and a Punch

On the mantle of the sidewall fireplace in the president's master bedroom suite on the second floor of the White House sits a gilded Louis XVI tuquin marble clock gifted to President George Washington by the Marquis de Lafayette. The silent but steady motion of its pendulum has brought the big hand on its silvered face to the XII and the little hand to the 1. The president isn't able to fall asleep, he is still tense and anxious about what was said at the briefing late that evening. The PLAN has continued to escalate using a series of threatening maneuvers and demonstrations against America's allies in the South China Sea. They seem to be *provoking* a pre-emptive strike. Finally, he nods off into a fitful slumber.

He walks by a row of crude wood huts, smoke billowing into the darkness, the coughing and soft moaning of young soldiers, two of them dragging a mate out of one of the huts under a blanket; the body is limp and lifeless, its soot-covered feet are protruding, the dead youngster is barefoot. Out, across in a field, a fire is burning, soldiers around in a circle stooping, trying to stay warm, snowflakes falling heavily on their ragged caps and capes, and a chill wind. "I'll die on my feet before I'll live on my knees." He cries out in grief, "George, George, wake up, you're dreaming," prompts Eva shaking his shoulder.

At the White House, located in the West Wing adjoining the Oval Office, is the Cabinet Room, where the president is waiting to be briefed on the latest intelligence reports. On the wall, a portrait of Andrew Jackson watches over the gathering. The room is full of government officials. They are aligned in partisan groupings with an entourage of the joint chiefs of staff sitting together in a row of chairs behind the conference table against the wall at the far end. President Greene is gazing out the window looking at the Rose Garden, while across the table, his attorney general is reviewing some notes.

Sam Patton had earned his reputation taking on the Cali Cartel in West Texas. He had gotten the job done under the added pressure of having a cash bounty put on his head by villains across the border in Cali territory. And it was known that more than a few ruthless Sicarios, i.e., paid assassins, were rumored to be in the States trying to earn the bloody reward dollars.

Patton is ready to brief the president on the latest turn-of-events. He looks up from his notes and offers, "Mr. President, can we step outside?" Standing in an alcove out of earshot, before Patton can speak, the president offers "Sam, I told Eva about it, I told her that I think they've got some kind of underground coup going to try to get rid of me, and do you know what she said? She said, "I'll be praying for you." The president raises his hands above his head and sheepishly glances up at the ceiling as if he was looking for some kind of sympathy from above.

"I'm glad she's on our side, Sir. Anyway, Sir, I've got some good news, for a change, one of the staffers from my office received a call from a young man representing Greene's Geeks. He said that they knew just how to counter the hack into the voting systems. It's completely over my head, but how it was explained to me, here, I made notes to myself." Reading from the notepad in his hand, "They use an IBM Watson supercomputer with multi-calculus capability to analyze, detect, and identify virile sources, and to recognize and separate the real votes from the bogus ones. He described it as a cloud-oriented, anti-malware patch. It connects to the supercomputer to locate and trace to show whether it was a real person at a real voting precinct casting a real vote. It flushes out and validates the real votes using actual voter registration records, open source data, and social media. He said they will be able to basically reverse the fake results and prevent any future attempts to cyber-steal the election. He said that they should get results by tomorrow before noon. They're going to work through the night," assures the attorney general.

"Magnificent, get a hold of ASAC Seve Ariza at the Washington field office right away, I'm promoting him to Special Agent in Charge-National Non-Partisan Elections Liaison and putting him in charge of this, we'll find an office for him somewhere, probably the Executive Office Building. Get in touch with Dean Morrison, Turner's man, Lord knows, the size of that place, should find available space for us to use."

"Tell him his first priority is to dispatch every available field agent to the precincts, and not to allow *anything* to be removed or brought in to those buildings. Seve's a good man, he introduced himself at the last convention; he was in charge of the security detail. We're gonna do an end-run around the eleventh floor over there...those bastards. Now let's get back in there, our friends are waiting."

A vigilant Secret Service Agent has courtiously opened the door for them when the president's secretary of Homeland Security (HS) struts through the door at the other end of the room.

"Here comes the champ," the president exclaims, bringing a smile and an uptick in confidence at the sight of his secretary of HS approaching his chair at the conference table.

"Mr. President, sorry to keep you waiting, I had to finish up with Prime Minister Blumenthal, why, he mentioned how fit you're looking these days. I told him you're probably spending more time with the heavy bag?" prods the secretary.

The president's Cabinet selection for HS is a remarkable man. They met at a fundraiser for the Boy's Club at the MGM Casino in Detroit that was built where the old Tiger Stadium had once stood. Dr. Ray Walcott, a living legend and pride of Detroit's African American community, is a nationally-renowned brain surgeon who had grown up on Detroit's East Side. Prior to entering medical school, Dr. Walcott had been known for a sledgehammer of a left hook he had regularly demonstrated inside the Golden Gloves boxing rings of Detroit. He had been inspired to take up boxing by the success of an undersized heavyweight, a sharecropper's son, a quiet Southern Baptist from Beaufort, South Carolina by the name of Smokin' Joe Frazier.

Walcott had been trained by Emmanuel Steward at the legendary Kronk Recreation Center on McGraw Street in Detroit's southwest end.

Known as the toughest gym in the country, it was named after local Councilman John F. Kronk, who was of Polish heritage. Following the rioting triggered by the murder of Doctor Martin Luther King Jr., the demographics around the place changed. So Steward, the person who would make the establishment nationally-renowned, was of African descent, as were most of the champions he trained. And from the outside, it looked mean, really mean, surrounded by abandoned broken-down buildings; the red brick was blistered with bullet holes with rusting sheet metal covering the windows. Inside, down in the basement, the door to the boxing ring was opened with a finger through a hole where the doorknob was supposed to be. In there, the temperature was maintained at 95 degrees, mainly because Steward, the National Golden Gloves Bantamweight Champion of 1963, wanted his fighters to be able to sweat and withstand the heat, but also because there wasn't much he could do about it. It made Joe Frazier's Gym, where Joe trained in 1971 for "The Fight of the Century" on North Broad in Philadelphia, look almost inviting.

And at the same time, it was an all-American kind of place. After two of his fighters came home on leave from U.S. military service, they gave their red and gold service boxing robes to Steward. The original colors of the Kronk Boxing Team of blue and gold were then changed to red, gold, and blue, blending in the colors of the United States Marine Corps.

But the most popular champion in his stable was Thomas Hearns, aka the Motor City Cobra. Hearns won his National Golden Gloves title in Hawaii. Towering over most welterweights, Tommy Hearns' power was breathtaking. Entering the title fight, he was 24 and zero, only two of his opponents had been able to stay on their feet to hear the final bell. In the second round, the defending champ who had never been knocked off his feet, felt, but didn't see, the lightning right fist of Hearns' when he crashed to the canvass.

Hearns was the new Welterweight Champion of the World. But it was Hearns' commitment outside the ring that gained him a special respect from local fans and citizens. While he went on to successfully defend his title in the boxing ring, he also defended the citizens of his community in the streets by donning a blue uniform, strapping on a holstered .357 Magnum and handcuffs, and proudly wearing a silver badge as a reserve officer of the Detroit Police Department for free, at no charge to the public. He said that every kid, at one time or another, wanted to be a police officer when they grow up. And he was actually *doing* it; a man who had already earned national fame and fortune, was willing to stick his neck out to serve his hometown community and win for himself a genuine sense of citizenship.

At one point, the good doctor had to decide whether to take his chances pursuing a professional boxing title or use his God-given intelligence to pursue healing. In the end, he decided to use his hands to heal the human brain instead of using them to put them to sleep on the canvasses of boxing rings. And those patients, healed by his gifted hands, were happy that he chose medicine.

The president had his own experiences in Golden Gloves competition in New York, but after getting pummeled one night by an unheralded light heavyweight from the Bronx who he couldn't lay a glove on, his decision to hang up the gloves was an easy one. They were kindred spirits, both being fans of boxing history and enjoyed each other's company, sharing boxing stories and memories of famous bouts.

During a break in the meeting, they reminisced how in '68, their chests swelled with pride when George Foreman held up that little US flag in the center of the ring and gracefully bowed to each corner with that joyful smile and sparkling gold medal hanging around his neck. To this day, the former Heavyweight Champion of the World says that he waved that flag so people knew he was an American. And after receiving the loud applause, he said if he had to do it all over again, he would have had *two* flags in his pocket that day. He quoted Frederick Douglass, who once said "I didn't know I was a slave until I realized I couldn't do what I wanted to do. When you can do what you want, you're free."

"I just wanted people to know where I was from," said George.

Walcott tells the president, "And for us aficionados, you've kept the history of our sport alive as well as brought justice for one of our black pioneers, Jack Johnson. He was the Jackie Robinson of our sport. Your hands-on sponsoring of big events shows that you feel boxers can be heroes too, admired for their achievements like any other athlete."

"You've reminded people of the old taboo on interracial dating; it may be obsolete, but young people use their freedom to choose their partners, white or black, and take it for granted. Ol' Jack couldn't, he's up there smiling, Mr. President, thank you for that," said the secretary.

The meeting has resumed:

"The Taiwanese are tough SOBs, and you've got to give them credit; with1,000 ballistic missiles aimed down their throats, they're not showing any interest in becoming communists," wonders the president out loud. You've got to respect their pride in being Chinese, and yet, at the same time, refusing to be broken and subjugated by the dictators, willing to stand up in the face of overwhelming pressure for freedom.

"So what happened in the South China Sea yesterday? How close did we get to the islands, the Spratlys?" inquires the president.

"Mr. President, the Preble and Spruance came within no more than 50 miles of their runway installation on Fiery Cross Reef. It wasn't the one and a half miles exaggerated in the press. They tried to jam our communications, but our new counter-laser technology worked wonderfully. Our aircraft smothered it. Our two Arleigh Burke class destroyers sailed through smoothly; communications with Taipei went uninterrupted," explains Joint Chiefs Kevin Williams.

"What do we know about the range of their surface-to-air missiles, anti-ship missiles, sub-surface technology, and other systems we're tracking?"

He's looking up at a big-screen displaying a digital map of the South China Sea. "Which of the islands are deployed for offensive operations, any new installations capable of that? What length of runway will accommodate their new war planes, their supersonics?" asks the president.

Staring at the portrait of Jackson, "We must show Taipei that we support them. We'll not hesitate to exercise our freedom of navigation in these waters, the Spratlys, and Paracels," exclaims the president. "President Acuna assures me that Manila is with us, and Prime Minister Haji of Malaysia has been a friend with us on this." the president insists. "And Japan is on our side I'm certain, I'll be speaking with Prime Minister Ito this evening."

The meeting is over. As he is turning to leave, Secretary Walcott overhears one of the political officers mocking the president's unrefined manner of speech. A fortyish-aged uniformed lieutenant colonel, a muscular six foot three, former parade ground drill sergeant, and public relations man for the joint chiefs, was grouped in a corner of the room with friendly elitists holding drinks in their hands. He is sneering about a recent telephone call wherein one of the delegates for the United Nations had demanded clarification of the U.S.'s official response to accusations of rogue behavior.

The delegate suggested it be put in an intelligible form of the "king's English." Walcott turns and yells across the room, "Hey, Colonel, how's this for the king's English: you can go to hell." Feeling that he had adequately responded to the insult, Walcott strides toward the door preceded by Raymond Posey, his young intern-aide. Then he hears, from the same corner, "What a poor excuse for a statesman...pathetic token." Walcott stops in his tracks, then glances at his aide before nodding at the door. Posey gets it instantly, with a grin, he shuts the door with a resounding click. You could have heard a pin drop as the secretary spins and stalks toward the offender in the corner.

As Walcott reaches the group, he stands face to face with the offender and says, "We were hearing rumors of outspoken remarks made by you people about having, oh, what should I call it...*displeasure* with our military policy concerning communist China? Why, that kind of talk might be construed by some to be borderline mutinous..."

"I don't know what you're talking about, now get out of my face!"

"Don't have the slightest, huh? Well, at least you won't mind apologizing for your remarks from a minute ago, not to me, but to the dignity of the Cabinet office of the president."

The lieutenant colonel glares at Walcott, seething with contempt. Walcott says casually, "Yeah, I thought so, it takes a man to apologize and admit that his remarks were out of line." Walcott slowly turns to walk away when he sees peripherally the big fist launched toward his ear. He instinctively ducks under it and comes up firing. The aggressor has left his chin exposed like a lighthouse in a storm. Walcott's left knuckles crash into the officer's jaw, lifting him up off his feet backward, where he lands with a thud onto the blue carpet. The man is on his back as he struggles to lift his head, dazed, wondering what hit him.

Walcott looks down at him and says, "Guess this hellbender had too much to drink at lunch, he can't even stay on his feet. Wishing he could have at least shown us a token of respect. Let's go, Raymond." As they pass through the door into the hall, Posey quips, "Don't think he was quite aware of your pugilistic background, Mr. Secretary."

Shoals and Supersonics in the South China Sea

At the heart of the tropical Island of Hainan in the South China Sea rests its highest mountain, Mt Wuzhi; its highest peak rises to 6,102 feet. Its coconut-palm coastline is 950 miles long with golden sandy beaches favored by tourists. The shallow blue depths of its sea grass-bedded shoreline is a popular spot for swimming. It is China's farthest southern province, only a one hour flight from Hong Kong and two hours to Taipei, the capital of Taiwan.

Exposed during the last ice age, this stretch of shoreline is a part of the Asian continental shelf. The seabed gradually slopes away from the beaches to a point called the shelf-break, where the seafloor begins a steep descent to the dark ocean depths of the abyssal plain. To the tourists lounging around the hotels at the adjacent Yalong Bay National Resort District, it all appears to be peaceful. But they don't see the underground caverns. The caverns are meant to be concealed from view because inside their submerged spaces are nuclear submarines, at least twenty of them, armed with intercontinental ballistic missiles.

It is Yulin Naval Base of the PLAN, the second largest Navy on the planet. The naval base is a work in process; the Chinese have been building an artificial harbor there to accommodate air-craft carriers, the over a thousand feet-long goliaths of any assault fleet. But hidden away, floating in an artificially expanded cavern, is a Leviathan, secretly built for a secret purpose. Its flight deck is enormous, capable of carrying over one-third more fighter jets, a superior number of the most advanced military aircraft to overwhelm any conventional number of fighters set against them.

The Paracel Islands are 150 nautical miles away, and the Chinese command the Paracels and the archipelago of The Spratlys, and next, the U.S. territory of the Marianas.

Aboard the PRC flagship destroyer Nanchang, it is cruising along on a training mission in the contested waters of the South China Sea. On the bridge, with a Zhonghua cigarette dangling too close to his white Naval uniform shirt collar, Rear Deputy Admiral Wu Tiānguó reads from the monthly People's Military Journal to the admiral standing alongside him, "Hey, Commander, listen to this: 'We shouldn't overstate the importance of a Chinese company operating the Hanjin shipyard in Subic Bay,' said so-and-so, an expert specializing in U.S. defense strategy at the American Enterprise Institute. He wrote: 'Just because a Chinese company operates the port and shipyard does not mean that Chinese military vessels can dock there - the same is true with the Port of Long Beach, California, which is now operated by a Chinese firm.' They look at each other and laugh out loud.

Just look at a map and one can see why the Taiwanese have reasons for concern, national security reasons. And Beijing has drawn its own map, a self-serving one called "The Nine-Dash Line," it is the line of the Dragon. And the Spratlys fall within this water-borne boundary line. A fire-breathing ring that defies the water that it encircles.

What does it take to make an island? Or what does it take to make a new dry island to build a military station? The Chinese military is making new islands out of submerged reefs and coral rock piles using sand. And the articles of international laws of the archipelago are not slowing this ominous build-up of white sand. China claims that they have a right to create these islands to harvest tuna to feed their people and build oil rigs above the surface to drill for crude, but satellites are seeing and saying otherwise: ballistic rocket pads.

The dredging vessels being used to build the islands, like all of the vessels of the PLAN, have a dual purpose; in this case, to provide an advanced watch guard and listening post for future military operations.

But, the PRC doesn't see it that way. Speaking in Beijing, Chinese Vice Foreign Minister Zhou Tang said, "China is the real victim in the South China Sea as 'dozens' of our islands and reefs in the Spratlys have been illegally occupied by three of the other claimants," Tang said.

"The Chinese government has the sovereign right and the capability to take back the islands and reefs illegally occupied by neighboring countries," Tang said. "But we haven't done this. We aim to preserve peace by great restraint, and in this noble way, preserve stability in the South China Sea." Tang said China's island building was not about militarization but a neighborly gesture of sharing .

He also repeated Beijing's standard line that while China's island expansion work is for defense of the mainland, its primary purpose is commercial. "First and foremost, China strives to be environmentally conscience. By building ecologically safe co-op facilities like lighthouses for regional countries to use, we prove our intentions of sincere community fellowship," Tang added.

From their oceanic observation station on Scarborough Shoal, their high-powered telescopic, an instrument made exclusively in Shenzhen by DJI, is focused on the active U.S. training mission in Subic Bay. Behaving more like a hovering Huey helicopter, a U.S. Fighter Jet has just executed a perfect vertical landing on the deck of a regal battle-gray super carrier. They can read the name plate of the pilot climbing down the ladder from the cockpit of the

U.S. Navy F-35C Lightning II Joint Fighter jet. It says: Captain Mark McKinley.

It is cruising effortlessly on a level plane in a sea of blue, with tailfin upright and steady, flat silver steel-gray. Its razor-sharp weapons concealed under its acutely pointed nose. Up ahead, an object is moving at a distance that is out of the range of its vision, but it uses the sensors embedded in its skin to detect and recognize it. The beast homes in and sets itself on a path, rapidly closing in. In the blink of an eye, the beast tilts its fins, and with a sudden burst from its tail, it is streaking vertically; there is a blinding explosion of white and red as it pounces on its prey, and its prey is no more.

But this is not the Pacific Ocean and the beast is not a Great White Shark. The sea of blue is the wild blue sky of aerial combat, and the beast is an American supersonic fighter jet that has tracked down and fired a "kill shot" to obliterate an unsuspecting enemy aircraft.

They are parked on the deck of the USS Carl Vinson, arranged in two tight rows, wingtips folded, noses pointed inward, slate silver-gray, seeming harmless enough. Yet they are the ten most lethal machines in the world, ten F-35C Lightning II Joint Fighter jets, ten supersonic killers. They are designed for stealth, and they are deadly, touting the most advanced weapons system in the world; and they can strike an enemy like a lightning bolt from a cloudless sky seemingly coming out of nowhere.

These modern marvels do just about anything, from an incredibly short takeoff, and it's showtime! Afterburner speed-over one and a half times the speed of sound, pulling 7 Gs' force of pressure pressing you, the pilot, back against the fighting chair, landing at night, talking to yourself 15 to 18 seconds of hyper-focus, downwind, time to calm yourself down. This 5th generation machine brings the latest in techno-stealth to the fight, one special kick-ass airplane, creating a surrounding invisible to the enemy with touch screens projected in front of the pilot's face, one dynamic engine, and if the engine quits, then just dead-stick the aircraft onto the landing field. And then, when it is armed:

A four-barrel 25 mm GAU-22/A Gatling gun fires 3,600 rounds a minute, and when arranged in "Beast Mode," the hard points of the wingtips carry either an AIM-9X Sidewinder short-range air to air missile or a heat-seeking "fire and forget" AIM-132 ASRAAM. Affixed to the inner wings are AGM-158 Joint Air to Surface Stand-off Missile (JASSM) cruise missiles. Sleekly embedded within or mounted outside its body are eight AIM-120s and two AIM-9s. The payload of its weapons bays hold six two-thousand pound bombs. In its belly, a special internal carriage secures a B61 nuclear bomb.

Only 30 pilots fly the F-35c; looking to the morning sky above, a flight group of five zooming jets look to be almost touching in the dim light, they look riveted together.

This elite squadron of pilots sport half-million dollar headgear. They can see the flight and combat information televised on the visors of their helmets. This high-tech vision system puts eyes in the back of their heads. They can see and process an enemy threat approaching from 100 miles away, no matter which direction they are facing. With their infrared night apertures, they have X-ray vision, being able to see through the aircraft and like a ball-handling magician, from their wingtips, they can fire their deadly missiles on target in a no-look position with the nose of the jet pointing in the other direction.

The nuclear-powered supercarrier that hosts them has been deployed to Subic Bay, a harbor made famous during World War II when, following General MacArthur's fulfilled promise to return to the Philippines, Clark Air Base was a key staging area that sent bomber after bomber from its airstrip to defeat the war machine that was Imperial Japan.

But they are departing, the international training exercise is over...

Demons in the Darkness

The Cameron County Jail looks forbidding, a place where you wouldn't want to spend the night. A six-foot chain-link fence topped with coiling razor wire sits on top of a staggered twelve to fifteen-foot high whitewashed cement block wall. The driveway entrance is secured by a rolling steel-gridded door targeted by surveillance cameras. Next to it, under an overhanging outside roof, is a smoking area with a faded red picnic table. A Coke machine partially obscures a black paint stenciled warning: "DO NOT BLOCK DRIVEWAY." Riveted on the wall above is a rusting tin sign that says "JAIL," with a fat black arrow pointing to the left. Directly below it is another newer sign in red block letters: "ALL PRISONERS," with an arrow pointing to the right. The International Bridge over the Rio Grande is less than three quarters of a mile away.

The bridge is a very short distance away from the pressurized atmosphere of the command post inside the county jail. And though time and distance are factored into every logistical problem to be solved, to the *thing* that is coming, it isn't a problem.

Originally, God's gift of bilocation was designed to be truly unfathomable, just one of those mysterious powers that was meant to be used for the good. One of several documented accounts occurred in the extraordinary life of the beloved Saint Padre Pio of Pietrelcina. While many saints received that mystical gift, only a few suffered the wounds of Christ's Passion in his own flesh... the stigmata.

Emma Meneghello, a very pious young girl of 14, was afflicted with epilepsy, which threw her into fits several times a week. One afternoon whilst in prayer, Padre Pio appeared to her and placed his hand on the bed sheet, then smiled and vanished. The cured epileptic arose to kiss the place where the padre had placed his hand when she noticed a small cross of blood soaked into the sheet. (A small square slice of the sheet, with the bloodstains is conserved to this day in a glass picture frame.) "Through the intercession of Padre Pio," writes this miraculously cured girl, "I have obtained other graces, especially for dying babies." Even Padre Pio didn't comprehend the phenomena that surrounded him. He said, "I recognize that I am a mystery to myself."

But the phenomena of bilocation does not manifest itself only in the supernatural realm of the paradisiacal angels, but also in the dark domain of the fallen angels, for their prideful leader, the subject with the goat-like face and horns tattoo, is a specter who has been seen at two separate locations at the same time; he is conjectured to be a spawn of Aka Manah from Zoroastrian legend, who controls the hydra tempter of the mind, such as sexual desire, envy, and greed, and other forms of depravity that distract people from being wholesome and good. Taking form in a ghostly replica of an accursed Indian from an earlier time, it has the power to replicate itself. This is the evil form of bilocation, bringing about harm or death to the person who is doing good, having demonic control over people like a phantom puppeteer.

"Tony, this can't be right, you gotta look at this; check the time and date stamps on these photos, and then look at the dude wearing the gold hoop earring with the black hair. Then look at these close-ups of his face with that horned goat's head tat on his forehead. This looks like the same guy," said Louis. "No way, what are you talking about?" Tony picks up the photos and looks at them closely, his eyes focusing on one and then on the other.

"But these photos were taken in Mexico City and these others at Matamoros...on the same day at the same time...are you kidding me?" exclaims Tony, astonished at what he is seeing. They deposit the strange imagery in the recesses of their memory banks and reset.

Louis reads from a torn-off sheet of paper: *Intelligence reports from U.S. DSS indicate higher-level threat of incursion into the U.S. at Texas border by foreign hostile pseudo-military via South America.* "What does *that* mean?" asks Louis.

"What part of the border are they talking about? Hell, the Rio Grande Valley and El Paso sectors by themselves are enormous. Not to mention the Big Bend Sector, where roughly 500 border agents cover more than 500 miles of the river border. Most of that is rough, wide-open backcountry. The patrol chief at Presidio told me that his small station is responsible for 113 miles of the river. We just can't cover it, it's impossible, we just don't have the people."

But I've got a hunch that they don't want to take the risk of being exposed out in the open. I think they are going to target the bridges because of the populations around them. I think they are going to take on an urban persona at the border towns where they can hide in plain sight."

Something demonic is lurking outside in the shadows, waiting, a specter, a goat's face tattoo. They're sitting at their computers engrossed in reading their emails when they receive the radio transmission from Sheriff McClaws that the border at Brownsville has been breached. An explosion at the Juarez Border is thought to have been a diversion, drawing attention away from the other sites of penetration. He will give them the details when they get to the bridge.

Louis and Tony burst out through the door and down the steps to the sidewalk, running to their vehicle parked down the street along the outer jail wall. As they approach the vehicle, Louis is moving toward the driver's side when Tony, at the passenger side, looks across the street and sees *it* standing in a vacant lot, a figure aiming a shoulder weapon at them. "Louis, hit the ground!" he screams. At that instant, the top of the wall explodes behind them, sending cement and barbed wire fragments in all directions. Louis is laying on the ground stunned, pieces of shrapnel have hit him in the legs, luckily, he has been mostly shielded by the vehicle. But Tony is also down, he is moaning, and his wounds are serious.

Katie McDermott, an emergency room nurse, is on her way home from the midnight shift at Brownsville Medical Center. She hears the explosion coming from somewhere nearby, for no other reason other than intuition, she turns off of Jefferson Street north onto Seventh. After a couple of blocks, she sees and hears a police cruiser with its siren wailing and lights flashing cross the intersection in front of her, speeding east on Harrison. She turns to follow it, and a few blocks down the street, she's forced to stop at a stacked-up line of vehicles in front of her. She sees flashing lights ahead and a commotion, people running from the jail to her left toward something happening down the street ahead; she pulls over, gets out, grabs her emergency kit from the trunk, and walks briskly toward the sounds and frenzy. Smoke curls dimly under a streetlight as she begins to see chunks of debris on the sidewalk and in the street; a smell of gunpowder. She senses that people are injured. She begins to trot toward a chaotic scene, people yelling. She sees one victim lying in the street next to a parked vehicle, being attended to by two deputies, she sees wounds to the legs, checks to make sure that a major artery has not been severed. She quickly moves around the vehicle to another victim lying on the sidewalk, with two police officers kneeling at his side. Katie sees, immediately, a sucking chest wound. An officer is pressing a rubber gloved hand over the wound, his trouser leg is covered with blood. Tony is gasping for air, and has a panic-stricken look on his face as she tells him that he'll be okay; asking the officer to keep his hand in place, she gets to work. From her kit, she removes a set of latex gloves and quickly puts them on and removes a dressing packet, tears it open, and uses a pad to wipe the blood from around the wound. She asks Tony to breath out. She centers an adhesive dressing over the wound, pressing down to make it airtight. She's told that an ambulance is en route, but an officer tells her that the response time is uncertain. She asks if a police cruiser is available and the officers reply with an affirmative yes, theirs is good to go. One of the officers runs to the cruiser, yelling to clear the area for the evacuation. The other officer, with the help of two others, gets ready to lift Tony into the cruiser. The cruiser pulls up, and Katie runs around to the opposite side and gets in the rear seat with her back against the door and her knees raised. They place Tony's back angling semi-upright against her knees; they're off and away with lights and sirens on a rush to the emergency room at Brownsville Medical, a critical nine minutes away.

Louis' leg wounds are field-dressed, and twenty minutes later, an ambulance arrives where Louis is put on a stretcher and hoisted by the EMS team into the vehicle for transport to the hospital. He's in pain, his ears are ringing, but he's lucid at the moment. He's strapped prone onto the stretcher; Louis is able to reach his hand over his front pants pocket, feeling for his rosaries; he feels the beads underneath and squeezes them. He begins to pray, *I believe in God, the Father Almighty…the Rosary*; not for himself, but for his friend and partner, Tony. He fades out, dreaming.

As he reaches under a promising rock, a deer that had been watching nearby bounds away downstream into the thickets…

The next morning at the hospital: "I told Teresa that you were about twenty rosaries away (Teresa uses the duration of one prayed decade of the rosary to measure time), bruised and banged up a little bit, but safe and in one piece." Hannah tells her husband over the phone. She didn't get more than a couple of hours of sleep last night. The most stressful part was not knowing the extent of Louis' injuries. Hannah knew about the possibilities that it could happen to Louis at any time, the world had become so violent, but she avoided thinking about it. For the children's sake, she had put on a brave face and only let go of her emotions after they had been put to bed. After receiving the phone call from Louis' supervisor that he was going to be okay, she had fallen to her knees in thanksgiving. Her husband's life had been spared and the terrible ordeal is coming to an end, she hopes.

She heads for the shower to prepare herself to start the new day. After feeding and dressing the children, she loads them into the family van to attend morning Mass at the chapel, a Mass being said for a special intention: for the healthy recovery of her husband's partner, Tony.

Guarding the Border

Originally known as Camp Eagle Pass, it served as a temporary outpost for the Texas militia, which had been commanded to prevent smuggling across the border during the Mexican War of 1846-1848. Henceforth, Eagle Pass became the first United States settlement on the Rio Grande.

Sheriff Julio "Tuco" Ramirez has put together a task force of seasoned law enforcement officers, all of them familiar with the panoply of criminal activity: murders, rapes, robberies, assaults, burglaries, auto thefts, and arson that funnels across the river from the City of Piedras Negras, Coahuila, Mexico, which lies three and one-half miles to the southwest. Ten years ago, he had to deal with a major problem with Mexican Drug cartels crossing the border to kidnap local teenagers and force them to smuggle the cartel's illegal drugs into the U.S. He handled that well, and after a long conference call with the governor of Texas, he feels confident that he is up to the task. He is grateful to be trusted enough to be placed in command of this operation. His deployment consists of three teams; he will command Team One, assigned to the bridge. His two other teams are deployed at either side and are led by trusted friends of the Texas Rangers, both former military, Screaming Eagles of the 101st Airborne.

He has been assured that this assignment is a top national priority, an Air Force National Guard unit stationed at Kelly Air Force Base, 143 miles to the east, is on alert to support him at a moment's notice. Additional military ground support units are put on standby to be mobilized if he needs them.

His assembled complement includes men from his own department, the Maverick County Sheriff's Office, local officers from Eagle Pass, federal officers of the Immigration and Naturalization Service, and his favorite LEO, Special Agent Diego Ramos of the Union Pacific Police Department. Officer Ramos has a partner, ever ready, always eager to please, tirelessly watching his back.

But his partner is young, only three years old. His partner's name is Hero, a sleek black velvet-coated German shepherd. Two summers ago, Hero had become famous. At the Eagle Pass depot, concealed within a plastic crate in a boxcar, he had sniffed out a cargo of captive young women, many of them unconscious from asphyxiation and a lack of oxygen. They were being shipped north to be sold in Chicago as grist for the brothels. Hero was a lifesaver. For his good deed, a banquet was held in his honor at the downtown Veterans of Foreign Wars Hall. Officer Ramos accepted, for Hero, a key to the city. Amidst all the fuss, Hero appeared to appreciate more his honorarium of a year's supply of Classic Old Mother Hubbard dog biscuits.

In times past, there did not exist a ready-made unit of law enforcement that could be mobilized in a moment's notice. The lawmen of those cities, towns, and districts consisted of local sheriffs and one to two deputies, depending on the size of their territory. When the sheriffs were faced with a particularly dangerous outlaw or gang, they needed more men to hunt down and arrest them. And so was born "The Posse."

One character who became the subject of a posse's primary interest was a bandit who came to be known as Railroad Bill. Bill McCoy terrorized the small towns along the rail lines in southern Alabama and northern Florida. Around 1895, a grimy-faced Bill displayed his superhuman strength by jumping out of a boxcar to steal a handcar at gunpoint from a railroad crew working on the tracks. He single-handedly pumped away with it to the stunned amazement of the stranded railroaders. Bill plied his illegal enterprise alone and was clever enough to exploit the imaginations of the local townspeople. He intimidated and beguiled enough to make the locals think that he could be anywhere and everywhere. But he had a softer side. Legend has it that along the way, he sold his ill-gotten cargo to needy folks well below the going rates.

Railroad Bill enhanced his larger-than-life image by out-fighting a posse of twenty men who had cornered him in the sleepy southern Alabama town of Bay Minnette. Bill escaped, but he left behind the bullet-riddled corpse of Deputy Sheriff James Stewart.

By now, his was a household name throughout the region. For the locals, the very mention of Railroad Bill brought about a tingling sensation and weird admiration for a criminal whose legendary feats brought fresh excitement into the otherwise ho-hum existence of their everyday lives and day-to-day boredom consumed with sundry chores.

But Railroad Bill's days were numbered. He met his demise at a train stop on the Mobile and Great Northern Railroad line at the Florida border, called Atmore. The Posse, led by Constable J. Leonard McGowan, included a number of Pinkertons who had gained fame as Abe Lincoln's bodyguard. And this time, they were playing for keeps. Bill was lured into the town's general store wherein he was gunned down in a barrage of bullets, including buckshot from the shopkeeper's shotgun. The date of his demise: March 7th, 1896.

In death, Railroad Bill's magnetic personality brought curious crowds of gawkers willing to pay twenty-five cents to view his bullet-riddled body put on public display on the porch of a saloon. But his frightful image lives on.

To this day, there are claims of sightings along the Alabama-Florida stretch of tracks of the Louisville and Nashville Railroad. One of the most haunting legends that made its way through the rail towns is the image of the dim glow of a single light, far off in the distance, that grows bigger and brighter as it approaches in the gloaming. Most witnesses to the phenomenon claim that they never hang around the station long enough to see up close the menacing specter of Railroad Bill furiously pumping away on his ghostly handcar.

Yesterday has been uneventful, but after the sun sets and day turns to night it is now pitch black with midnight approaching, the witching hour. Save for a lone coyote howling in the distance, all is still and quiet. Seemingly too quiet. The normally loud orchestral buzz of summer insects has ceased all of a sudden. Officer Ramos is set up on the bridge with Hero squatting at his side. Other team members are positioned along the U.S. side of the river. All are squinting across the river and listening for any unusual sights and sounds that would signal trouble.

Officer Ramos feels the leash tighten and sees that Hero has his ears straightened and is straining on the leash to see something over the edge of the bridge, down in the brush below. A glint of steel, his eyes refocus, Officer Ramos sees the moving objects below the bridge. He changes the channel on his radio from direct signal to the command post at Brownsville to wide-scan to send a general alert to all teams on the border. As soon as the knob clicks, his radio emits frantic voice traffic, but his transmission is stepped on by the exchanges back and forth. Again and again, he talks into the radio, "Breach of the border at Eagle Pass, numbers unknown." But his transmissions are snuffed out by the frantic voices from the team in El Paso, there has been a massive explosion at the river under the northbound Puente Río Bravo truck bridge from Ciudad Juárez.

The Texas border has been breached in multiple places. From staging areas across the border, from due northwest at Piedras Negras to Reynosa and southeast to Matamoras, international bridges have been the targeted crossing sites for the invading expat led cells. Undermanned squads of border patrol agents using speedboats and drones have been occupied with a group of migrants who have crossed the river west of the McAllen bridge at Madero headed northwest into the vast cattle ranch lands of Laredo, while a cell of invaders has successfully breached the border at the bridge and is making its way into McAllen.

At Brownsville, a cluster of deserted buildings in the No-Mans-Land stretch of U.S. soil between the river and the border fence is secured as a bridgehead by a cell of invaders who have crossed the river in instant inflatable rafts in preparation to scale the fence and advance into Texas. The surveillance cameras mounted along the top of the fence are shot away using silencers before the rappelling hooks are tossed up and secured at the top of the fence. The number of invaders scaling over the fence and where they are headed remains unknown.

Safe Harboring: Destination Virginia

L ocated within the bucolic Hampton Roads region of Virginia, it sits on leased fields of an abandoned antebellum tobacco plantation west of Smithfield, overlooking a northern bend of the Pagan River, adjacent to where the Fortune 500 company of Smithfield Farms operates as the world's largest hog and pork producer. With a strategic long-term purpose in mind to keep its people fed, this covertly concealed venture is owned and operated by the communist Chinese government of the PRC. It is the targeted destination of the MSS, a staging area for a number of coordinated attacks on the nation's capital, only 178 miles up Interstate 95.

About the only thing that could have raised suspicion is the account told by a couple of newlyweds to their friends. The couple had recently hiked through the woods on an excursion down to see the river and discovered a new chain-link fence interspersed with rotating surveillance cameras fixed atop interior steel poles. The security fence ran along the eastern side of the property to the end of the plateau overlooking the river and appeared to extend westward, out of sight along the woodland, at that point. They didn't investigate any further, rather, paying heed to the warning signs posted on the fence: DANGER–KEEP OUT; ELECTRIC VOLTAGE; RISK OF SHOCK.

Meanwhile, on the southern border, a two-person team of male and female expat escorts have found secure refuge for their cell at the Rattlesnake Inn, a drab garden-style hotel on Paredes Line Road, a couple of miles north of Brownsville. The female expat hikes back two miles to the Hertz car rental franchise on the city's North Side. She rents a windowless commercial van with optional bench seating.

On the sidewalk of a highway rest stop, a group of teenage vacationers attempt a polite greeting to members of a cell of hu-bots walking by, but they get no response, the kids think nothing of it, maybe they can't understand English, they surmise.

Several miles west of Smithfield, Virginia, a seldom-used road, overgrown and choked with weeds, its crumbled bitulithic pavement all but degraded and decomposed, winds eastward off of VA Route 10 before rising gently to a plateau overlooking a bend in the Pagan River. On this site, eroded from over two centuries of exposure, but still standing, is the framework of an antebellum period tobacco and wheat plantation. What was once the residential building, the plantation house is not a sweeping spiral staircase mansion of Southern novels, but a more common example of the practical style of the times.

A long and rectangular design of whitewashed quarter-sawn boards, only one and a half-stories tall; four main rooms are situated across the ground floor, while four evenly spaced windowed-gables jut out from the gradually angled peak in the roof, providing light to the confined sleeping quarters above. At ground level, five evenly spaced seven-foot-high wooden posts, in front and back, support the overhanging bottom end of the roof, which serves to cover the front and back porches with wide wooden board flooring built a step up from the ground. On its flanks, from the ground up, two large brick chimneys shaped like long-necked bottles are built to serve both ends of the house.

A hundred or so yards away from the house, a line of ten slave cabins still stand as a vestige of the forced labor of the era. Following the war and operating up until the late 1940s, the plantation was converted to a beef and dairy farm, a herd of short-horned cattle grazing within the fences of the surrounding farmland.

Larger barns were constructed, and metal-sheeted silos were erected to store the feed, while some of the slave cabins were used for storage and chicken coops.

In early 1862, the second year of the Civil War, the plantation was liberated by the invading Yankee army. Several of the freed slaves would volunteer to serve in U.S.-colored regiments and prove their valor in combat during the later stages of the war.

When the executive front office of Smithfield Farms heard about a new lease being reserved on the acreage adjacent to corporate property, it was perceived that the Chinese enterprise behind the lease was like any other of the innocuous foreign investment companies bringing commercial interests to the area.

On paper, it appeared perfectly legit. Out of nothing more than to satisfy a senior legal counselor's curiosity, a female summer intern was given the assignment to do online research on the company's credentials. Her findings turned up nothing more than a basic financial snapshot. The offshore limited liability company, known as Hotan International Investment & Development Co. Ltd., a Xinjiang-based privately-held company, owned a variety of agricultural technology and food production businesses, showing a net worth of $1.9 billion, publicly listed on the Shenzhen Stock Exchange under the ticker symbol 000666.

Stargazing in Hanceville

I
t is a blessing to be back home. Louis' uncle, Steve, has come over for a visit, bringing with him Louis' favorite beverage, a full case of Dr. Pepper. It had been a while since Louis was able to spend time with his aging great Uncle Steve, too long of a while. Uncle Steve was a WWII hero of seven campaigns, having been awarded two purple hearts, one of them as a result of German artillery while operating as a sergeant in charge of a mortar crew on Omaha Beach. Louis remembered the family scrapbook, which contained a faded newspaper article published after the war wherein his uncle was quoted about his birds-eye account of the view from his LST as they were approaching the beach: "It looked like Dante's Inferno."

To round out an incredible piece of soldiering, Uncle Steve served under General Patton during the march through the Rhineland. The one chapter that caused his uncle to pause and become emotionally silent was the day of his company's discovery of the Nazi concentration camp at Ohrdruf. An aged, twice-wounded soldier with both silver and bronze stars was reduced to tears when recalling that young orphaned boy's face, about five years old, wearing a G.I.'s field cap, trying his best to smile for the camera while his sweet innocent eyes welled up with tears.

He remembers when Uncle Steve read to him the military adventures of Robert E. Lee, who once had been honored in school books as an American soldier, a military hero, a commander of that fratricidal war where brother fought against brother, he commanding the losing side. And after profligate bloodletting, the country came to be unified again. And all of a sudden, it seemed that historical Confederate war icons of the South had become anathema to any discussion treating them as bygone American combatants. The history of Billy Yank vs. Johnny Reb was no longer discussed in the mainstream, not in public anyway. The book given to him by his Great Uncle Steve, to most, nothing more than a politically incorrect obsolete narrative, but to Louis, it was a chronicle of American history. Louis' most treasured family heirloom is Uncle Steve's WW II dog tags that he had worn around his neck as a young combat soldier, carefully wrapped around the Miraculous Medal.

Father Joe remembered it was there, at the Franciscan House, where he experienced a firsthand account of the demonic. It's one thing to hear certain things talked about, and another to experience them yourself.

Secretary Walcott's chief of staff notifies Louis, who, from his bed, alerts Father Joe to the threat linking the intruders at the Texas Border to the approaching Chinese Navy attack fleet in the Pacific. Father Joe has connected the dots to the ubiquitous involvement of the supernatural character with the goat-like face tattoo. He has enlisted the help of Sister Helen and the nuns at the Shrine in Hanceville. Sister gathered together the nuns and the three children and explained that their country, the United States, and the preservation of freedom and everything else the country stands for, was in desperate need of prayers.

That morning, in his bathroom at the Franciscan House in Washington, Brother Arthur prepares to shave in front of the mirror. He takes his electric razor and looks at himself in the mirror. He sees, in horror, plastered on his forehead, a horned goat-faced tattoo! Aghast, in revulsion, he dashes out and flings himself face-first on his bed and begins to sob.

At the house in Hanceville, Louis' nerves are starting to fray. In exasperation, "Things are crumbling all around us, we're under attack from everywhere, from foreign invaders and even our own government, from countries that our supposed to be our friends, and lately, I'm thinking that I must be dreaming, demonic forces from hell too? How can this be happening to us?"

"Gimme a break, Louis!" Father Joe shouts. "This isn't the time to be letting things get to you. There are more with *us* than there are with *them*. Saint Michael, our patron saints and guardian angels, remember? They're on *our* side. Things are *supposed* to seem like they're crumbling all around us! We'll be all right, God himself is in control of all of this. We can only do our best, we can't give up. Keep fighting the good fight. Too many people are counting on us, brother. I've asked Brother Arthur to come down and stay here at the Shrine; there's more than enough room for him. I *believe* in this place," implores Father Joe.

"Considering its supernatural powers, this is no ordinary demon; it had to have entered the earth from an open portal to the netherworld, which must be bigger than normal, and in that respect, probably located somewhere more isolated, where it is either unseen or overlooked. We need to find it, we need to gather a prayer group to find it, *wherever* it is," instructs Father Joe.

After Father Joe leaves, Louis explains the situation to Hannah, who agrees to take Teresa to the Shrine with her tomorrow to join in the morning prayer vigil. He tells Hannah to tell Teresa that Father Joe said that the children will be there. Louis will stay home with Joshua and Jaida.

The morning sunlight is lighting up the front-left side altar with an array of colors filtering in through a stained glass window. Her gold filigree crown is magnificent, the crown of Our Lady of the Angels. The three children and Teresa are kneeling in front of a stunning statue of the Mother of God. From her pedestal, she seems to be lovingly gazing down at them. The nuns in their umber-brown habits have filled five pews and are on their knees, their rosewood rosary beads dangling over the cherry wood benches in front of them. In rapt attention, their eyes are fixed upward on the golden monstrance in the shape of a cross suspended above the altar, a consecrated host is exposed within its transparent crystal jeweled center. Their unvarnished lips are engaged in unison, praying the Glorious Mysteries of the rosary... the mysteries of the miracles.

The Little One is whispering something to the others. They return to the rear vestibule where Teresa says "It's the Star, Mommy, follow the star."

"Hannah asks her daughter, "What star do you mean?" Teresa tells her mother that The Little One has seen it in the sky, a special Star, it can be seen at nighttime.

"But there are so many stars in the sky, how can we see the special one?" her mother asks.

"Why, Mary's finger is pointing down from it."

"Mary? Do you mean the Blessed Mother?"

"Oh yes, her finger is made of light!"

Hannah hugs her daughter and says, "We'll, have to let Daddy know right away."

Hannah steps outside and calls Louis. Louis, after listening to Hannah's report of the conversation with Teresa and the children, says, "Well, what do we have to lose, I'll let Father Joe know."

Father Joe has returned to the priest's house at the Shrine and is on the phone speaking with his brother. "I think the Star that they're describing sounds something like the Star of Bethlehem," says Father Joe. "Let's check the weather report for cloud cover."

From his recliner, "I'm looking at it right now, looks like clear skies for tonight," informs Louis.

"Well then, let's go outside tonight and have a look, I'll be looking from here. You tell Hannah to be outside with me at the Shrine tonight to do some stargazing, I've got a feeling that it is the key vantage point," replies Father Joe.

At home with the family at supper, Hannah asks Teresa if she'd like to count the stars in the sky with Father Joe. "So cool, Mommy, will we need telescopes?" Teresa asks innocently. "From what you told me, Teresa, I don't think so, if that Star is like The Little One described it, it should shine up there for us to see and know that it's the special one," Hannah explains. "Can't wait to find the Big and Little Bears, Mommy," says Teresa. Hannah hugs her daughter and smiles, realizing that her homeschool lessons about the constellations have taken root. "Sister Helen is bringing the children from the Shrine." affirms her Daddy.

Just past sunset, standing in the courtyard beside the pillar-mounted statue of the child Jesus, they gaze up at the doorstep to heaven. In the cool of the night, a silvery moon hangs to the east, illuminating the earth around them; the skies are the color of black ink with sparkles. Teresa points her finger to the heavens. "Look, Father Joe, that's the Big Bear (Big Dipper), and that's the Little Bear (Little Dipper); do you see them?" she asks excitedly.

"Where? No, uh, oh now I see them, thanks Teresa, they're beautiful..."

"And that's the Bull (Taurus) over there," Teresa points excitedly.

Hannah asks Teresa, "Teresa, can you find your brother and sister up there?"

"Of course Mommy, The Twins (Gemini) are right there in the middle!"

Peering through his binoculars, "But that's not Sirius because Sirius is over there behind us," says Father Joe, turning back around.

"Oh, that's one of my favorites, The Doggy," says Teresa.

"Well, this one is super bright, and it's sending off a beam of light toward the earth, do you see it?" asks Father Joe, pointing west.

"That's it! That's the special Star, and that light beam is the Blessed Mother's finger!" exclaims Teresa. Sister Helen is holding the hand of The Little One, who, with her two cousins at her side are gazing up at the Star and nodding affirmatively.

Back inside the priest's house Father Joe pulls out his smartphone.

"Well, what do you think', bro?" asks Father Joe.

"Amazing, so, this star, from what Hannah just told me, it's visible to the west? Looking like something unusual, not a common star or planet of the Milky Way, huh?" asks Louis.

"Well, I'm no expert, but the beam of light streaming from it seemed distinctive; it comes and goes, is it a comet streak? I dunno, maybe there's a logical explanation for it. But it's up there, you have to be looking for it to find it, at least Teresa and the three children saw it clearly without binoculars, so we'll see, maybe not everyone is able to see it, did you get a hold of the planetarium at UNA?" asks Father Joe.

"I did, and Doctor Max remembers me, he's looking forward to meeting you there." It just might be you, Hannah and Teresa. We're stretched thin; this is definitely an irregular non-official lead in the scheme of things, but I'm feeling back in the game. They set me up with a classified laptop. Remember, I'm only a phone call away."

At home, Hannah promises Teresa that she'll be able to visit Leo and his sister Una (pronounced yoo-nah) on campus as part of the trip.

Miracles and Extraterrestrials

B eing safe from hostile Indian tribes but effectively cut off from the rest of the settled East Coast by the mountains, the settlers in Southern Appalachia became comparatively more impoverished as modern progress passed them by. These stout-hearted people of the hill country now had to contend with lowland and coastal elites, usually over coercive taxation.

The area continued to grow poorer, the improvements of roads, bridges, and railways were ignored, and the degree of trust dwindled with a government run by an establishment out of touch with their plight. At times, political parties formed to take advantage of citizens' dissatisfaction with the government, only for the people to again be betrayed by the same politicians who had promised to change things for them, the same forked tongue used against poor whites.

The land itself, and the natural things within it, provided the means that sustained the lives of people set on making this land their home. And these were coarse homes without indoor plumbing, impoverished, the homes of coal miners who risked their lives everyday just to make ends meet. They, to this day, mine the coal that provides the fuel that generates the electricity for everyday conveniences that are taken for granted, like opening a refrigerator or turning on a lamp.

One particularly diverse tract of land is found west of the Allegheny Mountains and south of the Ohio River. It lies at the foot of the Mussel Shoals on the north bank of the Tennessee River. Flowing by on the western side of the place is Cypress Creek, a fresh water stream from the Tennessee; on its banks were constructed cotton mills, woolen mills, and lumber mills. It was surveyed for the Cypress Land Company in the second decade of the 1800s by an Italian immigrant, and so it was named Florence after the capital of the Tuscany region of Italy. In the way of masterpieces, the exquisite architecture of the old part of town reminds one of the painstaking efforts in the creation of a Michelangelo "David" and da Vinci's "Annunciation."

But nearby, there is, in contrast, a structure with a sense of simplicity. Traveling south, just across the river, in Tuscumbia, is the birthplace of Helen Keller, the deaf-blind girl who was the subject of the story, "The Miracle Worker." Built in 1820, known as Ivy Green, it's a simple, white clapboard home designed in Virginia cottage-style architecture. Nestled under a cooling canopy of one hundred fifty-year-old English boxwoods, magnolia, mimosa, and other trees, accented by roses, honeysuckle, and an abundance of English Ivy, it has been a permanent shrine to the wonderwork that occurred in a blind and deaf seven-year-old girl's difficult life, a life that some would not value, would not appear to be worth saving, for divinity is *always* where you *least* expect to find it, sometimes in places believed unlikely to produce... a miracle.

Doctor Max greets them at the arched doorway to the hallway of the UNA Planetarium. His astronomical site is distinguished by a domed silver-gray retractable roof of the observatory and adjacent cylindrical-structured planetarium. The scientist gives the impression of a middle-aged Albert Einstein, a head of bushy salt and pepper hair with a set of wire-rimmed spectacles balanced on the bridge of his nose. He's wearing a white semi-rumpled lab coat with the UNA logo embroidered on it, a profile of a left-facing lion under the Wesleyan arch encircled with the university name and 1830, the date of its founding.

Doctor Maximilian Marshall is an astrophysicist well respected for his well-rounded approach, which is grounded in classic education in biology, geology, physics, and atmospheric science. Prior to earning his doctorate at MIT, he studied solar astronomy, spending years analyzing a single star, the Sun. His years of galactic observation and study, combined with a serious belief in Christianity, has shaped his theoretical approach to the meaning and order to the existence of the moon, stars, planets, galaxies, and phenomena of the universe. His reasoning does not ignore the ancient astrologers, who, without modern day technology, relied on what is today categorized as metaphysics, the study of that which is beyond the physical to explain a purpose for these heavenly bodies. He doesn't discount the ancient theory that the planetary movements influence the moments in time, and since mankind is part of the story of the universe, our moment of birth was thought by the ancients to be recorded on the celestial clock, like the Sun's annual journey through the Zodiac. Doctor Max is more than qualified to explain what could be a celestial phenomenon.

He gives them a tour of the planetarium. While Teresa is admiring the local school children's artwork of the planets exhibited on the circular walls, Father Joe inquisitively engages Doctor Max in a casual discussion of "The Big Bang Theory" of creation espoused by modern cosmologists.

"Take for instance the bumblebees. I heard that using the modern calculus of aerodynamics, the little creatures shouldn't be able to fly, carrying all that pollen, yet they do; somehow, someway, they get their honey," wonders Father Joe out loud.

"Actually, upon close study, the bees are observed to be flapping their wings back and forth, not up and down as was first believed, to create a force like a mini-hurricane to lift them themselves upwards. But how was a natural propulsion so unique as that designed? How could it have evolved on its own, out of nothing, out of cosmic gasses? I know the point you're trying to make. The more you examine the complexity of life, in any form, it makes you feel that you know a lot less than you thought you knew. The very existence of the sun, the star that supports all life, in milliseconds to billions of years, can't really be explained."

Walking through the passageway to the observatory, Doctor Max explains to them the concepts involved in the instrument they're about to see. Inside the observatory at a tabletop coffee machine he offers tea and coffee. Hanging on the wall is a plaque in bas relief depicting an old-time wig wearing Englishman holding an apple. The cast brass lettering reads: Annual Issac Newton Award For The Advancement Of Science. Hannah accepts the courtesy, and the Doctor steeps a tea bag for Hannah and pours coffee in a mug for himself. "An optical telescope is a telescope that gathers and focuses light, mainly from the visible part of electrical-charged particles, to create a magnified image for direct view, or to make a digital photograph, or with sensors to create an electronic signal from an image to collect data and search for extraterrestrial information that we can study." he explains.

"What does 'extra-tal-e-star' mean, Mommy?" Teresa attempts.

"That's extraterrestrial, it means something from a different planet, basically."

"I thought so, didn't they make a movie about one?"

"Yeah, ET, that goes way back. One of my parishioners restored a red '82 Pontiac Firebird Trans AM, the car he drove to the theater on his first date. He really enjoys tooling around the neighborhood in that thing," said Father's Joe.

"Refracting and reflecting light has been known since 700 BC. Development of lenses began in Assyria, Egypt, and Greece, and, then, in 1609, Galileo Galilei built his first telescope using curved glass and mirrors to bend light and see far beyond the boundaries of the naked eye. Galileo's telescope used a convex, or curving outward objective front lens, and a concave, or curving inward eye lens." He pauses to take a sip from his mug. "A good example of natural refraction is when light passes through raindrops, the shorter wavelengths are bent more than the longer ones, splitting into different colors, making a rainbow in the sky. While explaining reflection would be shining a flashlight on a flat mirror to see it bounce off in another direction," explains Doctor Max.

The doctor puts his right eye to the eyepiece of the Celestron 0.35m Schmidt-Cassegrain telescope. Adjusting the focus knob, "Based on what Louis told me about the object, I was able to preset the altitude and azimuth settings, this aligning, or fine tuning, we call collimation, let's see what we have here." Equipped with a fixed star diagonal, it allows him to look through the telescope perpendicular to the direction the telescope is pointing, or at a 45° angle. His eye opens wider, he steps away, blinks twice, and puts his other eye to the lens. "I just want to make sure of what I think I'm seeing," as he readjusts the knob.

"I see what you are describing as a downward shining beam of light. Doesn't look like cosmic gas; well, this *is* very interesting. Stars are formed, they change, and they die. But this seems to be something that came out of nowhere," exclaims Doctor Max.

"This computerized control room of ours is linked up with the Hubble Space Telescope. I need to send them the readings we've gathered. They have a cosmic outside-the-atmosphere perspective using infrared radiation and microwave, and even gamma-ray detection, to get maximum resolution on this object. I'd love to see the close-up photos they might come up with."

Doctor Max is seated at the computer inside the control room. "These are the coordinates: 35.777855 latitude and -84.259644 longitude; let's see where Google Earth puts us," he says.

Using the keyboard, he enters the coordinates, and within seconds...

"What? What is this-looks like a body of water? A lake, a dam, a reservoir, maybe? It's gotta have a name."

"Looks to be Tellico Lake, it's on the Little Tennessee River just above the main trunk of the Tennessee River, out toward the Smokies, near Knoxville; huh, we need to do some research."

Doctor Max prints out several copies of the results. Father Joe takes his copy and sits down to study the information doing searches on his smartphone. Doctor Max queries the area on the computer. After twenty minutes, there is a growing sense of excitement.

"That's it! The site, it's been underwater since 1979" (the Icehouse Bottom site has been submerged by Tellico Lake, an impoundment of the Little Tennessee River created by the construction of Tellico Dam. Excavations were conducted at the site in the late nineteen sixties and early nineteen seventies prior to dam construction, in anticipation of inundation).

"It was the excavation, the defilement of the sacred Indian burial grounds that opened the portal to the netherworld," explains Father Joe.

A Family Adventure

Brother Arthur has arrived at the Shrine, and Father Joe is waiting for him. Inside the sacristy of the chapel, Brother Arthur removes the dark sunglasses and khaki jungle hat. Father Joe dips his thumb in the small canister of ashes of blessed palm, and as he rubs the ashes over the tattoo on Brother's forehead, he recites, "Remember man that you are dust and to dust you shall return..." Returning to the priest's house, in front of the mirror, using a damp wash cloth, Brother Arthur wipes away the ashes from his forehead to no avail.

They got up early. Making the trip are Father Joe, Hannah, Sister Helen, Teresa, and her three little friends from the Shrine. Hannah has put together a babysitting kit for Louis, complete with handwritten instructions of where things are in the house and what Joshua and Jaida are used to having during their daily routine. Not that he needs it, she just thinks that it might make it easier for him to play Mr. Mom if things don't go as smoothly as planned.

Driving in the family minivan, they've already passed through the northwest tip of Georgia. They stop to have their picnic lunch at a roadside rest-stop in a Loblolly pine-grove outside Chattanooga. Peanut butter and jelly sandwiches for everyone but Teresa, who doesn't seem to mind that yesterday's chicken nuggets are on the cold side. After about an hour and several decades of the rosary, the Great Smoky Mountains appear to the east as they exit onto I-75 toward Knoxville.

At this juncture, considering the difficult scenario facing them, and headed to a site previously occupied by Native Americans,

Father Joe suggests that they invoke assistance from a very special child because, he says, "We can use all the help we can get."

She was a child of a Mohawk father and a Christianized Algonquin mother. At the age of four, she was the only member of her family to survive smallpox, which compromised her own health and left its telling pockmark scars on her face. At age eleven, this child's first encounter with white men would cause her to suffer pain, real physical pain from harassment and stoning, and threats of further torture causing her to flee from her beloved home in what is now Auriesville, New York. But this pain was different. It wasn't the kind of pain commonly known to be inflicted by white men in the years of seventeenth century occupation and expansion. It was a pain that she embraced willingly, a voluntary suffering that was a consequence of believing the teachings of missionary Jesuit priests, who themselves would suffer painful deaths from terrible torture.

Their teachings of the gospel of Jesus Christ, her Lord and Savior, would leave an everlasting impression on her, truly everlasting. Because three hundred and thirty one years after her death, a young boy, a basketball player, claimed that he was cured after he prayed for her intercession. After cutting his lip in a ball game, he was diagnosed with necrotizing fasciitis, a rare, flesh-eating disease. The bacteria was burning across the boy's face as if his skin was nothing more than brittle paper, and modern medicine held no answer.

Then, Sister Kateri came for a visit. That's right, a living nun who had taken her public vows and religious name in honor of the storied Mohican girl. The boy's great-aunt had invited Sister Kateri, who had with her a three hundred and some years old relic to pray with at his bedside. The nun placed the relic on the boy's bed and immersed herself in intense intercessory prayer. And like what happened four centuries earlier, when the scars on the

Mohican girl's face disappeared at the moment of her death, the boy's aggressive disease suddenly vanished.

Father Joe explains to the children that the little Indian girl began her journey to becoming a saint when she was their age. In unison, they make the sign of the cross, and Father Joe begins, "Let us pray to Kateri Tekakwitha, the Lily of the Mohawks: "favored child of North America, we come to seek your intercession in our present need..."

They see signs for Fort Loudon Lock W, and arrive at the dam of the reservoir in Lenoir City, Tennessee. They park near the boat ramp and walk along the paved trail paralleling the water. The day is sunny and bright and the birds are singing. Teresa and the three children have their eyes along the trail, looking to spot different wild flowers for their collection. As they take a small path to the water, they are startled by a blue heron as it flushes from the reeds. It is a large bird; in its flight, the great wingspan makes it look like it is flying away in slow motion.

At the edge of the water, Father Joe, resplendent in his bright white-under-black Roman collar, prepares to give battle; he is in his element. The Little One and her two cousins kneel in the grass while the others stand silently with their hands folded and wrapped in rosary beads. A wind begins to kick up and dark clouds begin to form, in what, up to this point, had been a clear blue sky. He opens his black leather satchel and withdraws a capped plastic soda bottle marked with a black Sharpie "HOLY WATER" and places it on the ground. At that moment, they hear a menacing growl behind them.

They turn to see, standing at the edge of the woods, a lone wolf, snarling, with its teeth bared. Its leering yellow eyes are fixed on them. Teresa lunges forward, hugs her mother around the waistline, and squeezes.

"It's okay, Teresa, he won't hurt us, Father Joe is with us," Hannah assures her.

Father Joe glares right back at the beast. He whispers to himself, "Aw c'mon, Satan, is that all you've got? You can do better than that! Yeah, that's right, I'm *bringin'* it to *you* today!"

The priest withdraws a silk stole, colorfully designed with scenes of the fourteen Stations of the Cross, which was gifted to him from Father Amorth, and drapes the vestment over his shoulders. He pulls from the satchel a small red jewelry case from the leather bag, opens it and removes the gold locket enclosing the splinter of the Cross, kisses it, and as he puts it around his neck, a rumble of thunder is heard in the near distance. With the increasing wind velocity, white caps are appearing out over the water.

Lastly, he bends down and withdraws a purple velvet drawstring bag and removes a black ebony crucifix. He folds his hands, bows his head, and prays silently, invoking the Holy Spirit to give him strength. Holding the crucifix in his right hand, with his arm outstretched toward the water, Father Joe begins the Rite of Exorcism.

With a voice of resolute authority, he demands: "Saint Michael, the prince of heaven, compels you!"

By now, they are draped in semi-darkness, the clouds that have surrounded them are turning black.

"Our Majestic Savior, the Son of God, compels you!"

Their hair and clothing, along with Father Joe's stole, is flapping with the increasing gusts of a howling wind; they are struggling to keep their balance while The Little One and her cousins remain on their knees.

"The Third Person of the Trinity, The Holy Spirit, compels you!"

A torrential downpour of horizontal wind-blown rain begins to sting their faces, and Father Joe is feeling a painful pressure building in his chest. He tries not to react to it.

He places the crucifix back in the satchel and picks up the bottle, twists off the cap, and shouts in a loud admonishing tone, "The blood of the martyrs compels you!" A deafening crack from a bolt of lightning causes the children to flinch and shudder as it lights up the horizon on the other side of the reservoir.

"God, Himself, compels you!"

The wind is howling. He staggers from a ferocious gust, in visible pain, yet with determination, he shouts, "In the holy name of Mary, the Mother of God, I *command* you!!! Leave, therefore, you rebel, you *deceiver*!!!"

As he bends to pour the holy contents into the reservoir, he feels another sharp jolt of pain in his chest. The adults see the small splash and tiny bubbles as the reservoir absorbs the full bottle of holy water, and the storm continues to rage.

Hold on now, the eyes of the children are lighting up, lighting up in wonderment. Teresa has put her hands over her mouth and her eyes are as big as saucers. The children's attention is moving from the entry point of the holy water, then slowly out and away into the deeper water as if they're watching something astonishing.

Astonishing indeed, like the Egyptian waters of the Nile touched by the tip of Moses' staff; right in front of the children's very eyes, the clear water of the reservoir is turning color and spreading steadily outward until the full body of water, as far as they can see, has turned... blood-red.

Over two hundred miles away, kneeling inside the chapel in front of the Blessed Sacrament, Brother Arthur feels a tingling on his forehead, and the pain in Father Joe's chest is subsiding.

Hannah and Sister Helen have bewildered looks on their faces. Only Father Joe has a sense of what the children are seeing, and now, up in the sky, a bright shining sun has broken through the clouds, and the birds are singing again, and then they notice that their clothes are dry.

The drive home to Hanceville is a quiet one; they are tired, arriving after nightfall. Father Joe has received a call from his brother informing him of the dire military intelligence from the White House, confirming the threatening encroachment of an enemy assault fleet nearing the Marianas. He realizes the grave implications, the sovereignty of the United States is in the balance. There is much praying to be done.

The next day, during the afternoon, the first lady calls Father Joe at the priest's house at the Shrine and asks him to find Sister Helen. Father Joe tracks Sister down at the convent and dials up Eva before handing his phone to the abbess. Eva directly explains that her concern is the president. She asks for a special novena to be made, if it wouldn't be too much trouble. Sister Helen tells the first lady that the nuns are inside the chapel with the three children; she'll start from there. Sister goes on to explain how this morning, inside the chapel, she saw The Little One, whose face has been beset with a deep-set seriousness lately, kneeling at the side chapel in front of the statue of Our Lady. She appeared to be speaking in hushed tones with something unseen, all the while, the sisters, kneeling in front of the Blessed Sacrament, had been keeping vigil. "We'll all be praying for him," Sister Helen assures the first lady.

Somewhere in the Philippine Sea

The Seventh Fleet is anchoring the U.S. naval position in the Western Pacific, and a typhoon is brewing.

Typhoons, like hurricanes, are powerful swirling cyclones. They have winds that can reach well over 100 miles an hour. And they can span up to 1000 miles in diameter. But Azure is no ordinary typhoon.

At Anderson Air Force Base on the southern tip of the Marianas Island of Guam, the rain is screaming sideways, rata-tat-tattling off the multi -paned window of the air control tower; thick sheets of water are relentlessly pounding everything, wobbling the wings of grounded B-52 Bombers and "The Bones," the supersonic B-1B Lancers, which are exposed on and around the airstrip. The howling wind is bending the palm trees on Guam to their breaking point, waves are crashing into the shoreline, sending white water thirty feet in the air. To step outside in these winds is to risk being lifted and spun around blindly like a top.

Meanwhile, the BRP Andreas Mactan FF-150, the first missile-capable frigate of the Philippine Navy, is burning and sinking in the middle of the San Bernardino Strait. And the Chinese People's Liberation Navy attack fleet is sailing east at 35 knots.

For the past 19 hours, the Tritons have been flying at an altitude of ten miles circling the Philippines. Their radar detected the last recorded bearings of the Chinese attack fleet somewhere east of the Philippine Trench. The deployment of its Leviathan nuclear supercarrier has not been detected. It is flanked on each end of the flotilla by four escort vessels sailing fast, toward the Mariana Islands. Their nuclear submarines are moving below the fleet, spaced at one quarter-mile interval, unseen beneath the increasingly agitated surface of the sea.

But on radar screens everywhere, the radiated energy signals had gone dark; for the first time, the Chinese fleet has implemented its ultra secret project Sǎn, translated in English to UMBRELLA. It acts as a miles long invisible canopy, a dampening field, protecting the fleet from high altitude drone and satellite surveillance, shielding its emissions entirely by eliminating the telltale clues to its location.

The total distance involved in The People's Liberation Navy's attack plan is 1,655 nautical miles, from Subic Bay to Guam, via the Philippine Sea.

Somewhere in the Western Pacific, the USS Theodore Roosevelt nuclear aircraft carrier, aka the "Big Stick," is being escorted by a guided-missile cruiser and five destroyers, each packing nearly a hundred missiles. The Ticonderoga-class guided-missile cruiser USS Bunker Hill is the main escort for the Carrier Strike Group, coordinating the exceptional defense of the aircraft carrier. The Bunker Hill is equipped with an electronic guidance Aegis/AN/SPY-1 Radar Combat System deployed against enemy ballistic missile threats. In addition, recently installed on an area of the ship that used to support a pair of long-range cannons, is a compartment housing a novel anti-missile system never heard of before until today.

Guided-missile destroyers USS Russell, USS Rafael Peralta, USS Paul Hamilton, USS Pinkney, and USS Kidd comprise the other main warships of the escort. Lurking somewhere nearby, under the waves, are the nuclear-powered attack submarines protecting the rest of the strike group from subsurface threats. The

Theodore Roosevelt Carrier Strike Group is on a mission, its objective: to intercept and destroy, if necessary, a hostile Chinese Naval attack fleet threatening the Mariana Islands.

The day before, under a blue cloudless sky, a fighter jet landed on the great supercarrier. The "F/A-18XT" Super Hornet is assigned to the "Black Knights" of Strike Fighter Squadron (VFA) 154, and it is piloted by Lieutenant Ronnie Greer. He is a descendant of the legendary Tuskegee Airmen, an elite group of African American pilots of World War II. The pilots of the 332nd Fighter Group, wanting to distinguish themselves, boldly painted the tails of their P-47 Thunderbolts a fiery red, their war paint included red-tipped propellers and red bands on the noses of their P-51D Mustangs, and so their nickname, the "Red Tails," was branded in history.

Status Doubtful

G reer is a legend within the U.S. Naval Air Forces. He was a two-time All-American tailback for the midshipmen of the U.S. Naval Academy at Annapolis. Coming out of high-school from Alabama Christian Academy in Montgomery, because he was relatively small and underweight, the big schools showed little interest. But during the late summer debut of his freshman year, those who watched him play from the sidelines had never seen anything like him. He seemed to float on air and change direction at full speed, causing the players trying to tackle him to stumble and miss badly, as if flailing at a phantom. His enduring fame came during his senior year when he had sat out most of the second half of the season due to painfully torn ligaments in his ankle.

It is late autumn, and the Game of Games is approaching, the epic rivalry against Army, the Black Knights of the Hudson. It was to be a game that college football fans would not soon forget. Up to kick-off, his playing status is still reported as doubtful.

This November Saturday has dawned cool and gray over Yankee Stadium, with Navy slated as a five and a half-point underdog. When number 33 is seen coming out of the tunnel with the team, suited up and ready to play, the brigade of midshipmen on the Navy side of the field erupt, yelling madly, wildly thrusting their white hats in the air.

The game is a slugfest, with neither team willing to submit to the will of their opponent. Late in the third quarter, with Army up by a field goal from their own twenty-yard line, Navy is punting the football away. Through a gap in the middle of the line; a Black

Knight rockets through and blocks the punt, the ball is bouncing end over end backward toward the Navy goal line; players in black and white jerseys are diving for the ball, but it squirts free, a trailing midshipman landing on it in the Navy end zone. The referee clasps his hands over his head signaling a safety, two points for Army. The score remains gridlocked with neither team threatening to score.

With Navy down by five and the clock winding down, the play that will be etched in everyone's mind happens. Greer has been held in check all day by a gritty Black Knights defense. He just doesn't seem to be himself, lacking that famous burst of speed, unable to elude the defenders and shake loose.

With less than ten seconds left on the clock, it's fourth down, and Navy is huddled up with the football deep in their own territory. Their head coach overrules the play-call from the booth for a deep pass and wants a screenplay. Taking the snap, the quarterback fakes to throw toward one side of the field and then turns and delivers a swing pass on target to Greer, who catches it in stride near the Navy sideline. With two teammates out in front, Greer crosses the line of scrimmage, and with a wiggle of his hips, he makes the defensive back miss, he then jump-cuts left sharply toward the center of the field, causing two defenders to collide; he is streaking diagonally up field toward the Army sideline when a surging strong-safety puts a hard lick on him, spinning him around, seeming to knock him to the ground; a loud groan from the crowd...game over.

Not quite. Somehow, by sticking his hand in the ground, he has maintained his balance and keeps running; he is heading for mid-field with an Army defender closing fast, but a Navy wide receiver darts over and picks off the would-be tackler; now Greer is at the fifty-yard line and sees nothing around but daylight; everyone in the stadium and those watching on television can see what is about to happen, and they can hardly believe their eyes, and then, pandemonium; in the stands and on the Navy sideline, they are going berserk, teammates are jumping up and down, helmets and arms shoved in the air, a terrific roar swells from the crowd; in the corner of the end zone, Bill the Goat is leaping out of his costume; Navy's play-by-play man is on his feet, shouting: "he's at the forty, the thirty, the twenty, the fifteen, he's going to score!!!!! Can you believe this?!! Touchdown, Navy!"

The radar screens and weather barometers indicate that atmospheric pressure is plummeting and the winds are increasing. The weather instruments on the Philippine mainland at Luzon are recording wind gusts in excess of 50 miles per hour. The fighter duo of Lieutenant Robbie Greer and his wingman Lieutenant Andrew Kim are sitting in the carrier briefing room, attentively absorbing the recon mission. The commander is interpreting the most recent Triton data while their oxygen masks are being checked on the table-top monitor. A Chinese assault fleet is headed toward Anderson. They have volunteered for this mission, an extremely hairy one, to seek and find what appears to be a fast approaching full-scale Chinese Naval attack fleet, to observe with eyes-on, to assess and report the logistics and details of its lethal intent.

They trot out to the flight deck, and in the company of two deck crew in earphones and goggles, conduct a routine walk-around inspection of their airplanes. They deliberately scale the ladders, and each, with the help of a crewman, buckle themselves into their fighting chairs and shake hands. The side number of Lieutenant Greer's Super Hornet is 204 and his tactical call sign is "Paydirt."

Andrew is a Korean American. He is a competitive golfer, setting the record for the lowest single-season scoring average in Naval Academy history. Andrew was a late bloomer, using grit and determination to make it as a walk-on to the Navy golf team. His idol was Ben Hogan, another gritty late bloomer who won the United States open after sustaining life-threatening injuries to most of his body, including his pelvis and legs, a pro golfer's essentials; injuries so severe that there was doubt that he would ever be able to walk again.

On the early morning of February 2, 1949, on a foggy road in West Texas, they were headed to the next tour stop. With his wife Valerie in the passenger seat, nearing a small bridge, a speeding Greyhound bus suddenly crossed into the dimness in front of them; at the last second, Hogan flung himself across the seat in front of his wife as their Cadillac collided head-on with the bus. He had saved Valerie's life, but nearly ended his own. After the accident, no one gave him much of a chance to resume his professional career, let alone try to compete in the major championships, which, back then, involved a physically demanding final round of thirty-six grueling holes.

A little over a year later, on a hot June afternoon at Philadelphia's Merion Golf Club, with his legs bandaged tightly under his pants, in excruciating pain, with only three holes left to play, Hogan appears to falter; staggering, he reaches out for a fan to help him stay on his feet. He summons up the strength to knock a one iron from the middle of the fairway onto the 18th green to clinch it. Hogan had overcome the pain and willed himself on to finish victoriously. It was called the Miracle at Merion, one of the most heroic and inspirational accomplishments in U.S. sports history.

Andrew used Hogan's inspiration to develop a reputation for coming through in the clutch. He was always pitted in the last incoming match, with everything on the line, with everything left up to him.

His interest in becoming a fighter pilot was triggered by the history of the squadron to which he belongs. The Black Knights VF-154 dropped 470 tons of bombs and expended 1,500,000 rounds of ammunition against the communist enemy in Korea, and in June 1953, the Black Knights flew 48 sorties on a single day, setting a record for a Navy squadron. Seared in his memory, he will always see, in his mind, the smuggled photographs of those starving children in North Korea; wide-eyed, looking like little skeletons, the innocent victims of a callous Marxist regime.

His is proud of the patch sewn on the shoulder of his flight suit. It is a unique insignia, designed on a black field, a silver Crusader knight standing at attention, in full armor; a contrasting silver Christian cross standing out on a black mantle over the tapered torso, a combat shield, and big broadsword stuck in the ground at the warrior's side; a slayer of dragons.

Lieutenant Kim's side number is 206 and his call sign is "Iceman."

From a small glass-windowed cabin room, high above on "The Island," towering seven stories above the 1,100-foot-long flight deck, the Pri-Fly team of watchstanders are anticipating the F-18 Super Hornets' next moves.

Greer clears his mind and gathers his thoughts. He activates the electronics to start the engine and hand signals with a thumbs-up to the plane captain that he is ready to fly.

On the flight deck, there is danger all around. The blast force of a modern jet engine can blow an unsuspecting crewman into the sea. Or moving a couple of steps in the wrong direction, one can be sucked off his feet into the front air intake side of the engine.

With a thumbs-up, a crewman in salty yellow gear, vest helmet, and gloves takes control. The crewman signals with his arms for the chocks and chains that are holding the aircraft in place to be removed. On signal, Greer taxis around to the next yellow jacket, who guides him with arm signals, walking backward in front of the jet, while deftly stepping over the four arresting wires on the deck as it turns starboard toward the stern and final launch position. The light on the island glows red: four minutes to launch, visual checks completed. Greer receives the arm signal from the yellow jacket to spread the aircraft's wings.

Greer makes eye contact with a lanky crewman wearing a worn red vest and helmet. His nickname is "Det," short for Detonator; with both hands, Greer makes a cocked-gun gesture to Det, who loads the aircraft with the lethal battle ordinance. With a thumbs-up from Det, Greer is armed up now. The red light turns amber, the two minute warning, as he responds to the yellow jacket's signal and idles slowly forward to align the launch bar on top of the shuttle, taking up tension to hydraulic catapult number one. Two green-jacketed crewmen hook up the jet to the catapult and scramble away, making the thumbs-up sign.

Into his mask, Greer calls out "tension," and talks his way through his last-second instrument checks. He toggles the throttle forward and aft, left and right, takes his feet off the brakes, and calls out "Are you ready?" The marshal replies, "Good to go." The light flashes green. His pulse quickens. The ocean is steadily swelling, and the deck is beginning to pitch.

A "shooter," also standing in yellow gear, has taken over on the deck in the right front of the aircraft. He's waving his right arm furiously above his head, making a "raising the roof" gesture; his palm pushing up toward the sky, he's now signaling the 'select afterburner' for combat. Greer complies and hits the switch, finding his balance in sync with the moving angle of the deck, the shooter points two fingers directly at Greer, who activates full military power. A hundred flight deck personnel freeze in place; they become spectators and hold their breath.

With the tip of his right Nomex glove, Greer touches his helmet with a final salute and places his hand above on the towel rack bow of the canopy, and braces himself. The shooter returns the salute, bends his knees and touches the deck, and in a forward-leaning crouch, he extends his right arm, pointing toward the bow signaling the launch; nearby, a fellow crewman punches the button on Cat 1, and in seconds, with a deafening roar in a searing blast of heat like being shot from a cannon, aircraft number 204 catapults off the deck into the increasing force of a headwind.

In the blink of an eye, his airspeed gauge reads 180 miles per hour; he elevates by pulling hard on the throttle to activate the afterburners, he banks slightly and is soaring over the ocean as all those watching exhale in relief. He climbs to 15,000 feet in a holding pattern, waiting on his wingman.

Kim's Super Hornet 206 is launched to follow the leader into the darkening afternoon sky. In a matter of seconds, they are out of sight.

At an altitude of 25,000 feet, they are cruising at 777 miles per hour, bearing west, soaring toward the Philippine Sea. Andrew has Ronnie's "6"; he has his back. Ronnie's mind is concentrated on the big picture, on the mission, on getting them there. It's going through his mind: *how will he react when he spots the enemy fleet?* He is keenly aware of his wingman, trying his best to maneuver gently, knowing not to go to any flying extremes that Andrew is unable to respond to.

Andrew has his head on a swivel, constantly looking for unfriendly aircraft. They're keeping radio talk to a minimum, relying on hand signals, knowing that they will be heard by the enemy. After years of practice, they are flying as one. Andrew uses visual reads to respond to any changes or turns by Ronnie. In pursuit of their mission to get on path, Andrew is constantly responding to Ronnie's dips and rolls, Ronnie, dipping toward Andrew, Andrew, rolling away to maintain position. A roll by Ronnie causes Andrew to climb before dropping his nose down to move back to the level, optimal position with Ronnie. From time to time, Andrew is careful to reduce power using visual checkpoints so as not to get inside Ronnie's turn or to be sucked back too far. With power adjustments, pitches and rolls, their dynamic skills make them look like they are moving simultaneously.

At 10,000 feet, they maneuver to parade formation; wingtip to wingtip, they are flying fingertip close, ten feet apart. Andrew's adrenaline increases, his senses are heightened, keeping one eye on the instruments and one eye on the leader.

The pilots are feeling stealthy, flying with confidence that their newly installed Infrared Search And Track Pods (ISTP) will enable them to detect enemy aircraft a long distance away before the enemy will detect them; it means that the good guys are able to shoot first. This new protection relieves some of the anxiety from flying without their sister aircraft, the EA-18G Growlers.

These under-mounted radar beam-jamming pods send out electromagnetic pings to attack and disable the radars of enemy aircraft, making Ronnie and Andrew practically invisible to the missile lock-by-laser capabilities of hostile fighters. Their increasing tension is warranted because they know that flying toward them, in the foggy distance, are an unknown number of Chengdu J-20s, the air-superiority jet fighters of the People's Liberation Army Air Force; nuclear lethal, a chiseled-nosed dagger capable of traveling at a speed of over two and a half-miles per second; bringing fear with them...the Mighty Dragons.

Bandits on the Horizon

B ut they fly on. The last reported sighting of an approaching fleet was somewhere in the vicinity of Palau Island heading east at approximately 33 to 35 knots. While the Chinese attack fleet is approaching from the west, the U.S. fleet and its submarine's directional movements, heading east to counter it, are being watched. Their location is being digitally streamed to the Chinese command base at Yulin. The Chinese are monitoring the feedback sent by acoustic sensors and buoys installed on and around Yap Island, 526 miles southwest of Guam. And the robotic "underwater gliders" deployed below the Marianas are deployed to detect the presence of U.S. submarine movements, putting them on a collision course with the enemy in an ever-growing tempest of the Western Pacific Ocean.

"With me, Iceman?" radios Ronnie.

"Roger that, Paydirt is visual and then some," responds Andrew.

"Might have to go flat hatting, Iceman; fog-impaired," calls Ronnie.

"Spooled up, you lead," responds Andrew.

"Feelin' warm and fuzzy with these ISTPs," chortles Ronnie. "Not Growlers, but I'll take 'em, Paydirt," replies Andrew.

Formed in a two-ship wedge, Ronnie leads Andrew in a descent to the danger level, an under the radar altitude of 1,000 feet, but it is their only choice, what with visibility at a minimum and the strange ineffectiveness of the U.S. satellite and Triton radar systems. Nearing the estimated position of the enemy fleet, their dim glow-green slime lights are switched off. Ronnie and Andrew can see each other's infrared anti-collision lights through their night vision goggles. Their mission has taken on a harrowing bent, lending real meaning to the phrase, "fog-of-combat."

Lights are flashing on their panels, their ISTPs detect a swarm of aircraft up ahead in the distance, one hundred miles away, headed toward them, traveling at a speed of 650 miles per hour at an altitude of 40,000 feet. Their radar warning instruments remain normal, indicating that, so far, they haven't been detected by the aircraft flying above them, but what is appearing as a distinctive blip at the heart of the main object on their grids appears to be a confirmation of a group of what the Chinese have code-named N20, the top-secret production of long-range supersonic stealth bombers, each carrying ten tons of nuclear hell.

And cruising undetected, under the Chinese surface fleet, are several Type 094 nuclear submarines carrying 12 JL-2 intercontinental ballistic missiles.

"Are you picking up what I'm picking up, Iceman?"

"Rodger that, Paydirt, that massive blip looks like more than a recon sortie of bandits. That's a whole different configuration. Could they be bombers?"

Then, nothing but white static is seen on their televisors. "My radar just went bent, Iceman, seeing snow!"

"Roger that, Paydirt, nose cold, I've lost it too!"

"One minute and we'll be in front of whatever naval force is cruising below them; let's keep an eye on our instruments, slip underneath to have a look, Cherubs 3," radios Ronnie.

Shielded with their ISTPs, they dip under the thick bottom layer of gray-black cloud cover, and streak above the white caps of the angry ocean toward the enemy fleet. They are flying Cherubs 3...three hundred feet above the Pacific.

"Tally, tally, Iceman! Do you see what I'm seeing?!"

"Roger that, incredible..."

They have discovered the south flank of the enemy flotilla; visible on the surface are at least two Type 055 destroyers and other escort vessels.

Ronnie makes a wing flash to signal the 90-degree turn across the rear of the flotilla, and Andrew responds perfectly, rolling to his right, then re-positioning his plane's nose abreast of Ronnie's right wing and just enough below it to have a full range of vision.

They both see it at the same time, a vessel centered in the middle of a fast-moving flotilla, dwarfing the escort vehicles surrounding it.

"Firewall, Iceman, Buster to Mother, RTB, let's get out of here..."

Ronnie executes a hook turn, and Andrew swoops around alongside; they pull back on their throttles, heading home, on a direct line to the carrier.

"Marshal, 204 and 206 are RTB to Mother," Ronnie calls into his headset.

Andrew, who minored in American history, trying to fight off the jitters, plays a game in his mind: *It's April 1775, and we're Paul Revere and William Dawes, galloping hard over the dawning New England countryside, only we know that they're coming, and it's up to us to warn them...*

Snagging the Spaghetti

At night, alone and unafraid, in the middle of a raging typhoon, Lieutenant Greer was made for these conditions. But he is human and the inside of his helmet is drenched with sweat. And above the noise, he can hear his heart pounding. He and his wingman, Lieutenant Andrew Kim, are returning home to the carrier, home to "Mother." They have radioed the shocking recon Intel to the Roosevelt the oncoming Chinese fleet's position and its wide lethal footprint on the ocean's surface.

Situational awareness, it was the vital lesson hammered into them by their instructors. After so many hours of flying, they had come to realize it on their own, it was the intangible factor above all else that counted because now the situation facing them is wreaking chaos. Now they not only have to recognize the dangers of their predicament, they have to automatically react to them to make the correct lives-on-the-line, split-second decisions.

There has been a high duration of radio communication with the controllers up in the island; the extreme weather conditions are dictating it. Over the radio, the pilots hear the call "POWER" again and again as the controllers try to bring in other planes attempting to land up ahead.

The conditions are way beyond precarious now, the 405-acre, 260,000 horse powered vessel is at the mercy of the sea, like a toy being tossed about by an unseen giant playing in his bathtub. The lights on the scattered-wide screen of escort vessels are ducking up and down under the waves like fishing bobbers. The deck of the ship, normally hard enough to negotiate in calm conditions, now appears to be tilting up on its stern, the bow pointing up out of the water; a huge wave causes watchstanders in the island to be thrown against the aft-side glass of the cabin.

Traveling at 150 miles per hour, they must hit the deck precisely to snag their tail hooks into the "spaghetti," one of the four hydraulic-controlled arresting wires spaced fifty-feet apart on the flight deck. The wires are sequenced aft from the stern forward, numbered one to four. It is nothing short of a controlled crash... under normal conditions.

His aircraft slows, blinking instruments are registering a stalling of the engine, but the aircraft's computer system quickly corrects, and Greer breathes again, regaining full power. He's desperately fighting the elements. A sudden gust of wind is forcing Greer's plane downward, and he's losing altitude. Desperately, to stop the rapid descent, he pulls back hard on the throttle, abruptly increasing the plane's climb angle, barely avoiding contact with the crest of a thirty-foot wave.

Then, all of a sudden, the winds begin to cease and the waves begin to settle; the weather is calming, the carrier is rolling in the swells; they have entered the eye of the storm.

The pilots do not have a moment to spare, they will have only one chance to execute a safe landing before the raging wind force of the eye wall smashes into the ship again.

They adjust their airspeed power from severe gust level to a normal steady wind. The captain of the ship calls down to inform AIROPS that he is fighting the crosswind, trying to turn the ship to find a suitable bearing. Ronnie and Andrew realize that the ship is turning, preventing them from landing. Ronnie gasps, "What are they doing?!"

Andrew recites the Memorare in his head over and over, "Remember, O most gracious Virgin Mary, never was it known..."

Both pilots have attempted to land on the teetering deck, but have failed to hook one of the wires, skipping and bolting away airborne under full military power to circle for another attempt.

With fuel dangerously low, and the carrier in the middle of the ocean, the pilots are not within range of a divert airfield, meaning that the only place to land is onto the surface of the ship. A radio transmission is repeated, "We're flying Blue Water Ops." The flight deck is their one and only hope.

Ronnie, on his second attempt, has snagged the wires, the deck crew scrambles to his aircraft to clear the deck for Andrew. Ronnie has made it home safely. Now all he can do is wait, wait and hope for his friend and wingman, Andrew, feeling helpless like everyone else.

Andrew is up there alone and running out of fuel.

Controller: "206, expect CV-1 recovery Case III approach, altimeter 29.92, marshal on the 240 radial, 6, angels four, your fuel is Bingo! Push time, EMERGENCY!"

Andrew: "Iceman 206, marshal on the 240, 6, angels three, Bingo!"

Andrew is 3 miles from the ship as his aircraft picks up the "bulls eye." Displayed on his visor telescreen, he sees a 'fly-to' needle gauging his final bearings.

Andrew checks for full military power, makes an act of contrition, and braces for the jolting plummet toward the carrier.

The controls have been passed to a Landing Signals Officer (LSO) on the deck.

For the last few seconds Andrew gets off the instruments and switches to a visual approach; he's dropping in a 70-story free-fall toward the ocean, his eyes are piercing through a steady downpour, focusing on the up-and-down motion of the glowing glide-slope indicator fixed on the port side of the ship. The glide slope, the angle at which his aircraft is descending and landing, by the naked eyes-in-his head tracking of a bright amber light, his rapidly descending maneuvers are moving it to line up with a row of green lights; a sort of traffic light that is helping him avoid a high-speed, fiery crash into an unforgiving wall of metal. His eyes are riveted on the "Meatball" to fighter pilots, "the Ball."

Controller: "206, on course, on glide path, ¾ mile, call the Ball!"

Andrew: "206, Iceman, Ball, Bingo!"

As large swells engulf the ship, the stern is dropping, pitching the bow up above the horizon. Another swell causes the reverse; the bow is going down and the stern is rising in front, like a cold steel curtain. The moving deck surface is playing tricks on Andrew's brain; it's confusing him!

LSO: "Roger that, Ball, deck's moving, 206, you're a little low!"

Andrew's eyes pop as he sees the amber light floating below the green lights; the plane is coming in too low! At the last second, he pulls back on the control stick, creating a fraction of lift; he's holding his breath and bracing himself for the bone-jarring collision with the deck. As the wheels skid against the deck, a last-second roll of the ship has caused the plane to land off-center portside. He hears a faint pinging sound and feels a brief halting yank from a snagged wire.

But the plane's tail hook has pulled off of wire four, and the plane has slid across the landing zone onto the starboard edge of the deck with the right wing hanging over the side, its right wheel propped against the six-inch-low guard rail. A large swell raises the portside of the ship upward, shifting the crushing weight of the plane against the guard rail, causing the wheel assembly to collapse and the fuselage to slam onto the outside edge of the carrier.

Inside the cockpit, with a calm presence of mind, Andrew works the throttle to shut down the engine. This critical maneuver has turned out the lights, he is now strapped in darkness. Slipping and sliding, the fight crew rushes to the plane, but before they can harness it, the plane plunges over the side toward the Pacific sixty-feet below! As the aircraft tumbles downward, wing over wing, to Andrew, it feels like an eternity before it crashes into the water upside down.

Personnel up in the island look down in horror and crane their necks, keeping their eyes riveted on the plane as it sinks under the waves behind the whitewash wake of the onward moving stern. Deck crew toss their floating flashlights out over the side, hazarding a guess to where the plane hit the water.

But Andrew isn't panicking, a feeling of serenity comes over him as he is able to breath calmly through his oxygen mask and process his thoughts.

He remembers from training not to attempt to eject prematurely, it could be fatal, possibly launching him into the massive churning propellers of the carrier. Trusting that the plane is sinking at ten feet per second, he waits, with the patience of Job; he counts: ten, nine, eight...seven...six.

Putting his trust in God, he pulls on the ejection handle and shuts his eyes tightly...nothing...a split-second delay and the top of the seat bursts through the glass, jettisoning him downward, deep into the cold water beneath the sinking plane, the concussing force and pressure against the water has caused him to momentarily black out; a mouth full of saltwater brings him to his senses.

The force against the water has pushed his oxygen mask down under his chin. He is disoriented from being ejected in an inverted position. He spits out the saltwater, holding his breath. He feels something restraining him from swimming free, the parachute has activated and entangled with the chair. He grasps the fasteners to release the chute, kicking and ripping with his arms to free himself from the chute; still not being able to tell up from down, he is getting desperate, feeling for the toggles on his survival floatation device. This is the end. It was all meant to be, just like this...and then, with saltwater stinging his eyes, he glimpses a flicker of lights above him, not very far away, in the darkness...he is rising upward.

Andrew surfaces and gasps loudly, sucking in lungfuls of clean, lifesaving air. He's bobbing up and down on the surface; a gash in his knee from the cockpit glass is leaving a trail of blood in the water.

A search-and-rescue team from the Helicopter Sea Combat Squadron 15 "Red Lions" has scrambled onto an MH-60S Sea Hawk, lifting off from the deck of the carrier. The bright beam of a hovering search light finds the reflectors on Andrew's helmet. A frogman is lowered on a rope into the sea. Over the din of the rotor blades above them, he yells "Glad to meet you, sir; here, let's get this sling around you," as he helps Andrew slip his arms through the harness.

On the Roosevelt, the captain's eyes are widening as he stares at the radar in the control cabin. "C'mon Lions, move your asses!" He's seeing the fast-approaching eye wall, knowing what the ferocious winds will do to a helicopter trying to land on deck...blow it away like a dead leaf falling from a tree.

Kidnapped Off Campus

It's 8:30 in the evening, and Clarissa has been studying since noon. She is beginning to feel confident about the two exams tomorrow that will factor in significantly toward her final grades. Her stress level is subsiding, but she needs a break, and she is hungry. She walks into the kitchen area and opens a top cupboard next to the fridge: Cheerios, Trail Mix, and date-expired Oreo Thins. The cupboard next to it is basically empty, save for some leftover Saltine crackers. She wants something warm, and the cupboards are empty of her favorite soups.

She puts on a turquoise zip-up hoodie and grabs her purse; the convenience store is just a couple of blocks away on the corner. Stepping out the door, the daylight is fading, and because it is a Sunday, there is less traffic on the street. A normal line of various vehicles is parked along the curb. Within five minutes, she is walking out of the store with a plastic shopping bag containing a 12-pack of Maruchan Ramen Instant Chicken Noodle Soup and a Dannon Fruity yogurt, 4-pack.

She turns toward her house, and halfway there, she walks past a dark alleyway where she senses something hiding in the shadows. She keeps walking while turning her head, looking behind her to see if someone is following her. She sees nothing, sensing relief, but before she can turn her head around, she is grabbed from behind, a lung-sucking jolt of an arm squeezing her waist and a clammy hand over her mouth. In the blink of an eye, she is being shoved into an open side door of a blue minivan, where a stranger pulls her in and roughly forces her head down over his lap. The door slides shut and she has been taken, and whisked away to who knows where.

In the basement of the West Wing of the White House, a council of war is ongoing. The set-up of big-screen monitors covering the four walls of the Situation Room is blinking with static.

Prior to today, the Embassy of the People's Republic of China in the United States of America had a normalized statement on their public website: "The Chinese Embassy and Consulates-General in the United States have always been committed to the healthy and stable development of China-US relations to China-US exchanges and cooperation and to the two peoples' friendship."

As a matter of fact, things seemed to be going so well that the Chinese government has recently celebrated the opening of a new Chancery building located at the end of the north-south portion of International Place Drive NW, in the Northwest quadrant of Washington, D. C. The 116,800 square-foot structure was designed, with its symmetrical cement entrance layout and spatially sequenced floating flower gardens, to promote a harmonious balance between the concrete and the contrived.

But late last night, a message was delivered from the office of Foreign Ministry Spokesperson Zhao Teng. It is a two-fold ultimatum: 1) Beginning immediately, remove all unofficial assets from the Chinese People's Island of Taiwan, and 2) Cede over to the People's Republic of China, what, by natural law, is rightfully theirs: the archipelago of the Mariana Islands of the western North Pacific Ocean, between the 12th and 21st parallels north, and along the 145th meridian east... to include the unincorporated colony of Guam.

The latest U.S. naval reconnaissance reports reflect the full fury of an enemy assault fleet approaching the Marianas, and this council of war has been going on for the past two hours. The room is thick with growing tension. One by one, commanders of the various branches of the U.S. military have been briefing the president on the latest military intelligence from the Western Pacific. The enemy's deployment of its "Umbrella" project is having its intended effect. U.S. satellite, drone, and long-range radar capabilities have been completely neutralized.

An anonymous general is standing in place at the conference table, speaking for the National Security Agency of the Defense Department. The rack of chest candy displayed on the left of his full dress uniform is a collection of rear-echelon, non-combat awards, opposite the single bronze Armed Forces medal awarded him for "significant activity" in logistical planning from a desk in Kuwait during the Gulf War. So far, his pathetic explanation for failed anti-encryption efforts on breaking the Chinese codes is making the case that the agency really does deserve, to an unflattering degree, it's moniker: "No Such Agency."

The acting official for the director of National Intelligence is sinking into the plush black leather armchair. Sullenly, he sits there, like a bump on a log. He's just delivered a confusing briefing on a compilation of the latest national security assessments from the seventeen intelligence agencies. From across the room, he can feel the vibrations from the president, who senses an act of betrayal.

President Greene is becoming surly; to him, the reports of the commanders are all but worthless gibberish to him. He's trying to make decisions. Where *exactly* is the enemy fleet and is that fleet military bent on a strike against the United States territories...*or not*?!

A Secret Service agent approaches Vice President Turner at the table, and bending over, whispers something in his ear. The vice president's facial reaction is one of consternation. He excuses himself and walks out through the doorway to the outer room trailed by the agent. Those sitting nearest the doorway see the vice president clamp his hands over the top of his head and briefly dip his upper body toward the floor before the door is closed behind him.

One thing is clear. There will be no concessions.

From the South Lawn to the Marianas

Underneath the East Wing of the White House, a contingent of Secret Service agents and United States Marines is briskly escorting the president through the doors of the PEE-ock, the Presidential Emergency Operations Center, also known as "The Bunker." The president was forced to take shelter there after linguists at the State Department had picked up irregular chatter sounding over the eavesdropping devices at the Chinese Embassy. Immediate interpretation of the deciphered text has set off alarms across the Nation's Capital; warnings of imminent danger. Homeland Security is frantically gathering bits and pieces of intelligence indicating that organized numbers of covertly disguised hostiles are in the vicinity of the White House, endangering the life of the president by unknown means.

A wide-eyed little boy is standing behind the fence, holding his hands over his ears. He's standing next to his daddy, who has his arm around him. Over the fence, he's looking at the biggest and noisiest helicopter he's ever seen. The wind force from its giant blades are pushing down the grass in the middle of a bright emerald-green lawn, the South Lawn of the White House.

It's Marine One, a green-bodied and white-capped Sikorsky UH-60 Black Hawk. The little boy watches, spellbound, as it rises vertically, lifting itself above and overtop the white-columned portico of the mansion. He sees it hover momentarily before heading toward the Washington Monument to hook around it and rendezvous with an escort from the HMX-1 Squadron of military choppers before roaring down the Potomac, headed toward Andrews Air Force Base in Maryland, eleven miles away. The big mechanical bird will be there in less than five minutes. The little boy thinks that the president is just taking a fun ride this morning with his favorite soldiers.

The USS Nimitz Strike Group, reinforced with destroyers and submarines from Pearl Harbor, is sailing fast, its present location just south of Wake Island and north of the Marshalls, 1,400 nautical miles east of Guam. Designated as Carrier Strike Group 11, nine squadrons of F/A-18E/F and F/A-18C fighter planes of the Carrier Air Wing are preparing for air combat. The force has been ordered by the president, in support of the USS Theodore Roosevelt, with an objective to intercept and destroy, if necessary, a hostile Chinese Naval attack fleet threatening the Mariana Islands. A preliminary reconnaissance report of an advancing enemy fleet's Order of Battle has caused Admiral Cooper to order the fleet at Threat Class A readiness-potent and immediate.

The threat axis, the estimate of the likely direction from which the enemy attack will come, will come from the west. As the fleet moves on a path of intended motion west to meet the enemy, the pressure on Admiral Cooper is increasing by the hour. He is astonished at the enormity of the threat pushing toward him. Earlier recon reports had warned of an approaching enemy armada, bringing with it assets of formidable military power. The latest reports are beyond anything he could have imagined. This extreme threat will require extreme measures. And to make an extreme situation more extreme, the eastern edge of Typhoon Azure is expanding on the radar screen in the area directly ahead of the them.

He issues orders for maximum combat readiness to prepare to give battle against all known means of military menace on the high seas, the deadly supersonic missiles fired from jet fighters, surface ships, and submarines. But what he is not prepared for is something he cannot prepare for, is a new evolutionary type of weapon, a weapon that can be aimed and fired on target, to any place on the planet in minutes. A weapon that travels fifteen times greater than the speed of sound, with no warning, no sonic boom, uninterceptable; a blinding and obliterating flash exploding with a force equivalent to four tons of TNT, a hypersonic missile delivered at hyper speed. But that threat is measured within yesterday's reasoning, conventional reasoning; what is coming this day is unreasonable...unreasonable and nuclear.

But the Chinese military is not the only one doing never-ending and painstaking work to build a better mouse trap.

Isolated on the southern coast of the 49th state, sitting down at the bottom of a bowl between the ice-covered Chugach Mountains and tidewater glaciers of Prince William Sound, lies the fishing town of Whittier, Alaska. It was here in the wilderness, in a military installation carved out of the mountainside that was home to an ultra-secret project: Operation Boomerang; the effort to redefine modern anti-missile technology. It's one phase of a two-part scientific breakthrough that will turn the practice of Electronic counter-countermeasures (ECCM) on its head.

The U.S. fleet is sailing in a standard formation, deployed with layers of defense, designed to give maximum protection to the fleet's high value unit (HVU), the Navy's oldest and finest aircraft carrier, the Nimitz; named after World War II United States Pacific Fleet commander Fleet Admiral Chester W. Nimitz, who was the U.S. Navy's last living fleet admiral.

Furthest out in front, at 100 miles, are the picket ships, Arleigh Burke-class guided-missile destroyers with the USS John Paul Jones on the point, and the USS Dewey and USS Preble on the flanks. They are setting a silent anti-missile trap.

A deadly missile strike can be launched from over the horizon from a ship, a submarine, or a fighter jet 200 nautical miles away. This is an immense area to cover to be able to find an enemy's mobile launchers that are firing missiles traveling up to Mach 4 or faster, in a matter of seconds, to kill them before they kill you. The Aegis Ballistic Missile Defense system, combining multiple anti-missile intercepting radar with an arsenal of Raytheon-made missiles, is designed to knock down deadly incoming ballistic missiles; to intercept and destroy them high in the sky or take out cruise missiles skimming over the ocean. It can track up to one hundred at a time. Up to this point, the Aegis System, like the one now deployed on the Ticonderoga-class guided-missile cruiser USS Princeton, have tested well against most of the over-the-horizon training targets... *most* of the time.

So under the present circumstances, electronic warfare capability is at a premium if, and only if, the electronics are effective, only if they are not neutralized by the enemy.

But the most fearsome threat, from much less than 200 nautical miles away, much closer, below the surface, is the threat of an incoming heavyweight 650 mm wake-homing torpedo fired from an enemy submarine. The torpedo is designed to cross behind the stern and through a target vessel's backwash, using its built-in sonar to fix on and follow the stirred-up air bubbles in the wake, and then detonate its magnetically-triggered warhead beneath the ship's keel to "break its back," to break it in two, to break in two a vessel as large as an aircraft carrier. The spoken maxim of modern naval warfare: detect the mechanized killer fish before it detects you.

The USS Chung-Hoon, USS Sterett, USS Michael Murphy, and USS Ralph Johnson are positioned 20 miles out, forming the outer screen. They are to confront any enemy surface vessel or submarine that has bypassed the picket ships. They are engaged in anti-submarine tactics, sprinting ahead to a calculated position, and then drifting back dragging towed-array sonar behind them. The Princeton is coordinating the inner defense space five miles off the starboard side of the carrier. It will command the whole perimeter, dictating deployment of MH-60R Sea Hawk helicopters equipped with dipping sonar, MAD (Magnetic Anomaly Detection) devices, or command the deployment of sonobuoys to hurry them over the target to isolate the threat for aerial delivery of torpedo depth bombs should an enemy submarine penetrate the outer ring of defense.

Patrolling the deep dark waters beneath them are the Hunter-Killers, the nuclear attack submarines USS Charlotte and USS Cheyenne. They will operate independently, prowling in stealth mode; they have been issued general rules of engagement (ROE) for reconnaissance. They're deployed for an offensive action-reaction to detect electronic enemy emissions; first and foremost, the detection of the presence of a hostile counterpart submarine.

For the surface fleet, should a hostile submarine be detected, not everything has changed with technology. For just as it was way back during World War Two, the fleet will rely primarily on setting a zigzag course through the water to evade contact with the enemy's death-dealing torpedoes.

The teeth of the storm has passed them by. The foreboding reconnaissance report of Lieutenants Greer and Kim are now actionable. The Roosevelt strike group is coming alive. Within seconds of each other, a twelve-plane squadron of Black Knights, F/A-18F Super Hornets is catapulting off of the carrier. They are the interceptor aircraft; they are out to destroy the enemy launching platforms before they fire, intending on killing a number of missile threats in one launch.

This squadron of Super Hornets is an "aggressor squadron" armed with Stormbreaker glide bombs, a winged and tail-finned laser-guided smart bomb that can home in on moving targets in adverse weather conditions. A microwave radar-seeker gives the weapon x-ray vision to see through clouds, rain, and fog, and an imaging sensor gives it the capacity to tell a real target from something else, like an enemy decoy.

For the first time, these aircraft are equipped with advanced radar jamming-resistant laser pods fixed under the nose of the fighter jet. They can laser-paint a target on an enemy object for an ensuing missile launch against the most advanced EPM (Electronic Protective Measures) deployed to stop it. Knowledge of its development is kept airtight, on a need-to-know basis. Its "smart" technological capability is specially designed to operate in conjunction with a new secret anti-missile disabling technology recently installed on the deck of a combat-deployed surface vessel.

But the pilots would much prefer to be armed with more Stormbreakers. Amongst themselves, the combat pilots refer to these pods as "droppers." The moniker is not an attempt to liken their resemblance to a teardrop, but, in a real-world combat scenario, where dogfighting and visual targeting is a thing of the past, it's an inside sarcastic joke that this obsolete technology will do nothing more than aid them in *dropping faster* from the sky if struck by an enemy missile.

Their formation resembles a massive spear point as they soar in the sky westward. They will operate in a combat spread formation positioned 200 nautical miles out in the front and on the flanks of the fleet.

Hornets Versus Dragons

The squad leader, Eddie Kerner, is flying at the point of the spear. He's a gap-toothed twenty-eight-year-old Bears fan from the South Side of Chicago. He is best known for his hilarious impersonations of the executive officer types, the ambitious lifers that cause his squad mates to roll on the floor in laughter. His tactical call sign is "Brushee." He got branded with the nickname years ago after his bunkmate at the Academy caught him late one night in bed, caressing the fur of a course-haired teddy bear he had secreted in his duffel bag.

At one hundred miles out, another squadron of Super Hornets is rendezvousing en route with a group of Early Warning Unit EA-18G Growlers, providing a fighter escort to protect the Growlers equipped with radar jamming and radar decoy capabilities.

The remaining ship-based squadron of jet fighters is the fleet's main protectors. They're deployed on the carrier, ready to be launched to shoot down any enemy threat that has penetrated the outer ring of defense. They are best positioned to provide both layered and overlapping coverage of the fleet.

The order is broadcast across the fleet. EMCON C-offensive and unrestricted emissions, meaning radio systems are turned wide open. While his radar jamming aircraft are operating, by going fully active, the admiral brings on the vulnerability of being detected by the enemy, but the commander wants to have exact stand-by contact from the firing positions of his war ships. He senses that the enemy is fully aware of the positions of his vessels anyway.

Alongside the admiral, The CAG, commanding the air group, stands anxiously over the shoulders of the radio operators; they are listening to the strained transmissions of aerial combat. They are on edge...where are the early warning reports?!

Thus far, in the initial clash, the anti-missile decoys fired from the Growlers are doing the job; the Chinese missiles are taking the bait. Fiery explosions above the clouds, so many circles of smoke and raining debris make it difficult to estimate how many more waves of enemy missiles have yet to be launched, and they are soberly aware that they can't stop all of them.

Hundreds of miles out, they hear from multiple fighters: "Fence in, fence in!" The squadron has entered enemy airspace. "Gomers up ahead" Deadly contact with enemy fighters has been made.

On the pilot's control panels, the missile launch warning lights are lighting up like a Christmas tree; their systems are detecting smoke plumes from multiple fired enemy missiles.

Now, at ten thousand feet, the J-20 Mighty Dragons are swarming around and through a formation of F/A-18F Super Hornets at afterburner Mach speed.

"Roundman, I'm going tactical!"

"Dagger-break, break; I'm on-the-burner!"

"Check your six, Snapper, Check your six!"

Seated in front of one of the monitors in the Roosevelt's control room, a pretty female radar technician is using a tissue to dab the corners of her eyes. She is engaged to be married. She accepted her fiancé's proposal three days ago. Together, they just finished preparing the announcement of their betrothment to send to friends and family. A minute ago, she recognized his shrill voice in one of the pilot radio transmissions amidst the deadly aerial combat taking place in the skies above her.

"Indy, see Barney is Nordo."

"Roger that, Indy, I see him."

"Hurdler, they got music on me."

"Bama, taking a snapshot."

"Splash! That poor devil."

The enemy has fired another wave of rockets. The Growlers are running short on decoys, and the first squadron of Super Hornets are running low on fuel.

"Cowboy, I'm in Joker mode, one more pass."

"Stretch, me too, I'm going one more time!"

From the Bunker Hill, "Where in hell is the relief squadron? They need full-weapon support. They need it now, g-dammit!"

"Think two vapes got by us, Mother!" a pilot yells into his headset.

"Mayday! Mayday! I'm hit!"

"Stallion, punch out! Punch out now! Get out of there!"

A salvo of enemy missiles has penetrated the outer defense ring.

The commander on the Roosevelt hears the warning shouted in the control room: "Incoming!!" He steps forward to the radio, "Activate Boomerang."

Within seconds, the USS Bunker Hill responds, "Boomerang Activated."

Moments later, an explosion, a missile crashes through the top of the mast of the USS Kidd. An observer on the bridge is nearly cut in two by a flying piece of radar antenna that nicks the edge of the railing in front of him before crashing on the deck below him.

On the USS Russell, several crewmen on the deck are soaked by the wind-blown spray of a missile that has crashed into the sea fifty yards off the portside bow.

The radio transmissions are being relayed to the control room on the Roosevelt. Admiral Cooper is thinking fast. His extensive briefings on the new technology included a vital "what if?" What if the missiles keep coming? He realizes that the missiles, though still coming at them, are behaving erratically. He remembers the briefing, "when the lasers hit an approaching missile, it will either explode or keep traveling with it's primary electronic guidance system deactivated; the oncoming weapon should fly off course, defaulting to its backup system set to home in on the closest radar signal, or a signal *fed* to it."

These missiles are doing just that! The CAG knows what the admiral is going to say before he says it, and shouts out the command to his air group.

"Deploy Flashlight, deploy Flashlight!"

At a higher elevation, Eddie Kerner's squadron of Super Hornets is now circling thousands of feet above the enemy fleet. Pilots in the cockpits are filled with disbelief. Minutes before, confidently, they had thumb-pressed the weapons release buttons on their control sticks to fire the Stormbreakers. The missiles released successfully, rocketing toward the enemy target, but suddenly, they were intercepted by something invisible, causing them to abruptly deviate off-course, headed for nowhere.

Eddie hears the command, but can't believe it, "Deploy Flashlight?. Deploy the droppers?" Before he can *Roger* back, a smart guy chimes in from the cockpit of a Growler, "Sometimes you just have to reach out and touch someone."

After a momentary appreciation for the fearless timing of the remark, he speaks into the mic, "Roger. Tally-Ho. Follow me, boys, it's a target-rich environment down there; let's paint 'em up, let's give these bad boys a few coats of paint!" As he dips and dives toward the sea, he's followed, in precise intervals, by the rest of the squadron, they are stacked in formation...screaming downward.

At one thousand feet, the Super Hornets scatter. They are locking their lasers on any vessel they can see. Eddie makes eye contact with the most frightening sized ship he has ever seen. With his index finger, he squeezes the trigger underneath the head of the control stick and the laser locks onto the hull of the behemoth enemy carrier. But it's not only a laser, from the pod beneath his nose and those of his squad mates, from the "droppers," the simultaneous radiation of a circular force field, creating an expanding radio-waved web across the area to ensnare the outdated heat-seeking systems of enemy missiles.

And now, the explosive results of this amazing technology is readily seen and heard; the missiles of the enemy have, in mid-flight, turned completely around and are homing in on their laser-painted launch sites...on the Chinese vessels that fired them.

Ghillie Suits and Snipers

The Wi-Fi signal has been emitting from a site on the outskirts of the dense commercial district off Avenida Peralvillo, where the distinctive sounds of Chicano rap reverberate from the streets of the marketplace to the east.

The SWAT team has set up a loose precautionary perimeter. The cartel's "eyes" are everywhere. Well-paid youngsters are riding around on their bicycles with handy talkies Velcroed under the top tubes for easy access to radio an alert to the bunker. Late in the evening, two boys are riding directly over the pavement-covered culvert of the weed-choked catch basin adjacent to the bunker. One of the boys turns his head and looks right at them, and sees them, two snipers hidden in the weeds, but he keeps on pedaling because even though he saw them, he really didn't *see* them. The snipers leafed-out cameo face masks, BDU Ghillie suits and scoped .50 caliber rifles have blended in perfectly with the foliage.

They are lying prone, with the crosshairs of their scopes sighted on two Sicarios, about one hundred yards away. The Sicarios are sitting on wooden benches, inside a chain-link barbed wire-topped fence with a swinging gate. They are armed with Romanian-made AK-47s. The fenced-in lot is attached to a fabricated burnt-orange steel warehouse with a rust-splotched, corrugated roof. Between the Sicarios, next to a side door leading in and out of the warehouse, is an angled ground-level door or hatch leading to a cellar beneath the warehouse. A faded red awning with a white stripe is mounted above them on the outside wall, providing them shade from the sun.

A quarter of a mile away, the awning is also providing a visual reference for the binoculars of Colonel Cortes and members of the surveillance team who have secured the remaining upper floors of a half bombed-out brick commercial building. The building's grime-streaked windows provide a perfect sniper's perch to cover the front garage and pedestrian door of the warehouse.

The time is 0-dark-thirty, just before sunrise. The SWAT team has been in place for the last hour. Three members are sitting in a black SUV with tinted windows, parked around the corner from the warehouse. The main assault van carrying eight officers is parked and idling one block behind them. A pack of stray dogs, led by a big black one-eyed Rottweiler with an ugly pink scar across his neck, trots out from behind two abandoned automobiles and stops in the middle of the street in front of them. The Rottweiler turns his head to briefly check out the van before resuming to lead the pack to an alleyway, where they disappear from sight.

The sun is rising over the skyline to the east, just enough daylight to make out the targets. Through his binoculars, the colonel sees that all is still around the warehouse; the two Sicarios are sitting with their backs against the wall, hunched over, asleep on the benches.

Through his radio, he says softly, "Okay, let's roll." The SWAT van pulls up behind the SUV and bumper to bumper, they turn the corner and stop one-half block from the target, next to an old flour mill. The eight officers jump out and line up single file on the sidewalk against the red brick wall. The team leader in front raises his hand, motioning forward.

Crouching, with rifles trained to their front, they move along the wall in synchronized steps. They stop at the corner of the building where the team leader is able to quickly poke his head around to survey the scene. There is no movement. He turns behind him and points "Go!" Three squad members, one, a Breacher with bolt cutters, silently rush to the gate. The two officers cover their teammate as he cuts the padlock, grabbing the loose end of the chain, tucking it away from the gate posts. They trot back and get in line behind the wall.

Poking his head around the corner of the building, the team leader sees that everything remains quiet and still, the Sicarios on the benches are sleeping soundly. He turns back around to face the SUV in the street and raises his right arm and makes a pull-down motion to signal "ready to rock and roll."

The SUV goes into motion, rolling fast. It pulls up and stops in front of the far front corner of the building. A squad member jumps out of the backseat and tosses two flash-bang hand grenades over the fence, one toward the front door and the other down the side wall toward the sleeping Sicarios. He hops back in and the SUV speeds away. Within seconds, the flash-bangs detonate, two bright flashes and two loud bangs. Seconds later, poof! poof! The two Sicarios on the benches have been rudely awakened, and then dropped by bullets from the snipers' rifles in the catch basin. Moments later, the front door springs open, and two more armed Sicarios rush out and then drop in their tracks as they are taken out by marksmen firing from the upper floors of the colonel's surveillance site.

The SWAT team sprints through the gate, they split in half; four head to the front door and four head toward the side cellar door. Jumping over the dead Sicarios, they rush through the doors into the building, a muted crackling of automatic rifles, and then silence.

Juan is safe. He is found lying under a table with one arm slung over the back of the Sicario who aided him. The Sicario is shivering, face-down, next to Juan; he has one arm behind him, he's holding a cellphone on the small of his back, letting the SWAT team see the device that helped save both of their lives.

Rumblings and
Awakenings

I nside the air traffic control tower at Anderson, there has been
overheated radio traffic from desperate efforts to get as many
of the bombers off the ground and into the air as possible. Out on
the airstrip, the bombers are taxiing into position. Nose to tail, one
after another, airmen on the ground are furiously flagging away
to ground roll the backed-up line of planes down the runway and
into the air. Airman Chuck Cobb and the crew in the tower with
him haven't slept all night. "Did you see that out on the water, was
that lightning?" "No...that was a *red* flicker of light!!" A blinding
flash, an ears-splitting explosion, the concussion of the blast rocks
the tower; flame and smoke, debris from one of the blown-up
bombers, shatters the tower window.

They are totally unprepared for the onslaught that is coming.
A ferocious dogfight is happening in the clouds above, a con-
test between U.S.N. F/A-18F Super Hornets and Chinese J-20
Mighty Dragons. So far, in this era of advanced military technology, it's the Super Hornets that are breathing fire, the out-
gunned American pilots are bringing an advanced brand of heart
and guts to the fight.

On Air Force One, the president is hurriedly wolfing down a
sandwich while being fed a constant diet of frontline updates. Eva
is flying aboard as a precaution; the thirty-member flight crew is
nervous, and it is showing; they're making constant inquiries to
each other for unofficial updates. With a strengthened security

detail, Vice President Turner has remained in Washington to comfort his family.

Thoughts are racing through the president's mind; he didn't need this. He has earned more money in the commercial shipping business than he could ever spend in five lifetimes. Fame and fortune he already has. In the last decade, he had seen this great nation under God gradually disintegrating. But this is no time for that kind of thinking. He thinks about what his father taught him as a boy, "When the going gets tough, the tough get going!"

An antagonistic news media is generating panic. People are beginning to doubt; exploiting the cooperation of sympathetic major media outlets, leaders of the opposition are calling for his immediate resignation.

This is going on while a hostile Chinese Naval attack fleet with supersonic jet fighters and nuclear submarines is being engaged on the waters and in the skies of the Western Pacific, a fearful and formidable show of military strength to back up a cold-blooded ultimatum.

In the back of Eva's mind, she remembers Father Vit saying, "Divinity is always where we least expect to find it." Where *is* God, and what is He waiting for?

He isn't waiting long. Rumblings under the sea are shaking the Mariana Islands; the crescendo of a deafening roar, the surface of the ocean is beginning to chop and churn, an immense vortex is materializing on the water. To the west, out at sea, the vessels of the Chinese attack fleet appear to be reeling out of control...they are being sucked downward by the colossal green-blue walls of a massive whirlpool.

Afterward, in the words of the pilots who witnessed it, they couldn't say how long it took for the waters of the whirlpool to swallow the Chinese warships up before the maelstrom of cascading waters enveloped them. But from the best of their recollections, and what now can be only imagined, they think they glimpsed, far below, at the bottom of the hollow swirling chasm, Chinese warships and submarines spinning their propellers in ocean bottom muck, like a school of beached whales; and they still remember the Mighty Dragons... with no place to land.

And 8,000 miles away, in Washington D.C., around and inside the White House grounds, K-9 patrol guard dogs are barking and growling, straining on their leashes. What they hear and see are figures in dark clothing, mounted atop the fences, shouts and radio alerts from their uniformed Secret Service handlers ring out, and then, all of a sudden, the figures are seen to be dropping to the ground. The K-9 units that confronted them, testify that the intruders appeared dazed and stupefied, as if awakening from a terrible nightmare.

Clarissa has been drugged; she is tied up and gagged, balled up in the trunk of a car, which is approaching the International Bridge at Eagle Pass. She will be taken to a safe house in Piedras Negras, and from there, depending on the U.S. response to an ultimatum, she will either be released unharmed, or sold on the underground white-slave market. The silver Toyota Corolla is being driven by a fashionably dressed escort wearing cat-eye sunglasses, and seated next to her, in the front passenger seat, is a round stubble-faced Sicario, with tattoos of snakes and human skulls on the back of his hands, and a 9mm pistol tucked in his waist belt, under his shirt.

The backseat is occupied by two hu-bots, staring out the windows, but not seeing, the South Texas landscape. All of a sudden, the hu-bots begin to act strangely, grunting at first and then mumbling in a weird dialect, a dialect in Uyghur. Restrained by seatbelts, they begin to shift and squirm, when one of them reaches forward and puts his hand on the Sicario's left shoulder. The Sicario turns around to look at the hu-bot who's touching him; he gasps before screaming out, "Detener el coche! Detener el coche!"

The escort thinks, "Huh, what? Why stop the car?" She turns around and glimpses, only for a second, boring right through her, a look from the eyes of one of the hu-bots, a human look of anger. Ripping the steering wheel onto the shoulder of the road, she slams on the brakes as the car comes to a screeching halt, both front doors fly open and the two kidnappers jump out and run for their lives.

A patrol car, with its rooftop police light flashing, approaches and pulls up behind the car on the shoulder. The officers get out and cautiously approach the vehicle with its engine running and front doors wide open. What appears to be two individuals are sitting in the back seat. As they get closer they hear a muffled noise coming from the trunk. The two individuals, seat-belted in the back seat are commanded to stay right there. One of the officers trains his pistol on the trunk, keeping his eyes on the passengers in the backseat while his partner removes the keys from the ignition.

When the trunk pops open, the officers are surprised to see a young woman, tied up and crying, but ever so happy to see them. And the occupants in the back seat are happy to see them as well because, with God, everything is hackable...including Communist-implanted microchips.

On Air Force One, after being informed of what has happened in the Western Pacific, the president excuses himself, walks into his private study, closes the door behind him and falls to his knees. Afterward, Eva would tell those privileged enough to hear that it was at that moment that her years of praying and fasting had been answered, the miraculous moment of her husband's conversion. To this day, she frequently thinks of Mother Angelica, "If you have a problem in your life that you can't fathom or understand, you have to examine your prayer life, *not the problem.*"

News of the world-changing events has spread across the country, heralding the little shrine at Hanceville as the origin of miraculous things. A massive flock of newly-minted pilgrims have flooded through the gates to see it for themselves. The confessionals inside the chapel have been churning out penitents by the hundreds, and the waiting lines are streaming out the front doors onto the steps outside.

To handle the overflow, a temporary confessional has been set up in one of the side chapels consisting of a centered louver-paneled door with a priest's chair and a small table on one side and a padded kneeler on the other. Brother Arthur has finished his meal at the priest's house, and is heading toward the chapel to relieve one of his brother priests who have been hearing confessions nonstop since seven this morning. Brother Arthur is in a cheerful mood, finally able to feel normal again, his emotional ordeal with the grotesque tattoo, putting it behind him, considering it a trial of the past. He's amazed at the number of automobiles filling the parking lot, seeing license plates of states from halfway across the country.

He enters the chapel through a side door and walks through a hallway bringing him to a back door leading to one of the side chapels where the temporary confessional has been installed. He silently turns the doorknob and opens the door just a crack to see if the confessor is ready for his relief. As he peeks into the oratory, a first glance causes his heart to skip up to his throat; instinctively, he moves to the aid of Father Joe, who is laying prone face down on the floor. But before he can take another step, he is halted, frozen in place by a thumbs-up signal from Father Joe meaning that all is right and everything is under control. Brother Arthur retreats and quietly closes the door behind him. The seal of the confessional will not be compromised today. For on the other side of the confessional kneels a little girl, gleefully chatting away her innocent thoughts, known only as The Little One, bringing with her a presence of pure holiness, enough of a presence to cause, on the other side of the partition, a good and holy priest to prostrate himself face down on the floor...in divine adoration.

Following noon Mass, in one of the side pews inside the chapel, Hannah has remained to pray in thanksgiving for all of the blessings of recent days. The children are all there with her, hers and the three children from the Shrine. She promised Joshua and Jaida that after Mass they could each light a candle at one of the side altars. She opens her purse and takes her wallet out to pay for the candles. The aromatic drift of a distinct fragrance gets her attention as she glances toward the window ledge under the stained glass, expecting to see a flower pot filled with bright blooming hyacinth. She is startled to see an empty ledge. She turns back to look around the chapel for the source of the sweet scent. But where did they go? Why, a moment ago, The Little One and her two cousins had been sitting in the pew right over here! She turns to her daughter, "Teresa, where did the children go?"

With a wide smile on her face, turning toward the statue of Our Lady of the Angels, Teresa gleefully responds, "They went back to heaven, Mommy."

Sunsets and Salamanders

In the hospital, Louis is standing on crutches next to Tony in bed; they have been practicing. A nurse sticks her head inside the door, puts her index finger up to her lips, and scolds them for making too much noise. Now it's time to dial up Maria. "Okay, put it on speaker, Louis , I'm ready." Maria answers, "Louis?" In joyful unison they sing out to the Brooks and Dunn hit song:

"My Ma-reee-uuuh, don't you know I've come a long, long way
I been longin' to see her
When she's around she takes my blues away
Sweet Maria the sunlight surely hurts my eyes
I'm a lonely dreamer on a highway in the skies"

Tony has the refrain; screeching at his highest pitch, "

Ma-reee-uuuh," and Louis chimes in,
"Oh Maria I love you girl, oh my Maria."
"Ma-reee-uuuh, oh Maria, I love you girl,
oh my Maria, I love you..."

"I'm speechless, I love you guys," giggles Maria.

At the end of an emotional conversation about her brother's rescue and everything else that has happened, Maria's cheeks are streaked with grateful tears as they say their goodbyes.

"I think I'm going to ask her out," says Tony .

"Well, it's about time."

At the close of the day, Maria is sitting in her favorite Cancun chair on the back porch, sipping a Margarita from her favorite cactus-style glass. She doesn't do this often, but this is no ordinary time, it's a time to celebrate and give thanks. An array of gorgeous colors are beginning to materialize over the mountains. It's one of those rare romantic sunsets with a prism of flaming red, orange, and yellows that can take your breath away. She gazes over the desert landscape in the distance. She blinks twice. Can it be real? Maria is astonished to see that the scorpion has disappeared from the mountainside in Matamoros.

It is late summer already, and the leaves are beginning to turn yellow. The chirps of an exited chickadee pierce the quiet. The Devil's Den in Cheaha State Park is such a beautiful place to be this time of year. Louis and Hannah have spread the blanket underneath the branches of a majestic live oak. Joshua and Jaida are paging through two new nature books, looking at the pictures of plants and animals, hoping to match them up with live specimens they hope to find in the forest around them.

Louis' back is resting against the tree trunk, and his ball cap is pulled down over his eyes. Hannah is next to him, resting her head on his shoulder, watching Teresa with a fishing net and pink rubber boots, looking under a rock she has just turned over at the edge of the creek. Louis is dozing off, he's remembering the happy days of his childhood spent at this very spot, under this very same oak tree. He's just about to doze off when Hannah sees Teresa scoop something up from the creek and lift it up out of the water. Then, a joyful shout, "Hey, Daddy, I got one!" He jumps up to see, in amazement, Teresa holding up the dripping net with something wriggling inside it.

Teresa is excitedly jumping up and down looking at the catch she has made, which she has set down in the grass off the bank of the creek. It's a slender, squishy, mottled-in-mustard-brown creature, a smidge over one-foot long, with a keeled tail, and four toes on its front legs and five on its back ones. Two puny eyes, widely spaced, are peeping from the front part of its head; a real live Eastern hellbender.

After admiring the creature for as long as they can, they take a few pictures of Teresa holding her prize catch beneath a beaming smile. Louis helps her carefully pick up the little critter and carry it to the water's edge. She gently puts it down on the sandy bank, and the five of them watch in fascination as it slithers back home into the creek.

On the drive home, Louis is telling Teresa, for about the tenth time, how lucky she is; the creature is so rare and elusive, and to be able to catch one on her *first try*, well, it's just pure...Then he pauses, and with a proud smile, he says, "I'm sorry, Teresa, I should know better...*nothing* happens by accident."

References

Adams, Myra Kahn. 2019. "Shroud of Turin: Interview with Researcher Who Debunked the 1988 'Medieval' Dating." *Townhall.* November 3, 2019. https://townhall.com/columnists/myrakahnadams/2019/11/03/shroud-of-turin-interview-with-researcher-who-debunked-the-1988-medieval-dating-n2555665.

Al.com and Press Register Staff. 2012. "Bear Brant and His Houndstooth Hat (Sound Off)." Last modified January 14, 2019. https://www.al.com/sports/2012/02/bear_bryant_and_his_houndstoot.html#:~:text=Concerning%20Bear%20Bryant%20and%20his%20houndstooth%20hat%3A%20Bear,the%20owner%20of%20the%20Jets%2C%20gave%20Bear%20.

Aleteia. 2017. "The Devil Admits to Exorcist Fr. Amorth: 'I'm Afraid of the Madonna.'" Accessed May 2020. https://revelationstwelve.wordpress.com/2017/07/03/the-devil-admits-to-exorcist-fr-amorth-im-afraid-of-the-madonna/#:~:text=On%20the%20Libero%20website%20%28February%203%2C%202012%29%2C%20Father,The%20air%20became%20cold.%20It%20was%20terribly%20cold.%20and%20https://aleteia.org/2017/07/02/devil-admits-to-exorcist-im-afraid-of-the-madonna/.

"Appalachia." *Familypedia.* Accessed March 2020. https://familypedia.wikia.org/wiki/Appalachia#cite_note-abramson1-1.

"Appalachia (David Bradford)." *Sid Meier's Civilization Customization.* Last modified May 3, 2017. https://civ5customization.gamepedia.com/Appalachia_(David_Bradford).

Badass of the Week. n.d. "About the Author." Accessed June 2020. https://www.badassoftheweek.com/about.

Badass of the Week. n.d. "John B. Armstrong." Accessed June 2020. https://www.badassoftheweek.com/armstrong.

Badass of the Week. n.d. "John Wesley Hardin. Accessed June 2020. https://www.badassoftheweek.com/hardin.

Barillas, Martin M. 2019. "China Watchdog Reveals Horrific Allegations of Mass Forced Organ-Harvesting." *Life Site.* Last modified September 26, 2019. https://www.lifesitenews.com/news/china-watchdog-reveals-shocking-allegations-of-mass-forced-organ-harvesting.

Benedict, Raphael. 2019. "The Devil Admits to a Priest He Is Terrified of Mary and the Rosary, Here Is Why He Is Scared of Her." Accessed May 2020. https://catholicsay.com/the-devil-admits-to-a-priest-he-is-terrified-of-mary-and-the-rosary-here-is-why-he-is-scared-of-her/#:~:text=Fr%20Amorth%20remembers%20his%20first%20encounter%20with%20the,this%20demon%20that%20was%20looking%20at%20me%20intently.

Berntson, Ben. 2007. "Railroad Bill." *Encyclopedia of Alabama.* Last modified December 14, 2011. http://www.encyclopediaofalabama.org/article/h-1258#:~:text=The%20legend%20of%20Railroad%20Bill%20arose%20in%20the,song%20%28%20see%20lyrics%20%29%2C%20fiction%2C%20and%20theater.and%20%20%20https://en.m.wikipedia.org/wiki/Railroad_Bill%20and%20https://digitalalabama.com/

alabama-stories/alabama-treasure-legends/the-legend-of-railroad-bill/6214%20and%20https://www.findagrave.com/memorial/94786246/morris-slater#:~:text=He%20there-after%20conducted%20robberies%20on%20L%26N%20trains%2C%20wounded,and%20was%20killed%20at%20Atmore%20in%20March%201896.

Bowden, Mark. 2001. KILLING PABLO: The World's Greatest Outlaw. NewYork. Atlantic Monthly Press.

Bowman, Martin W. 2010. *Combat Carriers: USN Air and Sea Operations from 1941*. Charleston: Amberley Publishing.

Branch, Ricardo J. 2011. "Engineer Soldier Awarded Silver Star." *U.S. Army*. October 14, 2011.https://www.army.mil/article/35839/engineer_soldier_awarded_silver_star#:~:text=Scott%20D.%20Brooks%2C%2082nd%20Engineer%20Support%20Company%2C%2065th,award%20for%20his%20actions%20during%20Operation%20Iraqi%20Freedom.

Brooks & Dunn. 1996. "My Maria."Track 1 on *Borderline*. Arista Nashville, radio.

Brown, Michael H. 2018. "Soon-to-Be Saint Padre Pio Was Study in Most Inexplicable of Gifts: Bilocation." *Spirit Daily*. July 1, 2018. https://spiritdaily.com/blog/mystics/pio-bilocation#:~:text=In%20one%20case%2C%20a%20pious%20young%20girl%20of,on%20the%20sheet%20%28this%20stain%20has%20been%20preserved%29.

Carlisle, Jeffrey D. n.d. "Apache Indians." *Handbook of Texas Online*. Accessed August 2020. https://www.tshaonline.org/handbook/entries/apache-indians.

Casares, Oscar. 2018. "How Crossing the Bridge to Matamoros Got Complicated." *The New York Times*. February 7, 2018.

https://www.nytimes.com/2018/02/07/travel/browns-ville-matamoros-border.html.

Catholic News Agency. 2018. "Chinese Authorities Destroy Two Marian Shrines despite Vatican-China Agreement." *The Catholic World Report*. October 26, 2018. https://www.catholicworldreport.com/2018/10/26/chinese-authorities-de-stroy-two-marian-shrines-despite-vatican-china-agreement/.

Cheng, Evelyn. 2018. "Going It Alone: China Government Orders Farmers to Increase Soybean Acreage." *CNBC*. June 7, 2018. https://www.cnbc.com/2018/06/07/china-government-or-ders-farmers-to-increase-soybean-acreage.html.

China Daily. 2011. "Tofu Culture in China." Last modified February 2, 2011. http://www.chinadaily.com.cn/life/2011-02/12/content_11996892.htm.

China Travel Tour Guide. n.d. "Wuzhi Mountain." Last modified 2017. https://www.china-travel-tour-guide.com/attractions/wuzhishan-mountain.shtml.

Civil War Talk. n.d. "Notable Quotes of the Civil War." Accessed July 2020. https://civilwartalk.com/threads/notable-quotes-of-the-civil-war.83301/.

Courtois Stephane, Werth Nicolas, Panné Jean-Louis, Paczkowski Andrzej, Bartosek Karel, Jean-Louis, *The Black Book Of Communism—Crimes, Terror, Repression*. Cambridge, Massachusetts: Harvard University Press. 1999

Daily Mail Reporter. 2010. "Mexican Drug Carter Leader 'Tony Tormenta' Killed During Two-Hour Gun Battle with Marines." *Mail Online*. November 8, 2010. https://www.dailymail.co.uk/news/article-1327188/Mexican-drug-cartel-leader-Tony-Tormenta-killed-hour-gun-battle-marines.html.

Daily Mail.com by MailOnline Reporter. June 3, 2019. *China defends killing hundreds of unarmed students during Tiananmen Square protest, saying the country has made 'tremendous changes' as a result https://www.dailymail.co.uk/news/article-7099909/China-defends-killing-hundreds-unarmed-students-Tiananmen-Square-protest.html A look at key events in the 1989 Tiananmen Square protests By ASSOCIATED PRESS PUBLISHED: 21:13 EST, 29 May 2019 | UPDATED: 07:08 EST, 30 May 2019 Beijing*

Dictionary.com, s.v. "plata o plomo." Accessed May 2020, https://www.dictionary.com/e/slang/plata-o-plomo/.

Dodson, James. 2004. *Ben Hogan: An American Life*. New York: Doubleday.

Donecker, Frances. n.d. "San Antonio River." *Handbook of Texas Online*. Accessed August 2020. https://www.tshaonline.org/handbook/entries/san-antonio-river#:~:text=The%20stream%20was%20named%20for%20San%20Antonio%20de,understood%20the%20Indians%20to%20say%20was%20named%20Yanaguana.

"Doufu." n.d. Accessed June 2020. https://libguides.williams.edu/citing/chicago-author-date#s-lg-box-21699950.

Dye, David H. 2017. "Soto Expedition." *Tennessee Encyclopedia*. Last modified March 1, 2018. https://tennesseeencyclopedia.net/entries/soto-expedition/.

Echoes of the Void. n.d. "Patagonian Desert: A Desert with History and Agriculture." Accessed May 2020. http://echoesofthevoid.com/project/patagonian-desert/#:~:text=a%20desert%20with%20history%20and%20agriculture%20The%20

Patagonian,east%2C%20in%20the%20region%20of%20
Patagonia%2C%20southern%20Argentina.

Ellison, George. 2018. "Did the Southeastern Native Americans Take Scalps?" *Smoky Mountain News.* January 24, 2018. https://
www.smokymountainnews.com/archives/item/21571-did-
the-southeastern-native-americans-take-scalps.

Embassy of the People's Republic of China in the United States of America. 2020. "The Statement of the Chinese Embassy in the United States for Taking Over the Consular Jurisdiction of the Consulate-General in Houston." Last modified July 24, 2020. http://www.china-embassy.org/eng/notices/t1800766.
htm#:~:text=The%20Chinese%20Embassy%20and%20
Consulates-General%20in%20the%20United,and%20coop-
eration%20and%20to%20the%20two%20peoples%27%20
friendship.

Evidence to Believe. n.d. "Shroud of Turin: The Burial Cloth of Jesus?" Accessed May 2020. https://evidencetobe-
lieve.net/shroud-of-turin/#:~:text=First%20In-depth%20
Scientific%20Examination%3A%20STRUP%2C%20
1978.%20It%20wasn't,from%20the%20image%20on%20
the%20two%20dimensional%20cloth.

EWTN Global Catholic Network. n.d. "Mother Angelica Live Classics." Accessed March 2020. https://www.ewtn.com/
radio/shows/mother-angelica-live-classics.

Feuerherd, Ben, Jason Beeferman, and Bruce Golding. 2020. "Victor Alvarez, Conspirator in 1992 NYC Terror Plot, Set for Release." *New York Post.* July 30, 2020. https://nypost.
com/2020/07/30/victor-alvarez-conspirator-in-1993-nyc-
terror-plot-set-for-release/.

Fort Mims Restoration Association. n.d. "The Casualties." Accessed May 2020. https://www.fortmims.org/history/history03.html.

Fort Mims Restoration Association. n.d. "The Massacre." Accessed April 2020. http://www.fortmims.org/history/history02.html.

Gobetz, Wally. n.d. "San Antonio: The Alamo-The Chapel." *Flickr.* Accessed August 2020. https://www.flickr.com/photos/wallyg/42172403704.

Graves, Jim. 2015. "The Shroud: Not a Painting, not a Scorch, Not a Photograph." *Catholic World.* March 27, 2015. https://www.catholiceducation.org/en/controversy/other-topics/the-shroud-not-a-painting-not-a-scorch-not-a-photograph.html#:~:text=In%201978%2C%20Schwortz%2C%20a%20technical%20photographer%2C%20was%20invited,was%20a%20painted%20image%20from%20the%20Middle%20Ages.

Gryboski, Michael. 2019. "China Destroys 3,000-Seat Church, Detains Pastors." *The Christian Post.* October 21, 2019. https://www.christianpost.com/news/china-destroys-3000-seat-church-detains-pastors.html.

Haulman, Daniel L. 2012. "The Red Tail Origin." Accessed July 2020. http://tuskegeeairmen.org/wp-content/uploads/Origin-of-the-RedTails.pdf.

Hearn, Chester G. 2007. *Carriers in Combat: The Air War at Sea.* Mechanicsburg: Stackpole Books.

History.com 2009. "Joseph Stalin." Last modified September 19, 2019. https://www.history.com/topics/russia/joseph-stalin.

Hoshur, Shohret. 2013. "At Least 15 Uyghurs Killed in Police Shootout in Xinjiang." *Radio Free Asia*. August 25, 2013. https://www.rfa.org/english/news/uyghur/shootout-08252013134303.html.

Hubbs, Todd. 2020. "Soybeans Rally despite Record Yield Forecast." *Farmdoc Daily*. August 17, 2020. https://farmdocdaily.illinois.edu/2020/08/soybeans-rally-despite-record-yield-forecast.html.

Hume, Andy. 2019. "The Market in Tepito, One of Mexico City's Most Feared Neighborhoods." *Mexico News Daily*. August 14, 2019. https://mexiconewsdaily.com/mexicolife/the-market-in-tepito/.

IMDb. n.d. "Mother Angelica." Accessed March 2020. https://www.imdb.com/name/nm0029565/bio.

InSight Crime. 2010. "'Tony Tormenta' Leader of Gulf Cartel, Dies after 6-Hour Battle in Matamoros." November 12, 2010. https://www.insightcrime.org/news/analysis/tony-tormenta-leader-of-gulf-cartel-dies-after-6-hour-battle-in-matamoros/.

Jacobs, Andrew. 2013. "Plans to Harness Chinese River's Power Threaten a Region." *The New York Times*. May 4, 2013. https://www.nytimes.com/2013/05/05/world/asia/plans-to-harness-chinas-nu-river-threaten-a-region.html.

Johnson, Todd R. and Jeff Briggler. *The Hellbender*. Accessed February 2020.

Knight, James R. 2009. *The Battle of Franklin: When the Devil Had Full Possession of the Earth*. Charleston: The History Press.

Lambeth, Benjamin S. 2005. "American Carrier Air Power at the Dawn of a New Century." *National Defense Research Institute*.

https://www.rand.org/content/dam/rand/pubs/mono-graphs/2005/RAND_MG404.pdf.

Lay, Jeffrey and James Lurie. 2012. *Topgun on Wall Street, Why the United States Military Should Run Corporate America*. New York: Vanguard Press.

Lone Star Junction. n.d. "The Texas Rangers." Accessed May 2020. http://lsjunction.com/facts/rangers.htm#:~:text=The%20Rangers%20date%20back%20to%201823%20when%20Stephen,area%20of%20Austin%27s%20colony%2C%20protecting%20settlers%20from%20Indians.

Luukanen-Kilde, Rauni-Leena. 2000. "Microchip Implants, Mind Control, and Cybernetics." *Illuminati Conspiracy Archive*. December 6, 2000. https://www.conspiracyarchive.com/NWO/microchip_implants_mind_control.htm.

MacCormack, John. 2019. "Border Immigration Surge Reaches the Big Bend." *San Antonio Express-News*. June 10, 2019. https://www.expressnews.com/news/local/article/Border-immigration-surge-reaches-the-Big-Bend-13962823.php.

"Mammoth Primigenius (Woolly mammoth)." Accessed March 2020. http://www.prehistoric-wildlife.com/species/m/mammuthus-primigenius-woolly-mammoth.html.

Martin, Malachi. 1976. *Hostage to the Devil: The Possession and Exorcism of Five Contemporary Americans*. San Francisco: HarperOne.

Martina, Michael. 2015. "China Says Has Shown 'Great Restraint' in South China Sea." *Yahoo! News*. November 17, 2015. https://news.yahoo.com/china-says-restrained-south-china-sea-could-taken-044008937.html#:~:text=But%20China%20was%20the%20real%20victim%20as%20it,except%20

Brunei%20have%20military%20fortifications%20in%20 the%20Spratlys.

Marvel, William. 1994. *Andersonville: The Last Depot.* Chapel Hill: The University of North Caroline Press.

Masayko, Sarah. 2014. "Execution of Robespierre." *French Revolution Timeline.* April 6, 2014. https://frenchrevolution-timeline.wordpress.com/2014/04/06/execution-of-robespi-erre/#:~:text=July%2028%2C%201794-%20Execution%20 of%20Robespierre%20Maximilien%20Robespierre,men%20 were%20on%20the%20Committee%20of%20Public%20 Safety.

Mauser, Eric W. 2012. "Boy's Recovery a Kateri Miracle." *The Catholic Register.* October 20, 2012. https://www.catholi-cregister.org/features/item/15267-boy-s-recovery-a-kat-eri-miracle#:~:text=Last%20Dec.%2019%2C%20Pope%20 Benedict%20XVI%20signed%20a,on%20the%20base%20 of%20the%20portable%20basketball%20hoop.

McConnell, Sarah. 2020. "Today in Texas History: Remembering the Alamo 184 Years Later." *The Texan.* March 6, 2020. https:// thetexan.news/today-in-texas-history-remembering-the-ala-mo-184-years-later/.

McDuffee, Allen. 2017. "Forget Twitter Wars, Andrew Jackson Challenged More Than 100 Men to Duels (But Only Killed One.)" *Timeline.* October 18, 2017. https://timeline.com/ andrew-jackson-duels-dickenson-f281c96fb9f8.

Mensching, Gustav. n.d. "Saint." *Britannica.* https://www.britan-nica.com/topic/saint/Saints-in-Western-religions.

Michaels, Kenneth. 2019. "Mother Angelica Describes Her Vision of the Divine Child Jesus." *Catholic Say.* Last modified

September 28, 2019. https://catholicsay.com/mother-angeli-ca-describes-her-vision-of-the-divine-child-jesus/.

Moriarty, Tom. 2020. "Leadership starts at the interview: How to make a strong impression with new recruits."

Moritsugu, Ken. 2019. "Chinese Spacecraft Makes First Landing on Moon's Far Side and China Lands Spacecraft on 'Dark Side' of Moon in a World First." *USA Today*. June 10, 2019. https://www.usatoday.com/story/news/world/2019/01/02/chinese-spacecraft-makes-first-landing-moons-far-side/2469915002/ https://www.ufodigest.com/article/chinas-chang-e-4-first-to-land-on-farside-of-the-moon/#:~:text=This%20probe%20can%20fill%20the%20gap%20of%20low-frequency,so%20that%20Change%204%20can%20send%20back%20information.

Mother Angelica. n.d. "Holiness Is Not For Wimps and the Cross Is Not Negotiable, Sweetheart, It's a Requirement." Accessed March 2020. https://www.inspiringquotes.us/quotes/m0nO_JPa6EZuG#:~:text=Mother%20Angelica%20quote%3A%20Holiness%20is%20not%20for%20wimps,cross%20is%20not%20negotiable%2C%20sweetheart%2C%20it%27s%20a%20requirement.

Movieclips. "The Power of Christ Compels You - The Exorcist." YouTube Video. 2:35. May 26, 2011. https://m.youtube.com/watch?v=lpyg94OzHK0.

National Park Service. n.d. "Major Participants in the Creek War." Accessed April 2020. https://www.nps.gov/hobe/learn/historyculture/major-participants-in-the-creek-war.htm#:~:text=William%20Weatherford%20%281780-1824%29%20-%20also%20known%20as%20Red,of%20the%20Red%20Sticks%20at%20the%20Holy%20Ground.

National Park Service. n.d. "Mission Antonio de Valero, The Alamo Spanish Colonial Missions of the Southwest Travel Itinerary." Accessed August 2020. https://www.nps.gov/sub-jects/travelspanishmissions/mission-san-antonio-de-valero-the-alamo.htm.

"North Alabama Hauntings." n.d. Accessed March 2020. http://www.angelfire.com/music4/hauntedbama/northernala-bama.html.

Olohan, Mary Margaret. 2019. "China Harvests Organs From 'Prisoners of Conscience' and Religious Minorities, Tribunal Says." *Conservative Daily News*. September 26, 2019. https://www.conservativedailynews.com/2019/09/china-harvests-or-gans-from-prisoners-of-conscience-and-religious-mi-norities-tribunal-says/#:~:text=%E2%80%9CForced%20organ%20harvesting%20from%20prisoners%20of%20con-science%2C%20including,a%20video%20published%20on%20the%20China%20Tribunal%E2%80%99s%20website.

Ottum, Bob. 1981. "The Dreamer." *Sports Illustrated*. April 20, 1981. 24.

Pardo, Luis and Alejandra Inzunza. "US Police Corrupted by Mexico's Cartels along Border." *InSight Crime*. October 21, 2014. https://www.insightcrime.org/news/analysis/us-police-corrupted-by-mexican-cartels-along-border/.

Parton, Charles. 2018. "China's Acute Water Shortage Imperils Economic Future." *Financial Times*. Accessed May 2020. https://www.ft.com/content/3ee05452-1801-11e8-9376-4a6390addb44.

Pfanz, Harry W. 1987. *Gettysburg: The Second Day*. Chapel Hill: The University of North Carolina Press.

Phillips, Michael M. n.d. "Inside an FBI Hostage Crisis: A Stolen Boy, an Angry Loner, an Underground Bunker." *The Wall Street Journal.* Accessed July 2020. http://graphics.wsj.com/hostage/.

Plant Services. 2020. "Impression with New Recruits." October 7, 2020. https://www.plantservices.com/articles/2020/human-capital-leadership-starts-at-the-interview/.

Poor Clares of Perpetual Adoration. n.d. "The History of Our Lady of the Angels Monestary." Accessed March 2020. https://olamnuns.com/history-olam/.

Pray to God. n.d. "The Amazing Dialogues Between the Devil and a Vatican Exorcist." Accessed May 2020. https://praytogod.catholicshare.com/amazing-dialogues-devil-vatican-exorcist/.

Probe for Answers. 2006. "Colonial America." Accessed May 2020. https://probe.org/american-indians-in-american-history/.

Quora. 2015. "What Is the Meaning to This Sentence 'I'd Rather Die on My Feet Than Live on My Knees'?" Accessed June 2020. https://www.quora.com/What-is-the-meaning-to-this-sentence-Id-rather-die-on-my-feet-than-live-on-my-knees#:~:text=What%20Washington%20said%20was%20The%20thing%20that%20sets,behind%20the%20writing%20of%20the%20American%20National%20Anthem.

Reed, Lawrence W. 2019. "Francois-Noel Babeuf: The Marxist before Marx." *Foundation for Economic Education.* June 11, 2019. https://fee.org/articles/francois-noel-babeuf-the-marxist-before-marx/.

Research Laboratories of Archaeology. n.d. "Archaeology of the Appalachian Summit." *The University of North Carolina at Chapel Hill.* Accessed March 2020. http://www.rla.unc.edu/ArchaeoNC/AppSummit.htm.

Roach, Becky. n.d. "That Time St. Clare Defeated an Army with the Holy Eucharist." Catholic Link. Accessed August 2020. https://catholic-link.org/st-clare-eucharist-monastery-with-the-power-of-the-holy-eucharist/#:~:-text=Clare%20Defends%20Monastery%20With%20The%20Power%20of%20the,to%20devastate%20the%20encampments%20and%20seize%20the%20cities.

Roberts, Justin, dir. 2015. *No Greater Love*. Boston, MA: Atlas Distribution Company, 2015. Amazon Prime Video.

Root, Jay. 2017. "Border Patrol Agent's Murder Trial Begins This Week." *The Texas Tribune*. January 17, 2017. https://www.texastribune.org/2017/01/17/border-patrol-agents-murder-trial-begins-week/#:~:text=The%20case%20began%20in%20March%202015%20%20at,narrow%20bay%20between%20the%20island%20and%20the%20mainland.

Ross, Eleanor. 2017. "How and Why China Is Building Islands in the South China Sea." *Newsweek*. March 29, 2017. https://www.newsweek.com/china-south-china-sea-islands-build-military-territory-expand-575161.

Rubel, Robert C. "The Future of Aircraft Carriers." *Naval War College Review*. 64 (4): 13-27. https://digital-commons.usnwc.edu/nwc-review/vol64/iss4/4/.

Rust, Graydon. 2017. "On This Day in Alabama History: Rube Burrow, Gang Robbed Arkansas Train." *Alabama Newscenter*. December 9 2017. https://alabamanewscenter.com/2017/12/09/day-alabama-history-rube-burrow-gang-robbed-arkansas-train/.

Ruzicka, Joe. 2016. "How to Land a Fighter on an Aircraft Carrier on a Stormy Night." *Yahoo! News*. May 19, 2016. https://news.

yahoo.com/land-fighter-aircraft-carrier-stormy-200000628.
html#:~:text=Alone%20and%20unafraid-that%27s%20
the%20term%20Naval%20Aviators%20use,onto%20a%20
moving%20vessel%20belongs%20only%20to%20you.

San Antonio Missions. n.d. "Indian Groups at Mission
Concepcion." Accessed August 2020. https://www.nps.gov/
parkhistory/online_books/saan/campbell/sec2.htm.

Saraceno, Jon. 2018. "George Foreman: If I Had to Do It Again,
I Would Have Had Two Flags." The Undefeated. Last modified October 26, 2018. https://theundefeated.com/features/
george-foreman-american-flag-john-carlos-tommie-smith-
1968-olympics/.

Scofield, Levi T. 1909. The *Retreat from Pulaski: To Nashville, Tenn,
Battle of Franklin, Tennessee, November 30, 1864.* Cleveland:
Press of the Caxton Co.

Serafin, Faith. 2013. "The Legend of Railroad Bill-Alabama's
Robin Hood." *Haunted Haven.* August 27, 2013. https://
hauntedhaven.blogspot.com/2013/08/the-legend-of-railroad-
bill-alabamas.html.

Sheen, Fulton J.1958. Life of Christ. New York: Doubleday

Shiner, Linda. 2019. "Interviews." *Air and Space
Magazine.* April 2019. https://www.airspacemag.com/
military-aviation/f-35-faces-most-critical-test-180971734/.

Simek, Peter. 2017. "City Spotlight: Eagle Pass." *Texas Heritage for
Living.* December 6, 2017. https://texasheritageforliving.com/
texas-travel/eagle-pass/.

Skynyrd, Lynyrd. 1974. "Sweet Home Alabama." Track 1 on
Second Helping. MCA, radio.

Slone, Richard T. 2012. "The Early Years." Kronk. Last modified October 27, 2012. https://kronksports.com/history/.

Smithfield Foods. 2019. "Smithfield Foods Donates Land for Newly Opened Public Boat Ramp on the Pagan River in Smithfield, Virginia." *GlobeNewswire*. July 19, 2019. https://www.globenewswire.com/news-release/2019/07/19/1885384/0/en/Smithfield-Foods-Donates-Land-for-Newly-Opened-Public-Boat-Ramp-on-the-Pagan-River-in-Smithfield-Virginia.html.

Solimeo, Plinio Maria. 2012. "The Story of Saint Peter Claver, Apostle of Slaves." *The American Society for the Defense of Tradition, Family and Property.* September 5, 2012. https://www.tfp.org/the-story-of-saint-peter-claver-apostle-of-slaves/.

Starr, Penny. 2011. "Drug Cartels Cross Rio Grande to Kidnap U.S. Citizens for Smuggling Guns, not 'a Mile' of Border Secure, Says Texas Sheriff." *CNS News*. April 11, 2011. https://www.cnsnews.com/news/article/drug-cartels-cross-rio-grande-kidnap-us-citizens-smuggling-runs-not-mile-border-secure.

Sturdevant, Jay T. and David Bradford. 1999. "Still an Open Book: Analysis of the Current Pre-Clovis vs. Clovis Debate from the Site of Meadowcroft Rockshelter, Pennsylvania and Monte Verde, Chile." *Nebraska Anthropologist*: 31-38. https://civ5customization.gamepedia.com/Appalachia_(David_Bradford) and https://en.m.wikipedia.org/wiki/Meadowcroft_Rockshelter and http://www.rla.unc.edu/ArchaeoNC/AppSummit.htm.

Sunsigns.org. n.d. "Stephen Strasburg." Accessed May 2020. https://www.sunsigns.org/famousbirthdays/d/profile/stephen-strasburg/.

Telescope1609. n.d. "Galileo." Accessed July 2020. http://www. telescope1609.com/Galileo.htm.

Tennessee4Me. n.d. "Eva/Icehouse Bottom." Accessed April 2020. http://www.tn4me.org/article.cfm/era_id/1/major_id/27/ minor_id/85/a_id/307.

Tennessee4Me. n.d. "Dig Deeper: Read about Jackson's Duel with Charles Dickinson." Accessed April 2020. http://www. tn4me.org/sapage.cfm/sa_id/179/era_id/4/major_id/22/ minor_id/66/a_id/.

Tennessee State Militia. n.d. "Brief History of Tennessee Militia in the War of 1812." Accessed April 2020. http://tennesseestatemilitia. com/brief-history-of-tennessee-militia-in-the-war-of-1812.

Texas Mission Indians. n.d. "History of the Native People." Accessed August 2020. http://www.texasmissionindians.org/ index.html.

The Historical Marker Database. n.d. "The Mission Period: 1716-1793." Accessed August 2020. https://www.hmdb. org/m.asp?m=31015#:~:text=On%20June%2013%2C%20 1691%2C%20Franciscan%20Father%20Damián%20 Massanet,nearby%20spring-fed%20creek%20that%20 Ramón%20named%20San%20Pedro.

The Stuttering Foundation. 2015. "Bo Jackson." Last modified June 29, 2015. https://www.stutteringhelp.org/content/bo-jack-son#:~:text=Bo%20Jackson%20is%20the%20eighth%20 of%20ten%20kids%2C,being%20made%20fun%20of%20 by%20the%20other%20students.

Toomey, Michael. 2017. "Early Exploration." *Tennessee Encyclopedia.* Last modified March 1, 2018. https://tennesseeencyclopedia. net/entries/early-exploration/.

Travel China Guide. 2018. "Ancient City of Mallikurwatur and Yotkan." Last modified December 26, 2018. https://www.travelchinaguide.com/attraction/xinjiang/hetian/malikawate.htm.

US Department of State. n.d. "Diplomatic Security Special Agent." Accessed March 2020. https://careers.state.gov/work/foreign-service/specialist/career-tracks/diplomatic-security-special-agent/.

USS Wasp (LHD 1) Public Affairs. 2019. "USS Wasp, SPMAGTF 4 Arrive in the Philippines for Exercise Balikatan." *Commander, U.S. 7ᵗʰ Fleet.* March 31, 2019. https://www.c7f.navy.mil/Media/News/Display/Article/1801132/uss-wasp-spmagtf-4-arrive-in-the-philippines-for-exercise-balikatan/#:~:text=-SUBIC%20BAY%2C%20Philippines%20%28Mar.%20 30%2C%202019%29%20%E2%80%93%20The,March%20 30%2C%202019%2C%20in%20preparation%20for%20 Exercise%20Balikatan.

Vaccaro, Mike. 2019. "Looking Back at Tom Seaver's 10 Most Memorable Games." *New York Post.* March 10, 2019. https://nypost.com/2019/03/10/looking-back-at-tom-seavers-10-most-memorable-games/#:~:text=7.%20Oct.%2016%2C%20 1973%3A%20Reggie%20Jackson%20famously%20said,pitch-for-pitch%20and%20the%20Mets%20lost%20in%20 11.%208.

Walbert, James. 2012. "The Microchip Connection and You - Part One." Last modified 2019. https://organised-crime-of-covert-electronic-assault-nz.com/the-microchip-connection-and-you-part-one.

Waselkov, Gregory A. 2007. "Fort Mims Battle and Massacre." *Encyclopedia of Alabama.* Last modified January 11, 2017. http://www.encyclopediaofalabama.org/

article/h-1121#:~:text=The%20Red%20Sticks%27%20
assault%20on%20Fort%20Mims%20ranks,American%20
armies%20under%20the%20cry%20"Remember%20
Fort%20Mims.".

Wentz, Brian. 2012. "Viva Cristo Rey!" *Wait So That's What Catholics Believe?!?!* November 25, 2012. https://deaconbrianwentz.wordpress.com/tag/blessed-miguel-pro/.

Wragg, David W. 2000. *Carrier Combat.* Gloucestershire: Budding Books.

Wikia. 2020. "History of the United States Navy." Accessed August 2020. https://military.wikia.org/wiki/History_of_the_United_States_Navy.

Wikimili. 2020. "History of Tennessee." Last modified August 5, 2020. https://wikimili.com/en/History_of_Tennessee.

Wikipedia. 2020. "Aegis Ballistic Missile Defense System." Last modified October 27, 2020. https://en.wikipedia.org/wiki/Aegis_Ballistic_Missile_Defense_System.

Wikipedia. 2020. "Aegis Combat System." Last modified October 21, 2020. https://en.wikipedia.org/wiki/Aegis_Combat_System.

Wikipedia. 2020. "Alamo Mission in San Antonio." Last modified November 1, 2020. https://en.m.wikipedia.org/wiki/Alamo_Mission_in_San_Antonio.

Wikipedia. 2020. "Appalachia." Last modified November 2, 2019. https://en.m.wikipedia.org/wiki/Appalachia.

Wikipedia. 2020. "Battle of Horseshoe Bend (1814)." Last modified November 7, 2020. https://en.m.wikipedia.org/wiki/Battle_of_Horseshoe_Bend_(1814)#:~:text=Battle%20of%20Horseshoe%20Bend%20On%20March%2027%2C%20

1814%2C,begin%20his%20attack%20on%20the%20Red%20 Stick%20fortification.

Wikipedia. 2020. "Battle of the Alamo." Last modified October 31, 2020. https://en.m.wikipedia.org/wiki/Battle_of_the_Alamo.

Wikipedia. 2020. Bo Jackson. Last modified November 3, 2020. https://en.m.wikipedia.org/wiki/Bo_Jackson.

Wikipedia. 2020. "Eagle Pass, Texas." Last modified October 31, 2020. https://en.m.wikipedia.org/wiki/Eagle_Pass,_Texas.

Wikipedia. 2020. "Florence, Alabama." Last modified November 6, 2020. https://en.m.wikipedia.org/wiki/Special:History/ Florence,_Alabama.

Wikipedia. 2020. "Fort Mims Massacre." Last modified June 2020. https://en.m.wikipedia.org/wiki/Fort_Mims_massacre.

Wikipedia. 2020. "History of Optics." Last modified November 5, 2020. https://en.m.wikipedia.org/wiki/History_of_optics.

Wikipedia. 2020. "Icehouse Bottom." Last modified April 18, 2019. https://en.m.wikipedia.org/wiki/Icehouse_ Bottom#:~:text=Since%201979%2C%20the%20Icehouse%20 Bottom%20site%20has%20been,prior%20to%20dam%20 construction%2C%20in%20anticipation%20of%20inundation.

Wikipedia. 2020. "Ivy Green." Last modified October 8, 2020. https://en.m.wikipedia.org/wiki/Special:History/Ivy_Green.

Wikipedia. 2020. "Joe Frazier." Last modified November 9, 2020. https://en.m.wikipedia.org/wiki/Joe_Frazier.

Wikipedia. 2020. "Joe Frazier's Gym." Last modified May 3, 2020. https://en.m.wikipedia.org/wiki/Joe_Frazier%27s_Gym.

Wikipedia. 2020. "Lerna." Last modified November 4, 2020. https://en.m.wikipedia.org/wiki/Lerna.

Wikipedia. 2020. "Lernaean Hydra." Last modified November 3, 2020. https://en.m.wikipedia.org/wiki/Lernaean_ Hydra#:~:text=The%20oldest%20extant%20Hydra%20nar- rative%20appears%20in%20Hesiod%27s,serpent%20that%20 is%20slain%20by%20Heracles%20and%20Iolaus.

Wikipedia. 2020. "Meadowcroft Rockshelter." Last modi- fied October 14, 2020. https://en.m.wikipedia.org/wiki/ Meadowcroft_Rockshelter.

Wikipedia. 2020. "MS-13." Last modified October 27, 2020. https://en.m.wikipedia.org/wiki/MS-13.

Wikipedia. 2020. "Railroad Bill." Last modified August 21, 2020. https://en.m.wikipedia.org/wiki/Railroad_Bill.

Wikipedia. 2020. "Rube Burrow." Last modified September 2, 2020. https://en.m.wikipedia.org/wiki/Rube_Burrow.

Wikipedia. 2020. "Soviet Famine of 1932-33." Last modi- fied November 2, 2020. https://en.m.wikipedia.org/wiki/ Soviet_famine_of_1932%E2%80%9333.

Wikipedia. 2020. "Tenskwatawa." Last modified November 3, 2020. https://en.m.wikipedia.org/wiki/Tenskwatawa.

Wikipedia. 2020. "The Black Book of Communism." Last mod- ified November 2, 2020. https://en.m.wikipedia.org/wiki/ The_Black_Book_of_Communism.

Wikipedia. 2020. "U.S. Carrier Group Tactics." Last mod- ified June 18, 2020. https://en.m.wikipedia.org/ wiki/U.S._Carrier_Group_tactics.

Wikipedia. 2020. "VFA-154." Last modified September 2020. https://en.m.wikipedia.org/wiki/VFA-154#:~:text=VF-154%20dropped%20470%20tons%20of%20bombs%20and%20expended,the%20squadron%20had%20transitioned%20to%20the%20F9F-5%20Panther.

Wikipedia. 2020. "Wuzhi Mountain." Last modified Marc 1, 2020. https://en.m.wikipedia.org/wiki/Special:History/Wuzhi_Mountain.

Wynne, Stephen. 2019. "Pope Ignores Suffering of Chinese Catholics." *Church Militant*. May 30, 2019. https://www.churchmilitant.com/news/article/more-papal-spin.

Zwitter, Ion. 2010. "China First with Citizen RFID Implants." *Avant News*. March 19, 2010. http://www.avantnews.com/news/4413-china-first-with-citizen-rfid-implants.

CPSIA information can be obtained
at www.ICGtesting.com
Printed in the USA
BVHW041918210121
598357BV00004B/18

9 781662 804601